Once Upon A Time in Argentina

Frank Kidd

Free Ebook Version w/ Paperback Purchase

Thank you for buying paperback and thank you for reading.

One of life's many annoyances is not getting a digital copy with a paperback purchase. Well, here is one less annoyance.

For my beautiful and loving wife, you have done nothing but support me, give me space to do my thing, and encourage me carefully and quietly. It's appreciated far more than you know.

Praise for Frank Kidd

"I hated it."

— Jane Fonda (probably)

"Like the Wild Bunch on the high seas."

— Anonymous

"If he keeps writing like this we'll put him in touch with Taylor Sheridan."

— Unnamed and likely imaginary source at CAA

Part One

Chapter One

"The thought of suicide is a great consolation: by means of it one gets through many a dark night."
- Friedrich Nietzsche

If I left now, it would take me 34 minutes to get to the Dodge dealership. Maybe two hours for them to run a credit check and get me in a new Hellcat. After all, I wouldn't really haggle, or maybe I would. Really ruin the salesman's day before I left. Black, with a red interior, that's what I would get. Maybe even trade in my F-150—I wouldn't need it anymore.

From there I would run it hard, all the way up 101, the Pacific on one side of me, until I finally found a cliff.

I would throw it down a gear and stomp the pedal, and hit the guard rail at 130 mph. The car would buckle, but momentum would carry me over, and I would tumble through the air, a jumbled mass of fiberglass and steel. If I hit it fast enough, the guardrail wouldn't matter, and I'd make it to the water. I would disappear in the black maw of the ocean, lost at last to the sea, my body given back to the chaos, and I could be free.

This is what I had thought about every day for the last year. The most dramatic, most obnoxious ways to kill myself.

It was a game we used to play in the unit, this was how we wiled away the hours on a long deployment, or during night shift. We came up with the most intricate, obscure, and offensive ways you could kill yourself, and then trotted them out in front each other as if we were in show and tell. We would howl with laughter for hours, snorting and choking, at the images of our best friend hanging themselves from an industrial warehouse ceiling fan. On a long rope, of course, so that when they found the body, he would be whipping around the giant room. Suicide was like going AWOL, except they could never catch you. It was the only real way to say "fuck you" to the world. I think that was the attraction.

I had made my first suicide joke a week after I started at CORPOSUCKCOCK, and my new co-workers' reactions had been awkward requests to see if "I needed help," or was "doing ok." That was the first time I regretted leaving the Corps.

I stared at the fluorescent lights above my cubicle. They buzzed and flickered. Sometimes I swore they flashed messages, but whenever I noticed, they stopped, and the light held droningly steady. I resented being trapped there, held under artificial light while the California sun gleamed brightly outside.

The thing I realize now, is that in the Corps,

they were really just jokes. Out here they were an attempt at self-actualization.

I worked for a start up, they had moved out here a year ago, fleeing San Francisco. The company was called Artificial Spaces and was supposedly working on using machine learning to generate virtual spaces. I worked in the finance department, and they were bleeding cash, but it didn't matter. Most of America is an optical illusion that way, if you cross your eyes, and maintain the proper emotional distance to most of the buggery, you can sort of see what should amount to a culture and a country. Businesses don't have to be solvent as long as you can sell the vision.

Artificial Spaces had bought out an old aerospace building, and converted it to offices, so the windows were heavily glazed to prevent the soviets or whoever else they thought had been spying at the time from spying, but the Cold War had been over for the better part of 30 years now. So, it just dampened most of the natural light, and turned the inside into a depressing cave of fluorescents and cubicles.

I had worked here a year, and every day seemed a lifetime. The work was tedious. I spent most of my day answering emails, and chasing down spreadsheets, comparing cost proposals and receipts. I often wondered how I ended up here when I had so many other options. But in reality, all options had led to here, or a version of here.

"Let's meet in the Inspire room," Luke said, startling me from my thoughts. He stepped into the center aisle. He was a small man, with a well-trimmed beard, and dark rimmed glasses. He was also my boss. His hairline was receding, but I could tell he had not quite given up on it yet.

Three days ago, at a bar, he had confided in me that he was in an open relationship. I don't know why he did this, but he did, probably because he was sad and drunk, alone at a bar, and saw a familiar face. He also confided in me, that while his wife had slept with several new men, he had been unable to "score" at all. Even worse, he wasn't completely sure he wanted to. "I still love her," he had said. Although she apparently thought he was fine with the whole thing, he had only given in to her, because he was scared she would leave him. And who says men aren't the real romantics.

At the end of the night, he had tried to explain how freeing it all was, and that the experience had really taught him a lot about himself, and how to overcome his insecurities. How he desperately loved his wife, and letting her be with other men, was the surest act of faith in that love. He had told me this teary-eyed, and drunk, without the slightest hint of irony. That's when I realized the man had spent the whole night convincing himself of the idea. The experience turned my stomach. However, I had glimpsed a mirror image of myself in that instant. Always talking myself into the "right" course of action, the life that was expected, until I too, expected it.

"Actually, the Inspire room is already booked," Lisa said. Her voice was a cast iron grate scraping over concrete. Her perfume gave me a headache, and I imagined in several different lives she had been the girl to raise her hand at school and remind the teacher about the homework.

Luke looked exasperated at this scheduling mix up. I swallowed my disgust. He overreacted to everything. He acted neurotic, like a beaten woman, flinching at the slightest creak in the house.

"Ok, lets meet in the Believe room," Luke said at last, finally finished panicking. His voice weak and estrogenic, as if his diaphragm was perpetually compressed.

This was my manager. This was our fearless leader. A man in an open relationship. A man who feared the most basic decisions. He was made for middle management. Born to it, the way a Khan is to the steppe. If only he had ever read Jocko's Extreme Ownership then he too could command the platoons of corporate America.

The Inspire Room, the Believe Room, I don't even hear them anymore, it's normal now. The lights flickered again. They sent messages out in morse code. When I looked up, they stopped.

Everything in a corporate office, in corporate culture, in corporate anything is designed to extract your soul. I had heard startups were better, and if that was true, then I would likely not make it a day under the normal bureaucracy of a fortune 500. They break you down more thoroughly than bootcamp ever had, but never go through the trouble of building you back up. There was no crucible at the end of this mountain. Only a rock, that rolled backwards. An Outlook inbox that never filled. Call me Sisyphus. Somewhere in the distance of my mind's ear a hellcat savages pavement.

They pair brutalist architecture with stock images of sunrises and grassy hills, and then those are overlaid with inspirational words. Motivate. Learn. Achieve.

They give you pointless tasks. Approval loops that take a day to navigate before you end up back where you started. A tracker for updating the tracker. And then there is email. Thread after thread, of confusion, the shirking of responsibility. You learn other people's jobs just to tell them how to do it. Zoom meetings that go nowhere.

You think if you gut it out long enough, smile just right and talk at the perfect pitch you will get promoted. And often you do. But it's never for the reasons you think. It's never because you had a great quarter, or because you fixed a system and saved x hours of time. No. It's because you were there. It was your time. You were the one dumb enough to sign up for this, dumb enough to stick around.

And then you get promoted. A whole level. That's a step up. Your 70k a year becomes 83k a year. But somehow you only see $100 extra a paycheck. That can't be right, there is a mix up you think. But there wasn't. The step up puts you in a new tax bracket, which means the government gets its share, and since your health benefits are calculated on a company-wide curve, you are now expected to pay more of the premium compared to the company.

Your yearly raise will be 2-3% if you are lucky, and the company did "well." Whatever that means. But real inflation (use shadowstats.com and not that CPI calculated garbage) is running hot and has been year after year. If you calculate from three years prior, your dollars go 19% less far.

Quicksand. That's your life, and every day you are sinking.

But the one rule, and one rule only, is never bring any of this up to anyone ever. To break the illusion, just for a second, to shine a light in the dark corner, or mention that the king has no clothes, is a hard no. They are automatons and programmed to kill.

Why I can't disappear into collections of poorly made plastic figurines like everyone else, is a question I could never answer. They know it's bad. Caring just makes it worse.

The Believe Room is white walls, a laminate wood table, circular, the carpet dirty blue. My coworkers shuffle in, pick their spots with strategic precision. Which chair will let them extricate themselves the quickest.

Luke sets up the overhead projector while Lisa tries to help by giving him directions. Small men and wine moms are the slave drivers of the 21st century. They keep the machine moving. They are the ghouls that work for Master. Instead of whips they use empty smiles and nurturing voices, but eyes are empty, and bosoms cold.

"Today, boys and girls, we are learning about diversity, can anyone tell me why it's wrong to use N***** to describe Terrel?" my boss asked.

He didn't say this, but it's what I heard. My mind's ear again.

I make eye contact with Terrel. He had heard it too. I feel vindicated. Maybe, my boss did say it.

I zoned out for the rest of the meeting, bronze age warriors sack villages in my mind's eye. Red-bearded Scythian steppe nomads sitting atop squat, muscular ponies as their prey flees before them—the merchants, and the farmers, the self-domesticated. Scalps hang from their intricately decorated saddles, and their helms glittered with rubies. Swords flashed and men fell. One has a black-haired buxom beauty tossed across his saddle.

I wondered if my ancestors would disown me when I got to Valhalla, then I remembered that you had to die with a weapon in your hand. I'd have to rethink my suicide.

I should have died in Iraq. That had been my chance. But they had forced me out, I went to college on the G.I. Bill, after I was too jaded to enjoy it. I got a finance degree.

I had hated the Marine Corps, but in the way you hate a toxic girlfriend—you drive each other wild. She drives you nuts, keys your car, but when it's good, you are going eighty down a two lane road, smoking a cigarette, and her head is bobbing up and down in your lap. It's no long-term way to live, but it is a great way to die. She didn't have to break up with me.

Lunch was at my desk, and I spent the rest of the day sorting emails. When your job is wasting time, your time is wasting.

A black hand waved in front of my face. It was Terrel.

"Smoke?" he asked. Terrel and I were the only two people at the company that smoked.

"Alright, you got a lighter?" I asked.

"You know I do," he said.

"Cool."

We had to smoke fifty feet in front of the building. We knew this because we had been chased away from the front door more than once, by more than one sad, strong matriarch.

"This shit is gay as fuck, man."

I inhaled the cigarette. "I know, I hate it."

"For real, I would quit if it didn't pay so well," Terrel said.

He was doing the thing too, talking himself into it. Talking himself into life in the 21st century.

I PULLED up outside the Palm Vale Apartment complex and waved my key card in front of the access panel. The iron gate grumbled open, and I pulled inside. I drove my F-150 through a maze of drives, cell block after cell block towering over me. My own cell was nine hundred square feet of white walls on the second floor that I paid the jailer $1500 a month to live in.

I parked the car and rolled down my window. I lit another cigarette. The sun had reached that place in the sky, where the palm tree outside of my apartment shaded my specific parking spot, at exactly 4:05 p.m. when I got back from work. I figured it only happened once or twice a year like this. I took a long drag on the cigarette, basking in the serendipity of the moment. This was my summer solstice.

I found a package left by the front door. It was from MedTest Industries. For $150, you could take your own blood work. I set the package on the counter. Sarah had left a note asking me to get groceries. A little smiley face drawn at the end. Sarah was the only reason I was still here, in the country, in the universe, which were not great reasons to be with someone.

I tacked her list to the fridge with a magnet that said, "I love you". We hadn't had sex in a month and the problem was me. It had started a year ago, right when I switched jobs, my libido died, or at least that's what I thought. At some point later in this story I'd realize it was just depression, but alas. My junk works fine now.

I scanned the chore list and wondered why she couldn't do them. They were always simple things, things that could have been done in the time it took to write them down. Everywhere, my life was managed by women. Things that just a generation ago no woman in her right mind would dare suggest her husband do. But then again, a single man's job would have kept her fed, and clothes on her children's backs. I guess ultimately, this was the problem.

Instead, she worked a job. She was a certified girl boss, making twenty eight dollars an hour as a "manager."

I sat on the couch and googled low testosterone. I had tried it all, raw eggs, working out, vitamin D. Nothing had worked. I googled boxing gyms in my area. I found one ten minutes away, I would try it. Fighting would give me my life back. I ordered a pair of gloves on Amazon.

I boxed in the Marines. We even had to settle a few disagreements that way on deployment. All I knew was I needed something. I was dying. Withering. I could feel my soul leaking out of my ears and I had no way to stop it.

Sarah came through the door. "Did you do anything on the list?" she asked.

"No, I just got home," I said.

She huffed and disappeared to the bedroom.

I flicked the tv on and looked for a game. Every five minutes an ad for an antidepressant came on, and then one for a new diet, and then one with a mixed-race couple, the white guy cowering beneath the ire of his ~~beautiful~~ ugly afroed wife. Interracial marriage or sex, or whatever you want to call it, had never offended me until it was meant to be offensive, and by then it had become illegal to say it was offensive. What luck. Also what the fuck is with everyone in ads having vitiligo. I've never seen one in real life.

My gloves came three days later. I tore into the amazon box and tried them on. They were black, shiny, and new. Begging me to break them in. I gleamed.

The gym was in a brand-new shopping center. I pulled up and parked. I stared at it. My class started at 7 p.m.

Inside, there were rows of heavy bags. The place gleamed. Pop music blared overhead, and my heart dropped. It was full of women—yoga pants, and athletic wear—the entire gym reeked of antiseptic. I scanned the place quickly, there wasn't even a place to spar. This wasn't a boxing gym; it was Pilates with gloves.

"Welcome to Boxer's," the woman at the front desk said, "have you been here before?"

I glared.

But it was too late, I couldn't turn around now. I feigned interest in her droning, and ten minutes later I was signed up for three free sessions. Five minutes after that, I bobbed and weaved, as "our" homosexual Puerto Rican instructor led me and "the girls," through a series of routines. He wore an earpiece, his spiky hair gelled, and instead of actual work out clothes he bobbed around in an overly tight red polo shirt that had the gym's logo embroidered on it—Boxer's.

He looked like he should be selling ShamWow. I imagined the bag was his face. His energetic voice, frenetic over the gym's speakers, urged all of us on, and by the end of it I was convinced that this class was equal to, if not actual—sodomy.

I walked outside. My bubble of motivation burst, the wave that had given me new hope, dashed upon the fake and gay reality of the 21st century.

When I returned home, I threw my gloves in the corner. I pulled a glass container full of leftovers out of the fridge and sat on the couch. I had thrown all our plastic containers out three months ago and bought glass. I lived in fear of micro-plastics and waged a losing war on parabens. I refused to touch the receipts at the store, convinced that they contained dangerous phytoestrogens. Despite all this, my testosterone still hadn't improved, or so I thought.

I scrolled on my phone. Wondering why I did it. Every two posts was some sort of ad for a testosterone booster, or a course that would make you a millionaire. Every day, the answer box showed women how ugly they were, and showed men how poor they were.

Again, I googled boxing gyms in my area, but this time I pulled up a crime map of my city. I found a couple streets where the dots clustered, and then searched for a boxing gym in the triangle. I found it, Lion's Gym. That was my spot. That's where I would try next.

I TRUDGED my way through Walmart, gathering the things on the list. I went to Walmart because it was close, and it was cheap, but also because I am a masochist.

Small family-owned grocers gave their life for this. For cheap foreign made bullshit, picked over by white trash and their black neighbors. Obese women, freed from their duties to husband and family over fifty years ago, and given the authority a name tag carries, deputized by Sam Walton himself, now roamed the aisles, some would call them the commissars of a new age.

"Excuse me," a voice from behind me says.

I have zoned out in the middle of the aisle. I scooch my cart over awkwardly, the wheels groan and creak, I'm suddenly confused, as to how I was even in the way. But then I see the rest of her. She smiles at me as she passes, her smile another fold in her giant neck. She's a blob, a mass of flesh. A monstrosity of sagging skin stretched to its breaking point underneath pound after pound of pork fed flesh.

She waddled past.

At the front of the store, I went to the self-checkout. There were only two registers manned by human cashiers. Part of me longed for the days when you were forced to talk to an awkward teenager, or the lonely grandma, forced to participate in the community you lived in. Instead, they had replaced all of them with these infernal machines, the ones that beeped at you when you didn't put your items on the scale fast enough. I finished checking myself out, and bagging all my groceries.

I headed to the exit.

The commissar was there. I tried to avoid eye contact as I wheeled past her.

"Sir, I need to see your receipt," the woman said.

I stopped the cart, white knuckling the handle.

"The receipt is in that bag," I said, and pointed to the sack on top of the cart.

"Can you take it out for me?" she asked.

"No, you take it out," I responded. I have a thing about phytoestrogens remember.

"But we aren't allowed to touch your things," she said.

“Not really my problem is it," I said.

The woman huffed and picked the receipt out of the bag. She scanned it, pretending to check it, never comparing it to any of the items in the cart. She went to hand it back to me, but I pointed at the sack. She huffed again.

"How do you know that what is in the bags is on the receipt, if you aren't allowed to touch any of my stuff?" I asked as earnestly as I could fake.

She stared at me, her eyes glassy, and then said, "Sir, we do this at every Walmart."

"Why do I have to show you my receipt if there are CCTV cameras in literally every aisle?" I asked.

At this the woman grew visibly frustrated. "Sir, please leave," she said.

"That's what I was trying to do before you stopped me," I said.

"Sir, if you don't leave then I will call security," she commanded.

I wheeled my cart outside.

Chapter Two

Lion's Gym was sandwiched between a restaurant with Arabic letters and a massage parlor with Chinese letters. Trash was strewn across the cracked asphalt of the parking lot. Near the nail salon, a bum talked to himself. His green, gray shirt ragged, full of holes, he waved his arms wildly, lost in some deep, intense argument with the demons inside his head.

"I know buddy," I muttered.

This part of town was sketchy, which shouldn't have come as a surprise, seeing as I had picked it out based off a map of violent crimes. I thought about turning to go home. The lot was mostly empty, except for a black Chrysler 300 and a white Nissan Altima parked in front.

I grabbed my gym bag from the backseat and cracked the door. Cold winter air enveloped me with cleansing hands. Cali cold mind you. The cold air felt like breath of life in a dying world.

The gym's store front was made up of dark tinted glass. Lights were on inside, glowing purple through the dark windows. A large vinyl decal of red boxing gloves hung in the window on the right. On the opposite side, was plastered a second decal of a massive lion's head. The lion was golden and wearing a crown.

As I shuffled towards the door, I heard the static buzz of the neon sign above the door. It's warm red glow said they were OPEN.

The gym was a hive of activity, and much larger than I had expected. As I would eventually come to learn, almost nobody drove here, they all walked, or took the bus, and half of them were some shade of homeless. The whole gym was painted in varying shades of gold and black, the gym's colors. The floors were bare concrete in places, and in others, sported a rubberized coating.

"Welcome!" a large man shouted, and he approached me, arms raised as if he had been expecting me.

Heavy metal thumped over the loud speakers. Two men sparred in a ring in the center of the gym. The ring sat above the rest of the room like a real boxing ring. Row upon row of heavy bags hung in the back.

A group of guys worked through their combinations. Another guy jumped rope nearby. When he caught my glance he glared. His torso glistened, and every time he jumped, he splashed down in a puddle of sweat that had collected beneath him. The place stank of blood, sweat, and rusted pipes, but not antiseptic. I felt like I had come home.

"I haven't seen you before?" the man asked, stopping in front of me. "My name is Abdel Qassim, I own this place." He stuck out his hand, and I shook it.

"I'm Ryan McGowan," I replied.

"Ahh, Irish. So you are a natural," Abdel said.

"I've boxed before, wouldn't say I'm good though," I said.

"We will make you good, no worry."

Abdel was taller than me, about fifty years old, but heavily built. His powerful shoulders bulged beneath the yellow track suit. He had black curly hair, and a well-trimmed goatee. He spoke with an accent. I would later learn that he immigrated from Jordan, having left to make a life here. He had been a champion in his own country and now ran his gym the way he wanted.

"Where do you live?" Abdel continued. "How did you hear of this place?"

"I googled it," I replied, leaving out the crime maps.

He eyed me and then said, "Very well. See Juan, he will get you a locker. The price is one hundred dollars a month."

Juan jogged up to us. Juan was lanky, but carved out of stone. Every muscle in his forearm readily discernible.

Juan showed me to my locker. It was number 09, in a row of old yellow rust boxes. The paint was chipped and peeling. They didn't look like they had been retouched since the 50s. Juan handed me a lock, and I sat down on one of the wooden benches.

"Thanks," I said.

"It's part of your monthly fee," he replied.

"And when are those due?" I asked.

Juan smiled and said, "Every month, whenever you can pay in the month, but you better not miss a month, otherwise you have to go through the grinder."

"The grinder?" I asked.

"We are having one tonight," Juan said. "But I think it's better you just pay." And with that, he left. I finished getting dressed, wrapped my hands, slid on my gloves and walked outside.

As soon as I stepped foot outside the locker room, a whistle went off in my ear. I flinched, my head ringing. I recoiled. Juan shouted at me to take them off, to "get those gloves the fuck off." And like that I was back in boot camp. My fingers worked the Velcro on the gloves and when I had peeled those off, Juan still shouted, but now it was about the wraps. I tuned him out, and slowed my breathing, my fingers steady as I took my time unraveling the wraps. When I had all of it off my hands, the shouting stopped.

"You haven't earned gloves yet," Juan said. "Babies have to learn how to dance first."

Juan motioned for me to follow. I scrambled to scoop my gloves and wraps up off the floor, and followed Juan to a section of the gym set off from everyone else. It was a small area, the floor put together with big foam puzzle pieces and sectioned off by Fisher Price Playpen walls that looked like they were scrounged out of a dumpster. There was a tv on the wall in front of me, and above it scrawled in chalk, were the words "The Nursery."

"Babies stay in the Nursery until they learn how to walk," Abdel said from behind me.

I looked at him, and it must have been a tortured look, because he continued by saying, "Don't worry, you aren't special. Everyone has to do it."

Juan flicked the TV on and worked his way through the selection menu of a Zumba DVD. When he was done, I met my instructor. A bubbly black woman, in tight leggings.

"Now dance," Juan said. "And don't let us see you slacking. You'll never get out of the nursery if you slack."

I looked around. Half the gym stared at me, two hulking black dudes had stopped sparring in order to stare. They both grinned in anticipation, waiting for me to start.

"Abdel, you're wasting your time. Everyone knows you can't teach white guys to dance," one of them shouted.

I felt the red heat of embarrassment climb my body, and turned back to the TV, unwilling to let any one of them see my flush. And then I danced.

The embarrassment I felt here, dancing by myself in The Nursery, was nothing like the shame I'd felt at Boxers. This shame came without resentment, this shame was what one felt when they had expected a place in a brotherhood but had not yet earned it. This was paying your dues. This was how men made sure that you actually wanted to be there, that you could join their tribe, and that you wouldn't turn their sacred fraternity into Pilates with gloves.

I had worked through the first lesson twice before the whistle blew. Training was two hours for everyone, no matter when you showed up, or what you were working on.

"Grinder!!" Juan shouted. He blew his whistle again, and I watched as everyone stopped what they were doing and walked to the ring. Abdel slid inside, he motioned for a scrawny Mexican kid to join him. The kid scrambled into the ring looking forlorn and shamed.

"Rollo, didn't pay his dues last month," Abdel said. "Not with money at least, and that's fine, because I take multiple forms of payment. Rollo will pay with his own sweat and blood. Who wants to go first?"

A tall black guy, named Jackson, clambered up the steps into the ring. Abdel handed both of them headgear, and they adjusted their mouthguards.

Rollo and Jackson sparred for three rounds, and while Rollo held his own, Jackson's reach was such that he could jab from seemingly anywhere in the ring to tag him. When the three rounds were over, they tapped gloves, both out of breath and covered in sweat. But only Jackson left the ring, and when he did, he tagged another guy in.

That's why they called it the grinder. Rollo had to spar everyone in the gym in back to back rounds. As guys fought, they tagged their buddies in and then left for the night. After an hour of this, I was ready to go home but Juan shook his head no.

"You have to stay until you fight or it's over," Juan chided. "Since you are a baby, and don't know how to fight, you have to wait until it's over."

This was not the gym you joined if you had a 9 to 5.

The rounds went on and on, until Juan could no longer hold his arms up. Thick blue bruises welled up all over his body, they yellowed his skin. When he breathed it was with a rattle, and at one point his nose started to bleed. But through all of it, he kept going, he kept trying. When he had fought eleven guys in a row, he collapsed in a heap on the floor. At this Abdel waved his arms, and helped Rollo up. He gave him water, kept him conscious, and another coach started applying ice to some of his bruises. This was the grinder, this was how a man paid off his debts.

Sure that Rollo was being taken care of, Abdel turned back to the group and said, "that was a new record. He fought 11 of you!"

"So he's good now?" I asked Juan.

"He's good," Juan said.

Chapter Three

I'm leaving, I need some time to think.

— Sarah

⁂

That's what the note read when I got home. No "I love you." No list of chores. Nothing. Just that singular line.

I walked to the bedroom, my heart falling to my feet. I looked in the closet. She had packed most of her clothes and had left almost nothing. The strip of pictures pinned to the cork board above our mirror was turned around backwards so the picture side faced the board. I gently unpinned it, flipped it over, my own face smiled back at me, and hers. It was taken on our first date.

⁂

I HAD ASKED for her number a week before that picture was taken. I was at the bar to watch the game, by myself. She was wearing skintight black jeans, and a red flannel tied off in the front, underneath was a white tank top. Her blond hair was shoulder length and straight, cut jagged. She was attractive, and slightly mentally ill, which meant I was in love. She had walked in with two other girls, but they barely registered for me. One of them was the fat friend, and the other was fine, but had an overbite and her eyes bugged ever so slightly, which gave me stage five clinger vibes. Physiognomy was weird that way. I was proven right in my initial assessment, because later that friend caused a bunch of drama when Sarah started spending more time with me.

Sarah made eye contact with me, and I held it, and then smiled at her. She gave me a smile back and I turned around to continue watching my game. The next time I caught her looking, I walked over and introduced myself. It was over after that. We played pool the rest of the night. I had tried to get her to go home with me, but she had refused. She said I had to take her on a proper date first.

A week later I showed up at her house early, and the old Ford I was driving then, made a clunking noise when I slowed down. The cabin almost always smelled of exhaust. She hopped in, pulling herself up with the "oh shit" handle.

"Where we going?" she asked playfully.

"Dinner first, and then we will see where the night takes us," I said. I had been nervous at first, but the longer the night went, the more that faded.

"If you make it through dinner," she quipped, but she was only teasing.

Dinner had come and gone, and we found ourselves walking along the boardwalk. It was a tourist area built up along the river where one could browse the windows of the shops. We ended the night in a divey little bar at the very end of it all, and after several games of pool, she pulled me into the photo booth. We hadn't even kissed yet and she was sitting on my lap.

I don't even remember taking the pictures because I was so focused on getting to the kiss. When she turned her head to look at me, giggling at the photo that had just been printed out, it happened. That moment where it feels right, where you both move in on each other like magnets. When the body takes over, and your mind finally shuts the fuck up. She had full lips, and they were soft, but the way she kissed made me want more, a lot more. That first kiss had turned into several, and before we knew it, we were stumbling back up the boardwalk, horny and in a hurry back to my apartment. She moved in two weeks later.

I turned the picture over in my hand. I no longer recognized the people in the images. They didn't exist. They never had. They were artefacts of two people duping each other.

It was weird getting to know someone. You fill them up with your hopes and dreams. You show them the best version of yourself, and before long you believe your own bullshit. You think this time it will last, and then slowly, ever so slowly, you figure out that they are human, and you both weren't perfect puzzle pieces designed for each other in a heavenly factory. And they realize that you are mostly full of shit, and that you are mean when you get mad, and you've mostly only been mad now, and depressed, for the better part of a year. In fact, you can't remember the last time you weren't mad. You blame it on the world. You blame it on her. But you are the problem. You're just mad at yourself.

* * *

"FUCK ME," I muttered. I flicked the photograph at the wall. "Fucking cunt."

I was exhausted from the boxing class, which is probably the only reason I was taking it so well. That and the fact I had been waiting for it. I was secretly glad that she had left. In fact, if I was being totally honest, I was thrilled to be rid of her. Behind the slimy feeling was a giddiness that signaled new beginnings.

When you go through enough break ups, you learn how to take it on the nose. You learn not to lose yourself in the rejection, and sort of appreciate the process. Yeah, it sucked. And you missed them, but really you missed what they did for you. You missed not being alone. You missed not having to think about how and where you were going to get laid next. You missed the fantasies that you had built up in your head and projected onto them. And now you had an excuse. An excuse to get drunk on a weekday. An excuse to buy a pack of cigarettes. Now I had something other than the world or myself to blame my depression on. If I was really committed I could milk this break up for six months.

I started the water for my shower and stared at myself in the mirror. Four years from the military and I was closer to 30 than I was 20. I had gotten flabby. I used to be carved from stone. Now my pecs were starting to sag. I had some weight around my gut. Not a lot, but enough to say I drank before bed. I'd gotten sloppy. I was that guy. The vet that turned to a puddle of mush and romanticized about better days. FUCK... fuck. At least I didn't have a saggy eagle globe and anchor tattoo.

Tomorrow would be the real test though, when the soreness from today's workout set in. I hadn't worked out like that in a while, and tomorrow I would feel like I had the flu.

I remembered the package from Med Test Industries. I walked to the kitchen buck naked and pulled the little white box down from its place on top of the fridge. When I got it open, I found a little thing you were supposed to prick yourself with and a small poly vial to collect the blood sample with. The whole thing took less than ten minutes. I put the vial back into the box, and the box in the fridge, next to a six pack of beer, two empty containers of ketchup, and an old banana. The fridge smelled stale, like soured milk.

The directions didn't say that the blood needed to be refrigerated but it felt like the right thing to do. But if the blood did need to be refrigerated, then how was it going to make it all the way back to the lab unrefrigerated, and wouldn't the hormones, and chemicals breakdown in the meantime. The whole thing seemed like a scam. Blood tests at home. Did they just send you back some random results, because how would you double check them? The refrigerator beeped at me, telling me I had stood there with the door open for far too long. I stared into the white walls of the mostly empty box. Something was always beeping at me.

After my shower, I slipped into sweats, and retrieved a beer from the fridge. Ten minutes later, I just grabbed the whole six pack and sat back down in front of the TV. I flipped through channel after channel. Saturday Night Live. The news. Nothing could hold my interest. I finished my beers and went to bed. I barely slept.

ON MY WAY TO WORK, I stopped at the Post Office, and dropped my package into the blue bin outside. My results should be back in two weeks. It would be interesting to see if my results came back for low testosterone. Maybe I could get my doctor to give me roids. It felt like I had low test. I had no interest in sex, and even less in porn.

I pulled into the parking lot at work. It was already brimming with cars, so I drove straight to the back and started my search. I pulled in between a red Dodge Ram and an old beat-up Toyota Corolla. I gripped the steering wheel. The corporate headquarters looming in front of me.

"Fuck," I muttered.

I had become more and more neurotic since I started this job. Flashes of anxiety, caught up in what people were thinking about me. I had never been like this. I had never even experienced it. Even in high school, I had lived by my own rules and let the chips mostly fall where they may. And in the Marines, I had gotten along fine. Sure, I had gotten smoked, and I had even put boxing gloves on and taught my NCO a thing or two about leadership. I had survived fire fights and slept through rocket attacks. But here, here I drowned in anxiety, drowned in everything.

The thing was, I wanted to do a good job. I was a hard worker, and diligent. But here, there wasn't actually a job to do, there was a job to fake. Fake the tenor of your voice, cop the soft lulling rhythm of an HR lady. Pretend you care about diversity, equity, and inclusion. Pretend you tried to meet that deadline. Save all your email threads requesting help from another department so you could prove you tried. Send multiple emails a day, haranguing people to do their jobs, to give you the products they owe you. And then, when management laughs and shrugs it all off, when they show that they could give two fucks as well, you are still supposed to pretend that you care.

And on top of that, it wasn't a life. This wasn't what I wanted to do. I couldn't be miserable anymore. I just couldn't do it. I would rather be in Afghanistan.

I released the steering wheel and collapsed backwards into my seat. The office building towered ominously in the early morning sun. I rolled down the window and breathed in the fresh air. It was a cool 65 degrees out, and the air was salted and fresh from a slight breeze blowing in off the Pacific. I felt the sun warm the skin on my arm, and watched the golden rays light up the tiny hairs. San Diego had its problems, but it was still one of the most beautiful places in the world.

I called my boss. He picked up on the second ring, and I told him, "I'm not coming today."

"Oh, how come?" he asked. "Is everything alright?"

"Yeah, everything is cool, just don't feel like it," I said.

"Oh, well... you know, you are supposed to give a week's notice when you take PTO."

The correct answer to this was to claim a mental health day. To cop a defeated tenor and ask for it sheepishly... or fake a cough.

Instead, I breathed deeply. Everything around me was golden, and suddenly I felt it. I felt the fire I had not felt it in a very long time. It was an old spark that rekindled the fire of what was just moments ago a smoking ember.

"Hey Luke," I said, "how about you just start out processing me, because this is my two weeks' notice, and I'll be taking PTO for the next two weeks."

"Wait, what. You can't just quit like that!" Luke said. He was exasperated and flustered. "That doesn't give us time to find a replacement."

"Luke," I coaxed, "I'm quitting. It's your problem now, not mine."

He breathed heavily into the phone. Then said, "Can I ask why?"

"Because you're a cuck," I said, "and this place makes me want to blow my fucking brains out."

A long silence on the other end.

I hung up.

And like that a weight lifted off my shoulders. I was free. And the world was again mine. I put the F-150 into gear and pulled out of the parking lot. I hammered the gas pedal when I hit the street, squealing my tires. I smacked the knob on Ford's dash to turn the radio on, and the easy beat of *Take It Easy*, by the Eagles reverberated through the truck.

Today was a new day.

WHEN I RETURNED to the apartment, I pulled the notice off the fridge that I had received two days earlier. It said due to increasing prices in the area the apartment's rates were going up. They were going to charge $150 extra a month. I threw it in the garbage. I had a week before the end of the month, and because I would be breaking the lease, I would lose my security deposit.

But I didn't really care. I didn't give a single fuck. Fuck all of it.

I took out a piece of luggage and filled it with most of my clothes. Any that I didn't wear all that often, I shoved in a garbage bag, which ended up being mostly button ups and polos for work. Besides a tub of my scuba gear and wetsuits, I didn't really have much. The surfboard stood on end in the corner of the room. I hadn't touched it in two years.

I picked up the boxing gloves and tossed them in the tub with my wet suits. All in, I had about two totes worth of shit to my name, a surfboard, and a suitcase stuffed with clothes.

By the time I had gone through my shit it was almost 4:30 in the afternoon. I had worked almost all day, packing and sorting my stuff. Beck would be starting his shift for the night at Ol' Kydd's Tavern.

I PARKED OUTSIDE KYDD'S, just as the sun reached the golden hour, and I felt weightless. Mission Bay lay quietly behind it, a few sail boats rocking to the Marina's gentle lull. The Tavern was an old building. It had been around forever, since the 50's at least, although remodeled and rebooted several times, it still felt dirty and divey.

Inside was crowded, I weaved my way to the bar.

"Hey Ryan!" Meg called my name from across the bar.

I turned around and smiled at her, she waved to me, and then went back to her conversation with a customer. She was a little brunette, tight bodied, with dimples when she smiled and a bubbly personality. For the first time in months, I felt the beginning of arousal. She had tried to flirt for months, but I had ignored it being with Sarah and all, which had of course only encouraged her advances.

I sat down at the bar. Beck was already working. He greeted me with a smile.

"Oh shit, you are here early, and on a Tuesday," he said.

"I quit," I said.

"No fucking way!" Beck said. "Finally." He set two glasses down in front of me and poured a shot of Patron. I toasted him, and then tapped the glass on the bar, before throwing it back.

"I'm canceling my lease as soon as my shit is gone," I said.

"Are you leaving?" Beck asked, suddenly concerned.

"Naww, man. I'll sleep in the truck."

Beck held a finger up as if to say "hold that thought," and moved to the other end of the bar. He poured a drink for someone. When he returned, he said, "You know, I got an extra bed in the boat, and most nights I haven't even been there cus I've been shacking up with that Samantha chick."

"Dude, I'll be fine," I said.

"Seriously man, it'll be chill, like old times." Beck poured me a beer and set it down in front of me. Miller Lite. "Besides, what you doing for money?" he continued.

"No idea. Thinking about just being homeless to be honest."

"I could get you on here?"

I took a sip of beer. "How many hours?" I asked.

"Shit man, what do you want? Twenty a week? We don't need a lot, just someone to cover down."

"Yeah whatever, let's do it. See if you can get me on," I said.

I felt a hand slide gently up my lower back. I could already tell it was Meg, her citrus perfume encased me. I felt her tits press against the back of my arm, and then she leaned fully into me. Spearmint breath.

"Hey babe, hard week?" she said, cracking her gum.

I turned around in my seat. She moved closer

and put her arm around my shoulder, her hips brushing the insides of my thighs. I gave her a big smile, "Yeah, you could say that. What you doing later?" I asked.

She feigned shock at the question, "Aren't you with..." she cracked her gum again and waved her hand as if trying to remember Sarah's name.

"We broke up," I said, shrugging.

She shoved off of me playfully, and said, "We'll see. You might have missed your chance already." I watched her leave, and she put some extra swing in her hips, because she knew I was watching, and she knew I knew she knew I was watching.

I spent the next two hours letting Beck talk me into moving into his houseboat until I was finally drunk enough to accept the offer. Then I moved to the pool table and in between fetching drinks for her tables, Meg would come over and flirt.

When her shift was finally over, I offered to walk her to her car, but we never made it. Instead, we ended up in my truck. Her lips were soft and wet, and we kissed sloppily. I worked my mouth up and down her neck, inhaling her scent, the citrus perfume replaced with her warm musk. Her hands worked the button on my pants, and I felt her tits underneath her shirt. She peeled her shirt off, revealing a sports bra, and once that was off, I buried my face in her soft, round breasts. They were pale compared to the rest of her, and she had tan lines from a bikini. They were bigger than I had imagined, and natural, which was like finding a unicorn in California.

I fumbled for the latch on the seat and slammed it backwards clumsily. This drew a giggle from her. She fell back in the passenger seat, peeled off black skintight jeans, touching her knees to her face in order to get them off, and then crawled over to lower herself onto me. As she did, she bumped the horn with her ass, and two people smoking in the parking lot looked up confused. We both laughed and she dropped her head against my shoulder, before lowering herself onto me.

She moved back and forth, gyrating. She was warm and wet and knew how to move. The windows on the truck fogged.

When we were done, I lay there staring at the foggy windows. I always forgot that happened.

She got dressed, and I cracked the windows, the night air damp and fresh. We smoked cigarettes in the silence.

I SPENT the next week selling off my furniture piece by piece on Facebook marketplace. I charged almost nothing because it was saving me money not taking it to a dump. By the end of the week, my mattress was on the floor and the apartment was empty.

I gave management the heads up I was leaving, and they started to give me lip about some extra fees, because it was short notice. All I said was, "Fine. I don't care."

As I left the office, my phone vibrated in my pocket. It was an Instagram notification. I glanced at it; Sarah had posted a new picture. It was her and her "best friend" from work, Steve. She was sitting on his lap at some bar, and the caption said to new beginnings.

"How fucking long was that going on?" I muttered. I had felt bad about hooking up with Meg less than a week after Sarah had left but not anymore. Fuck her.

At Beck's houseboat, I unloaded my shit. It was a model straight out of the 90's and quite roomy. I felt like Mel Gibson in Lethal Weapon, or Travis McGee, or Brad Pitt in Once Upon A Time in Hollywood. I stowed my shit inside and then stashed my surfboard. The thing was a floating trailer. It had a sink with little prefabricated counters, cabinets with wood laminate doors crammed into every inch of available wall space. Beck used the oven as a pantry and did most of his cooking in a little air fryer and toaster oven combo. The backsplash was stainless steel, and he had a little magnetic spice rack attached. There was a decent sized bench "couch" in front of a small table with thin cushions. In the hold was a triple berthing, Beck said was the guest room, which was simply a cushioned triangle that could sleep three if you really wanted to and extra space for storage. That's where I set up shop.

I pulled a beer from the fridge and stepped out onto the front deck of the boat to watch the sun set. I took a deep breath. The horizon alight in pinks and oranges. Seagulls squawked overhead.

Tomorrow I would wake up, hit some waves, go back to Lion's Gym, and then start work at Kydd's.

But tonight, I would watch the sun set. I breathed easily. More easily than I had in several months.

My blood test had come back. I opened the

email and accessed the results. It turned out my testosterone levels were fine, if not above average. They say that animals, especially monkeys, only masturbate when in captivity. How much different were we? It seemed Test results and parabens and phytoestrogens were a neurosis.

I was free now. In the wind as they might say, and where I belonged.

Chapter Four

Six Months Later

I woke to the gentle rocking of the waves against the houseboat. It was pitch black where I slept. I groped around in the dark until I found my blue jeans on the floor, and then pulled them on. I walked upstairs and flicked the light on in the boat's kitchen. It was 5:30 am. I grabbed the stainless-steel percolator, a gallon of water from the fridge, and the little can of Folgers out of the oven. The oven acted as our second pantry as space was tight on the houseboat and the oven didn't really work all that well anyways. I shoved it all into a plastic sack, then loaded the surfboard into the truck.

Ten minutes later, I sat on the bed of my truck in the parking lot of Oceanside. The percolator attached to a small Jetboil, its propane flame boiling the water for my coffee. The sounds of the Pacific at my back. When it was done, I poured the coffee into a little cup and sat back down, just as the rising sun breached the horizon.

It took nearly three minutes for Helios to tear himself away from Terra. And then he just seemed to just hang there, resting, as if newly born. The sky was red and gilt gold. This happened every morning. And every morning almost everyone missed it in favor of a little more sleep, or because they were getting ready for work, or just because they didn't care, but not me, not anymore. Every morning a god woke from his slumber and climbed the golden steps of heaven.

I took a sip of my coffee, soaking in the fresh air and the new rays. When I finished, I put the jet boil and my cup away, pulled the surfboard free of its rack, and with the red sun at my back, hurried down to the beach.

The water was cold and took my breath away, but I controlled my breathing and ignored the discomfort. The chill energized me. Salt on my lips when the ocean splashed me, and I paddled outwards to the surf line.

When I was far enough out, I watched the waves break. I watched their timing, felt the rhythm of the ocean, and caught my breath. My whole body buzzed, tuned to the same frequency as the ocean.

When I had it timed, I paddled for the spot where the waves broke. As I neared, the water carried me on its gentle rise. I rode the ocean's rising crest, gaining speed. I caught the peak and popped up on the slick board. My toes gripped the foam. And then I was riding. I tensed my belly and felt my breathing slow.

The ocean took me into its trance, and we communed. I took the holy sacrament of life, of single mindedness. I had only ever found that sacrament so easily and readily acquirable in three places - while surfing, when riding a motorcycle, and in the blood heat of fight. Zen. Flow. Battle-calm. They were all the same.

I rode wave after wave, hypnotically, riding the ocean's pulsing thrum back to the sandy shore. Palm trees were my spectators; the morning sky brush strokes of pink and purple. I saw it all, felt it all, the world in all her chaos finely ordered. When I misread the ocean, or when I allowed myself to think, when I noticed her beauty instead of absorbing it, she punished me—she dunked me beneath the surface and held me there. But when I listened to her, she rejoiced, she rewarded me with long moments of silence and the thrill of perfect minutes. The Ocean, as any good seamen will tell you, is a jealous lover. She demands total attention. But, as many a good seamen will also tell you, she was the only woman that will ever reward you for it.

I surfed her for another two hours, and stopped about the same time the beach began to fill.

With the board loaded, I sat on the tailgate and dried myself off. I watched as a group of teens gathered in the parking lot. The girls preened while the boys howled with laughter, and I wondered what they were talking about, I wondered how simple their lives were.

I took a swig from my water bottle and tasted the salt still on my lips. Three "dudes" on skateboards rolled up to the original group of girls and boys, and the energy changed. Like a dark cloud, or a thunderhead on the horizon, the air went static, and the birds left the area.

They all knew each other, that much was clear. But how, I couldn't tell. And then with little warning, the smallest guy from the original group launched himself at the nearest skateboarder, and they all came to blows. A mess of sloppy punches turned to sloppy wrestling, and one of the skateboarders fell flat on his ass because he tripped on his own pants. The girls shrieked for them to stop and I looked for their savior.

A cop on a bicycle rolled up shouting and blowing a whistle, but before he could get off his bike, the teens broke the fight off and scattered in different directions. He tried to park the bike on its kickstand, but as soon as he let go, the bike fell over, and the cop cursed under his breath. He said something to the girls and then let them go. They wandered off shaking their heads and holding each other's hands, and when they were far enough away broke into gleeful skips.

The cop stood his bike up and rode in my direction.

"Did you see that?" he asked. He was overweight and out of breath. Red faced; his brow glistened with sweat.

"Yeah," I said simply, wondering where he was headed with all of this.

"Why didn't you break it up?" he asked in a huff.

"Why did you?"

He stared at me, dumbfounded.

Then he shook his head and pedaled off. I finished my water. Peeled off my suit and climbed into the F-150. With the windows down, I rolled slowly out of the parking lot, wound my way past the lost and forgotten, the teens, the bangers, the hippies, the homeless, and the crackheads. Passed the writhing mass of humanity, one left to simmer for too long on an open stove, and I gunned it down the open road.

AFTER I SURFED, I went to Lion's. I now paid half of my dues by cleaning. I would show up at midnight on Sunday and clean the whole place, spotless. Abdel gave me a key so I could let myself in. But during the days I came to train, there were already guys working out, there were always guys working out. The life of the unemployed.

"It's the Gringo!" Juan shouted at my entrance. "What are we doing today? More surfing? Maybe fishing?"

"Already surfed," I shouted back. I waved to Abdel, and he nodded back. He was holding pads for Charlie. In the locker room, I threw my duffel bag down on the bench. Changed into shorts, and a gray cut off, then wrapped my hands.

I warmed up with sprints, and then some calisthenics. My body was still buzzing from spending the whole morning surfing, so it really wasn't necessary, but it felt good. I was in some of the best shape of my life. Carved from stone. I had abs that belonged to a skinny sixteen-year-old quarterback who had just gone through puberty and had a metabolism that was overcooking.

After calisthenics, I put my gloves on and worked through combos on the heavy bag. I worked until my shoulders burned and sweat ran into my eyes. I worked until the ocean whispered to me, the shadow of her touch remembered, and my vision tunneled. Single-minded.

The five-minute buzzer went off and that's when I saw him. He was standing in the corner of the gym, leaning easily against the wall. He was middle-aged, maybe older, but fit, an easy six foot tall and broad shouldered. He wore gray joggers, and a sand-colored t-shirt. His forearms were thick, like a wrestler's or a farmer's. His hair cut in a close fade; he was military or former. Black bushy eyebrows, that almost made a unibrow sat below a furrowed brow, and somehow matched the thick, heavy handlebar mustache. We made eye contact, but he didn't break it. The buzzer went off again, and I went back to my heavy bag.

"Do you want to spar?" Abdel asked from behind me. He startled me, for I had been focused on the bag. My mind occupied by the weird stranger, I had forgotten form and function, and had instead taken to slugging the bag with wide, heavy hits that rattled the chains.

I looked up. The man was gone from his corner. Like a ghost he had come and went.

"That man? Who was he?" I asked.

"Who?" Abdel asked.

I pointed to the corner where the man had stood, "Over there. He was watching me."

"Ah, an old friend," Abdel said. "But if he ever asks something of you, you should consider it carefully."

"Ask me what?"

"It does not matter, he comes here to watch fighters sometimes," Abdel replied, and then he grabbed me gently by the shoulder, the way a grandfather guides a child. "Come, I need you to spar with Charlie."

Charlie was a lanky dude, black, and formerly a banger. He had given up the life though, had a baby now. Boxing kept him clean. It did the same thing for him, as it did for me, except he still lived in his war zone. He bobbed around in front of me, dancing rhythmically. Anyone who thought the black preoccupation with dance didn't help when it came to fighting, had never fought a black man.

I edged forward, bobbing to my own time, my footwork solid, but not fancy. I threw a jab, then a double. Charlie leaned backwards, just out of reach, his feet still moving. He threw a jab of his own and I blocked it. He had reach on me, at least a few inches. I catalogued all of this in our opening moves.

Then I advanced, throwing a double jab, and then a right cross to the body, which landed with a thlap and left the skin bright red. Sparring wasn't fighting. It was practice. And while I had landed a clean shot, I had still pulled my punch.

"Very good," Abdel said.

Charlie pulled away and we both reset. He was flustered by my last strike, and a bit angry, which was understandable. Anger had taken me a long time to control. Pain had been my switch. And when it was flicked, a red veil dropped over my eyes, I lost logic, and an animal emerged, an animating spirit, the chimps in my ancestry had likely known well. It was an instinct that had served them well, the chimps, and that had saved them many times when caught out on the flat ground of the savannah, a pack of hyenas cackling in the driving rain. Cornered and with nowhere to go, I imagined it was blind rage that had prompted that first chimp to pick up the nearest branch and convert it into a club, or grab a stone and cave in the mongrel skull of its nearest attacker.

Then, no doubt, emboldened by a successful first strike, and drunk on a blood fever, I imagined the chimpanzee had kept going, furiously stringing together a series of heavy blows, until the whole pack lay crippled and dying, howls sounding like screams, cries drowned out by the dull thud of an African monsoon. I wondered if my chimp ancestor had looked down at the bloodied stone in his hand and knew what he started. If he had known the age of weapons had begun. If he had realized the leap that had been taken.

Charlie hit me with a perfect jab. Snapped my head back and I stumbled backwards. Even with the headgear, I saw stars, and I tasted copper. Blood ran into my mouth. He followed up with two shots to the body, and after that I finally covered up, robbing him of any further wins. His eyes gleamed with honor regained, and I felt my own heat rising. My temple throbbed. I pushed forward, off balance, and fighting for control. Two more jabs landed uselessly because I was still covered up.

Then I launched my assault. A jab first, and then an overhand right that caught him square because he had bobbed into it. I followed up with two body shots, aiming for the solar plexus, aiming for pain. Killer instincts fought for control of the bridge, and I was loaded up for another strike, when the whistle blew.

"Reset," Abdel shouted. He knew me too well. He knew everyone too well. If there was ever a man who could push men just past where they needed to go without letting them break, it was Abdel.

We reset. Our eyes met, and I saw the fire of pride dampened. I offered to tap gloves and he accepted. The rest of the session was friendly.

AFTER LION's I picked up Chinese and ordered extra fried rice. On the boat, I scarfed down the takeout and then retired to the hold and passed out. I woke from my nap by 4 pm. Beck's shower wasn't working so I dived into the water, climbed out, used bar soap on my body, and then dived back in. I pulled on my black polo, with Kydd's embroidered on the front, a Yankee Clipper behind it.

I walked in through the back of Kydd's. Sam was bent over the deep fryer in the kitchen, and Pedro was unpacking stacks of little paper baskets, the kind that hold fries, white with red stripes.

"What's going on?" I drawled.

"Another day in paradise," Sam answered.

"Living the American dream!" Pedro hollered back.

I worked my way past the empty cardboard boxes strewn across the kitchen's yellow tiled floor and stopped at the double doors that led to the area behind the bar.

"Is Beck in?" I asked over my shoulder.

"He's in," both answered in unison.

I found Beck already pouring drinks for two blondes at the bar. They both flashed him smiles. When he turned back to see me, he rolled his eyes.

He wasn't getting tipped. I shook my head to confirm, and he nodded. We both started laughing without having said a word.

It takes about three weeks of working at a bar, before you can categorize almost all of humanity by the way they tip. There was the grinch, the guilty, the over eager, and the philanthropist. But my favorite, because it was so perfectly typical, so obvious, but I had never even been aware until I tended bar, was the barbie. Barbies, as Beck and I had nicknamed them, were a certain segment of the female population, who had internalized their looks and attention as being actual currency. How the exchange rate worked, I wasn't sure. But in their universe, a forced smile equaled a 20% tip; I couldn't imagine what a fake orgasm had bought them.

Not all was lost though, because I spotted a guy at the end of the bar. He was a suit. Which meant it was a toss up on whether he was a grinch or not, or at best the guilty. I glanced at him, his hair gelled up in the front, making a cliff of his face, just the way his boyfriend had left it.

"Grinch?" I asked.

"Always," Beck said.

"You know what a negative times a negative makes though?" I asked.

He cocked his head and squinted. I could see the wheels turning.

"A positive," I said grinning.

I asked the Grinch if he needed another, he nodded his head. When I put the beer down, I leaned over and said in a whisper so the girls at the other end wouldn't hear, "Hey buddy, Imma help you out. See those girls over there. They've been eyeing you up all night -"

"Didn't you just get here," the Grinch asked, cutting me off.

I looked at him stunned. "Well, they've been eyeing you up since I got here, what's it matter? Listen up man, I'm going to tell them that you bought their next round, but really, it's on me. Just to get you started, and the rest is all you buddy."

He held his hands up looking exasperated, "Really. I appreciate it. But I don't want you to do that."

"I got you," I said. Then I headed straight for the Barbies and asked them what they wanted; I told them that the gentleman at the end of the bar had agreed to pay for their next round.

"I'll have a vodka-water, w/ lemon," the barbie on the right said. She had a thick valley girl voice.

"And you?"

"Ummm, like let me think, how about a vodka cran," the one on the left responded.

"Cool," I said, ignoring how long it had taken her to come up with the only drink she had ever ordered.

After I slid the drinks onto the bar in front of them, they both leaned over in one synchronous motion and waved to the Grinch. He didn't look pleased, but instead rather resentful, which confused me immensely. He made no move to join the girls. After about five minutes, the girls joined him at the end of the bar, for fear they had been spurned and were now missing out on free drinks. We watched as the grinch suffered through the barbie's attempts at small talk.

At last, the dude stood up, red-faced and distraught, and said, "I didn't buy you those drinks. He did," and pointed at me. "I don't know what kind of scam he's trying to run but I just wanted to be alone. I just broke up with the love of my life," his voice wavered, and I thought he might start crying.

I stood there frozen, like a deer caught in headlights.

The Grinch dug around in his pocket and flicked his cash at me across the bar, then shouted, "I'm gay, you fucking asshole!" and promptly walked out.

The barbies, now the centerpiece of the bar's attention, but not in the way they had wanted, got up as well, and both strung together their own series of expletives revolving around, "what the fuck."

And then like that, they were gone. Beck and I looked at each other, in awe at how monumentally the scheme had blown up in our faces and then burst out laughing. The rest of the bar went back to their drinks and conversation. And the place began buzzing again as if nothing had ever happened. We slowly went back to work, trying not to crack up. Too stunned to fully commit to laughter. But as the minutes went on, and the whole situation replayed, it got funnier and funnier until we could barely look at each other without laughing.

The night drug on and was rather uneventful. We entertained our regulars with the tale of the barbies and the gay grinch.

It was late when I spotted him.

It was the man I had seen at the gym earlier. He wore a button up, with pearled buttons tucked into blue jeans. He looked like a real cowboy with the handlebar. He sat by himself in the corner of the bar, drinking a Miller Lite, and we made eye contact. I could tell he wanted to talk.

"Beck, I'll be back alright," I said.

Beck just nodded and kept working. The bar had thinned out by this time, so I grabbed two Miller's and walked over. He watched me as I approached.

"Sit down," he said in a friendly way.

I pulled out the chair and sat. Handing him one of the beers.

"I saw you at the gym, today," I said.

"And?" he asked.

"Arc you following me?"

"Depends. Are you looking for work?" he said before finishing off the rest of his first beer.

"Not really. Why?" I responded.

"You miss it don't you," he said.

"Miss what?" I asked, but I already knew what he was talking about. I played dumb, because I didn't like games.

"Cowboy shit. They tell you that you shouldn't like it, but we do, at least our breed does," he said.

"Still confused," I said.

"Argentina. It's on the up and up. It's going through the government down there. I'm getting together a group of guys. Can't tell you too much more. Not unless you are in."

"And you? Who are you?" I asked. "And in for what?"

"Mike Hudson," he reached across the table to

shake my hand. "The guys call me Colonel," he continued. I shook his hand. The grip was firm, but there was a glint in his eye. A spark, like I had shook hands with the devil. The man was a predator, and Abdel's warning replayed in my mind.

"Green Berets. Twenty years," he continued. "For twenty years I put up with their bullshit, paid for it with three marriages," he put the bottle up to his lips. "Now it's time to cash in," he said and pointed a finger upwards.

I drummed my fingers on the table. He was right, I did miss it, rather, I had missed it, but to sign up for wet work shit without a clue what I was getting into seemed like a bad idea.

"It was fucked up what they did to you," he continued. "I heard about it when I was getting out. I would have punched him too. Twenty years ago, shit... ten years ago, if you had done something like that, they would have given you a medal. But now, well you know..." he motioned outward to the rest of the bar. But he wasn't talking about the bar, he was talking about the world, and I knew what he meant. "...times change, but men don't."

"Six months ago, and you probably would have sold me, but I have a good thing going on here," I said. "It's been too long."

"Chasing broads, boxing, surfing... You do," he replied, slowly.

It irritated me that he knew so much about my life. It crawled up under my skin like a splinter I couldn't extract. That was his game though.

"But you still miss it," he continued. "You never got your day in the sun. Well fuck em, make cash instead. Shit, you could buy twenty house boats with the cash I'm talking about."

"I'll think on it," I said, and moved to get up.

"You got a passport?" he asked.

"Yeah, why?" I asked.

"You'll need it," he said, and slid a business card across the table. "Don't take too long making up your mind, I leave in two days."

I picked up the card and flicked it. "Cool," I said and walked away.

"Number is on the back," he called after me. "Download Signal first."

I raised the card between two fingers and shook it, acknowledging I heard him.

Back behind the bar, Beck worked a broom underneath the little ledge, fishing out dust bunnies and plastic rings from newly opened bottles.

"What did he want?" Beck asked.

I glanced at the stranger. "He offered me a job."

"Oh yeah. Did you take it?" Beck asked.

"Said I'd think on it."

Beck stopped his sweeping, "Hey uh, I've been meaning to talk to you about something. This might be a bad time, but..."

"Yeah, what?" I asked.

"So, the boat, I think I'm going to sell it," Beck said.

"Fuck me," I muttered.

"Hey man, I'm—"

"It's ok," I cut in. "Seriously, thanks for letting me use it. You gotta do what you got to do though. I get it."

"It's just me and Samantha..." he trailed off.

"You guys are gay for each other huh," I said, and punched him in the shoulder.

"Yeah, pretty gay," he said.

"Let me know how that works out for ya," I said. "I think I'm done chasing women. Well, not chasing, but maybe done catching em."

"Yeah man. I'd sell it to you, but—"

"It's cool. I'll figure something out. Besides, I kind of knew this would happen."

I watched the stranger leave. The Colonel. Dude was goofy, like he walked out of an action movie, or was putting together the A-team.

I pulled out the business card, it simply said ARES Consulting, and above it was the logo, a Spartan helmet, the kind that always showed up on bumper stickers with the words Molon Labe printed beneath. Shit was pretty hokey.

On the back, written in blue ball-point pen, was a phone number. I stuck the card in my pocket.

When I got home that night, I cracked a beer and sat out on the deck of the boat. I listened to the black void and watched the stars that danced above it. I pulled out my phone and downloaded Signal. I put the number on the back of the card into the app's contacts. I looked at the card again. Then I flicked it over the edge of the boat. I slid the phone back into my pocket without texting the number.

"Fuck me," I muttered.

THE NEXT MORNING, I skipped surfing. I was back in the gym. I moved back and forth beneath the string. Dancing, bobbing, throwing a left jab and then a right. So much of boxing was about movement. Being a good boxer wasn't about the hands or the arms, that was all secondary. It was about the feet, the legs, the hips. The hands and arms were merely weapons, the engine was the legs.

"Good morning," Mike Hudson said from somewhere behind me.

I bristled at his unexpected intrusion. I hadn't expected him to be here, hadn't seen him approach. I dropped my hands and turned around.

"Let's find out if you got it," Mike said, and he threw me headgear. His own hands already gloved up.

"Where's yours?" I asked.

"Don't need it."

I tossed my headgear aside as well, and followed Mike to the ring. I tried to hide my excitement. I was going to beat this guy's ass. I hadn't decided why I disliked him yet, or why I liked him, it was a bit of both. Something deep within me was reacting, the shadow of an animal that visited me in my dreams.

Mike was in forest green ranger pants and a loose white tank. He moved swiftly up the steps and dipped in between the ropes. The man was a cat, but still an old one. He warmed up, jumping up and down, waiting for me to follow.

"What's this about?" I asked and climbed into the ring. He smiled wide, like a salesman that had just set the hook.

"I beat you and we get on a plane tomorrow night headed to Argentina," he said. "I want you on my crew."

"And if I beat you?" I asked.

"Then you come, you stay. I leave you alone," he said.

"You leave me alone forever?"

"I'll do whatever the fuck you want princess."

"What if I renege?" I said, ignoring his manner. He was fishing for a reaction.

"You won't." Again, he grinned.

"How do you know?"

"Do you know what they do in zoos to keep lions from getting bored?"

I just looked at him, probably dumbly.

"They give them animal carcasses, puzzle feeders, they hide their food in logs. It's called enrichment. They try to mimic what it's like in the wild."

"Does it work?"

"Not really."

"What does that have to do with anything?"

He shrugged. "Feels self-explanatory."

There was a charisma to him, but also a maliciousness. Somehow, I found myself in the ring with him and not entirely of my own will. I was being led.

"Abdel, start the clock," Mike shouted.

I glanced at Abdel, his face stone. He had warned me. He seemed to know I was now dancing with the devil.

We both moved forward and tapped gloves. I glided backwards. He circled. We were two hawks colliding, fighting over the same field mouse. The small thing quivered between us, our honor, barely enough to feed one.

Mike moved in first and threw a sloppy jab. I bobbed and threw a double back, but he was already gone. He closed the distance again and feinted with the same punch. I counterpunched, but he was gone. Two body shots from my blindside rocked me, one in the ribs and the other in the gut. I stumbled backwards and covered up. Mike let me reset.

He was playing me. I felt that little thing inside me awake. The chimp. Back on the savannah, club in hand.

I marched him down, closed the distance, and threw a left-right-left but he bobbed away. He feinted again and went for another body shot, but I had been waiting—I ducked and rotated inside; his glove grazed me.

When I stood up it was just in time to meet an overhand right. The blow knocked me to the mat.

My head rang. My vision blurred and tunneled. I felt myself climb onto all fours. I was still conscious, just barely, he'd caught me off balance.

I pushed up to my knees.

Abdel counted loudly ringside.

On six I found both my feet and my wits. I stood up and at last understood my situation. Mike was good. He was better than me. I had underestimated the older man, and now he had me. We circled, and this time when he came, I played defense. He threw a jab and I slipped, he feinted, and I rotated.

We were dancing now.

I led him on, not punching back, drawing him closer with each attack until he smelled blood. When he finally pounced, I counter punched. The jab snapped his head back, and I moved in, landing a right hook that made him stumble into the ropes.

He covered up and I focused on the body. And then he had me tied up in a clinch, and it wasn't until he had me rotated around so my own back was at the ropes that I realized he had me trapped. The body shots came in hot and heavy. There was no escape, no room to move. I tried to cover up, lowering my hands.

"Grin and bear it," Mike said.

⁂

When I woke, it was Abdel kneeling over me.

Mike was there too.

Consciousness, bloomed, and I realized my predicament.

"Plane departs at 6:30."

I struggled to speak, to form words.

"How do you know I'll come?" I asked.

"Because you're sick of the zoo."

I watched him leave.

Chapter Five

THE FLIGHT from San Diego to Bueno Aires was 14 hours long. Mike had bought us both seats in business. My first deployment involved a similar, but longer odyssey. We had flown from Baltimore to Ramstein, Germany, and from there, flew to Kuwait, and then into Iraq. It was a two-day trip by the time it was over. Unlike my deployment, I was on this plane for all the wrong reasons, if that was any sign, then good fortune lay ahead.

The stewardess gave her speech about oxygen masks and life jackets, and I turned the paperback in my hands over and over. It was A Princess of Mars by Edgar Rice Burroughs; the book had taken on a special, and superstitious meaning. I had returned to it often. It was one of the few things I had shared with my grandfather. At other times, times like now, reading it had become a ritual, something I did before I embarked on some new season of life. The front cover was stained with what looked like coffee, only I knew that it was blood.

Mike stared out of the window.

"You said Cowboy shit?" I asked, "Cartels?"

"Not like that," he said, "Not like whatever you're thinking. Chinese fishermen. They want us to keep em out, teach them a lesson."

"Why us? They have a coast guard," I asked.

"They just joined China's Belt and Road Initiative."

"So?" I asked. I turned the book over in my hands, feeling the cracked spine.

"They were supposed to join back in 2017, but they didn't. In 2016, their Coast Guard sank a Chinese fishing vessel. It was fishing illegally in their territorial waters. China got mad, threw the whole deal up in the air. Used it as leverage. The illegal fishing is a big problem for Argentina, but an even bigger problem, is not having any capital for new infrastructure. So, they've been letting it slide ever since, but the people are starting to get mad. The fishermen are going to the press to complain. They say there's no more fish. The government is starting to get antsy, they're already sensitive about looking weak on China."

"So where do we fit in?" I asked.

"We're a deterrent."

"Will China know who we work for?"

Mike shook his head no.

"So, it's a black?" I asked.

"Like Africa," the man said. "Ghosts. Pirates. Whatever you want to call us. We're there to make the fisherman think twice and to not get caught doing it."

I felt a twinge of anxiety in my gut. This sounded like more than I'd ever signed up for.

I leaned back in my seat. The Boeing 747 taxied down the runway, and I allowed my mind to drift. The moment the plane left the ground, we were weightless. Mike closed the shutter to the plane's port hole. He wriggled a shot bottle of Jack Daniels out of his cowboy boots and downed it.

How had he got that past security?

"You don't like flying?" I asked.

He crossed his arms and sat back, "Not especially." He lowered his ball cap over his face.

I turned back to my book.

My first deployment had also been my last. It had started on a flight much like this one. In fact, planes had taken on a weird spiritual meaning in my life. I think by association rather than anything overtly spiritual. They had always led me to somewhere significant. At first it was Bootcamp, then it was selection for Force Recon, and after that it was to San Diego, where I was stationed with 2nd Marine Raider Battalion.

Special operations had always been my dream. The goal. And after three years in Infantry, I went through the MARSOC training pipeline. From there I was deployed to Japan, which was less a deployment and more a good ol' boys club, and then to Iraq. And Iraq was where my profession of arms was cut short, way short, but that was a story for another time.

THE PLANE SMACKED down on the tarmac in Buenos Aires. I had finished John Carter and several movies, but not caught a wink of sleep.

Mike gripped the arm rest as if he was prepared

for the whole thing to come apart. Instead, the plane glided over the tarmac for several hundred more feet before screeching to a halt.

"It's actually a good thing when they land that hard," I said.

"Yeah, and why's that?" Mike asked.

"When there is a heavy crosswind, they have to put her down fast and quick, really get those tires to bite into the tarmac."

He just looked at me. "Shut up."

"Now what?" I asked, trying to change the subject.

"We're here for the night. You meet the rest of the team. Then we all fly to Ushuaia tomorrow."

Outside the terminal, I spotted a vending machine and felt the urge to buy a Coke. Mike waved down a "Radio taxi," a little chevy hatchback painted black with a yellow roof. I had just taken out my credit card and was about to swipe it when Mike's baseball mitt of a hand swiped my card right out of my hand.

"What the fuck!" I said.

"Me, what the fuck. You, what the fuck. You can't use any of your own cards here," he pulled out a wad of Argentina cash and handed me a roll of bills. "What do you think this is?" he asked. "This isn't vacation."

"You said we were just contractors?" I asked. This all seemed extra, too extra for a bit of security.

"What didn't you get about black. Dark. Dark like Africa. What other cards do you have. Hand them over." Mike held out his hand.

I fished out my wallet, and he took the whole

thing. He shoved it into his pocket. "Don't worry, I'll get you squared away at the hotel."

The cab was surprisingly nice, a newer model, and even driving through the city I was impressed by Buenos Aires. It was a proper city. The streets were clean, and the people looked mostly happy. Old Spanish architecture lined the streets, some more than others. Mixed in, were buildings with sleek modern design. It conjured an old established feeling that one wouldn't find in any American city built west of the Mississippi.

Our cab pulled up in front of the Savoy Hotel, a baroque building near the city's center. I followed Mike up the front steps, duffel strapped firmly to my back. The hotel was originally designed and built in 1906 which gave it an old school Spanish elegance. The lobby was punctuated by several pillars, the tops of which were graced with carven scrolls and gilt in gold. I was sure it wasn't real gold, likely brass or bronze, but it was impressive, nonetheless.

“Meet me in my room when you are ready,” Mike said, and handed me the key card.

My room was laid out in a more modern style with modern looking furniture, which made sense, after all a hotel room was a hotel room. A small TV was placed in a corner of the room, and the bed faced two enormous outward facing windows. Opposite the tv was a corner desk with a glass top and an antique styled chair. The chair was the only piece that played on the theme of the hotel.

I tossed my things on the bed and ran my hands through my hair. I ran water for my shower and when it was hot enough, stepped in. After my shower, I laid on the bed and fell asleep.

I WOKE up to a rap on the door, I checked the clock. *Shit.*

I stumbled to the door, feeling like death. Jet lag had really taken it out of me. I looked out the peephole. It was Mike. I pulled on a pair of pants and then threw on the same t shirt I had on before, slightly irritated by the wake-up call.

When I opened the door, I found Mike flanked by six others.

"Hey there sleepy head," Mike punched me in the shoulder, "thought we would just meet here instead."

"Yeah, that's... cool," I said, off balance and still waking up.

Mike threw a black duffel on the bed and then introduced me to everyone. "This is Jim Bignell, we call him Tex."

He was a former ranger, short and skinny, and wore glasses. I shook his hand, after which, he pulled from his jeans pocket a small black box the size of a tazer. He unfolded an antenna, hit a button, a light blinked red, and then he started around my room, scanning the walls, the tv, the lamps.

Ben Schmidt, who they called the Hulk, had filed in behind Tex, and it was easy to see why. He was built like a heavy weight champion. An easy 250 lbs., and most of it frame. He towered above me, but his smile was generous, and he had eyes that lacked the wolvishness of the others.

"Ben, Hulk. Call me whatever you like, just not a son of a bitch," the man said softly. He grabbed my hand.

"I'll stick with Hulk," I said.

"Good man." He nodded his approval.

Mike pulled a skinny Arabic looking man towards me. He had black hair shaved close and a wild black beard.

"This is Bahrawar," Mike said. The man extended his left hand, and I reciprocated. "You can call him Psycho. He doesn't understand English."

"Nice to meet you," I said, and the man merely nodded in return.

The last two had already sat down, and Mike turned and pointed at the big blond and said, "That's the Nord. Unlike Ben, you can call him whatever you like." The Nord had long blond hair that reached his shoulders, and a short beard specked with red.

"Liam. Hey." The Nord said simply. He gave a small two-fingered salute.

"The other," Mike continued, "is Mex, because he's Mexican, which should be obvious."

He gave me a head nod, and merely said, "My real name is Angel."

"Alright, Christmas time," Mike said, grabbing the briefcase and unzipping it. "Phones on the bed."

Everyone threw their phones on the bed. I looked around, unsure what was happening, and then added mine to the pile.

"Great," Mike said. He scooped up all the

phones and put them in a Ziplock bag, which he handed to Tex.

"Do we get those back?" I asked.

"Not a chance," Mike replied with a smile. "Now, each of you get one of these." He ripped open the duffel and pulled an orange box out. "It has satellite capability. No calls home, and no contact with anyone you knew, at least not until we are done."

Mike pulled several more boxes from the duffel and tossed them to each of us. They were bigger than normal phones but not overly cumbersome.

"The phones are preloaded with everyone's number," he continued, pulling one of the boxes out. He clicked it on and waited for it to boot.

"This app," Mike turned the phone screen towards everyone, "the fire icon will wipe the phone and brick it if you get caught up."

Next, Mike pulled out paper plane tickets and handed them out. "We all fly down to Ushuaia separately so as not to draw attention. Argentinian intelligence will pick you up outside the airport. Look for a black sedan and a gentleman in a green ballcap. He'll take you to Ushuaia Naval Base, and from there we take a helicopter to our new home."

"How long is the gig?" Mex asked.

"Four months."

"What about passports?" Nord asked.

"Right here," Mike pulled a bundle of red booklets from his bag and undid the rubber band. He flipped each one open and then tossed them to their owners. "It's a new year why not a new you."

I looked at mine. Jack Randolph. That had to be the fakest name I had ever seen.

"Jack Ryder? Really?" the Nord asked.

Heads shot up around the room.

"You're all Jacks," Mike said. "My one-eyed Jacks."

"Jack Sanchez?" the Mex said. "Do those names even go together?"

"Now, we talk money," Mike said, handing each of us a business card with a QR code.

I turned it over in my hand. It was a string of numbers and on the back was a series of words. "That is your crypto wallet. Bitcoin will be deposited to your account as we pull jobs. An even million each when all said and done. Don't lose that, otherwise your money is gone. Better yet, sear it into your brain, because boys, there's no backup for those."

"Fuck me," the Hulk muttered.

Mike clapped his hands. "And or expenses, use these." Mike flipped each one of us a prepaid Visa.

I watched as the crew filtered out of my room. On the bed next to me was my new life. A new name, a new phone, and a new bank account. I spent the rest of the night memorizing my crypto account, and when I finally fell asleep, I dreamed the numbers and the words.

Chapter Six

Ushuaia was founded at the southernmost tip of South America. The Spanish had referred to it as "fin del mundo" or the "end of the world." The city itself sat on the bank of the Beagle Channel, named after Darwin's famous expedition. The entire island chain was called Tierra del Fuego or the "Land of Fire" by the Spanish explorers that had first observed an archipelago covered in native cookfires.

As the plane circled above, I stared out my window. It was all mountains and water punctuated by beaches and plains. A fantasy land captured in a bottle. The Martial Mountains towered above the strait. Clouds whispered over their peaks the same color as the whitewater below.

Once we landed, I stared out the window as the plane taxied to our terminal. The building, shaped like a very long and stretched out pyramid, was surprisingly small. Its roof was covered in blue corrugated steel and large glass skylights, matching the color of the sky behind it. Its eaves nearly touched the ground. Its architecture was surprisingly modern for a place sitting at the literal edge of the world.

That thought gave me pause, and a wave of sadness washed over me. The same dread whose cold clammy hand had brushed the back of my neck upon finding a Starbucks at the Cairo International Airport. Every day the world shrank a bit more. Place me anywhere on the globe and I would likely feel claustrophobic.

The same impulse that had driven man forward, that had tamed wilderness after wilderness, had been the very thing's destruction. Adventure was a primal desire for space.

These were feelings I had always had. It was the thing that had driven me and my friend into the woods behind our house.

Tye had lived next door to me, and since we were the same age, we had become fast friends. But something had happened to his Dad, so he only lived with his Mom, and my parents watched him quite often.

We would disappear into the little wood, and having found a spot where the earth was soft, take to digging into the side of a hill. Below us, what we called the river, was but a tiny drainage ditch. It was above this mighty river that we built our fort. We made a dugout in the side of the hill, no more than five feet wide and maybe a yard deep. We worked for weeks, shoveling dirt all day, and only took breaks to throw rocks at one another, or to form hunting parties and chase squirrels that ventured into our territory.

Eventually, when we had enough of digging, we would gather sticks and break them off at a similar length. We drove these sticks into the ground at the edge of our hole with an overly large stone, which we had dubbed Rock Hammer. These formed the walls of our fort, and when it was done, I remember having seen nothing as beautiful.

I dare anyone to show me a happier boy than me, sitting in a dirt hole dug into the side of a hill and peering over a rampart made of sticks and brush, wooden sword in hand, and imaginary enemies skulking among the trees.

Susy lived across the street, and she had once tried to join us in the woods, but as a matter of course Tye and I never let girls into our fort. We chased her off by waving sticks and throwing mud clods. We had let her younger brother come, but only on the condition that he followed our orders. It was our fort, and Tye and I had agreed to share leadership.

For some boys, whose energy wells up inside them, sitting still was as painful as pins and needles. Tye and I were such boys. At school we often acted out, playing pranks, at first upon each other, and then after they separated us, on whoever was nearest.

I remember punishment had been doled out via a system called red light green light. But the lights weren't lights at all, but colored strips of paper. Every day you started with a green strip under your name on the wall, and if you were bad then they gave you a yellow, and if you were even worse they gave you a red. We almost always ended the day with a red. But all that really happened was that the teacher called your parents, which always ended worse for me than Tye. But the funny part of this system, was that you could get your green slip back by doing something, "good." For me and Tye, this had often seemed an impossible task. With no imaginary monsters to slay, or fort to defend, the definition of good felt like a word for submission. The other children, realized "good," was often as simple as telling the teacher on me and Tye.

These are not things I could put into words at such an age, but in hindsight they made me wonder.

Eventually, my parents had said that me and Tye were no longer allowed to play together, and even worse the school moved him to another classroom.

One day, Tye no longer seemed the same. The light in his eyes was gone, and he no longer liked to play swords, or chase dragons. He told me that he no longer got in trouble, and that his mom had started to give him medicine. What medication this was I don't know. Ritalin probably. Slowly, we drifted apart, having less and less in common.

Tye committed suicide his senior year of high school. I joined the Marines a year later.

I had often felt guilty about him. If only I had never let us drift apart. I could have helped him. Looking back now I understood that Tye's fate could have been my own. I understood who killed him, and it had not been himself. I had watched it all happen in the slow motion of a decade. What had started as Ritalin and a hyperactivity disorder grew into a basket of SSRIs meant to treat his anxiety and depression.

And this is what I remembered as I looked at this monstrous pyramidal terminal. A temple to civilization. A temple to suffocation.

The plane lurched to a stop breaking my reverie, and I waited my turn to deboard, but my mind was still heavy with thoughts of Tye.

Inside the terminal, I asked a lady for directions to pick up, and she merely pointed at the glass doors in front of me. I was already there. Of course, I was. The place felt smaller once inside.

I scanned for my ride but didn't see a black sedan or a man in a green ballcap. It was a balmy 55 degrees outside, warm for here. I was still spoiled from San Diego. I rubbed my hands over the slick sleeves of my fleece lined jacket, but still the cold seeped into my body and hung in my pockets.

January through April was considered summer in the southern hemisphere, but down here, 700 miles away from Antarctica it always stayed somewhat cool. It was 6 p.m. and the sun had yet to reach the golden hour. It wouldn't set completely until after ten.

A black sedan pulled a U turn in front of me. I gathered my bags, a duffel and an overly large piece of checked luggage. All mostly stuffed with cold weather gear. A man in a green ball cap exited the passenger side door and motioned me towards the trunk.

I shoved my bags into the back of the car and said, "Buenos tardes."

The man muttered something to himself in Spanish, but I made out the words "spooks" and "gringo." He spat onto the ground, and yanked open the rear passenger door, motioning for me to get in.

His face was pock marked, brows thick black and bushy. His eyes pooled with a deep resentment I hadn't seen since Iraq. I hesitated, looking at the empty back seat. The driver of the sedan turned around to look at me and with a wide smile waved me in.

My eyes darted for a way out, but I was already in, propelled forward by some unseen force.

This whole thing wasn't about the money. It was about the edge. It was the edge of the wave just before it breaks, when the abyss hangs beneath you, and suddenly, life is about living and surviving, and if you are lucky—thriving—and everything else seems meaningless, because it mostly is.

The inside of the sedan was spotless but smelled like cigarettes. The soldier behind the wheel glanced back at me in the rearview mirror and chuckled. He was obviously enjoying the drama. His partner, sitting in the seat next to him, was still visibly upset and clearly disturbed by my presence.

"He doesn't like the compañía my friend," the driver said back to me.

His partner shot him a dirty look.

"Many here lost family to the compañía," my driver continued.

"Compañía?" I asked, holding up my hands.

"Si, Senor," the driver said, but he didn't elaborate.

OUR HELICOPTER WAS an AS332 Super Puma, old school and beefy. The others were already standing around outside of it when we arrived.

The sedan had barely stopped before I popped

open the door and rushed around to the trunk. I helped myself to my bags and caught the evil eye of green ball cap. I didn't break eye contact and he looked away.

"Thought you would never make it," Mike said.

"How long have you guys been waiting?" I asked.

"Only five hours," the Nord responded.

"I'll make sure you're the first one to fly out," Mike said, sarcastically.

"Fuck you," the Nord said.

"Ah looks like you'll be last one out then," Mike hit back.

"Yeah, that's what I thought," the Nord said.

I handed my bags off to the copilot who stuffed them in the cargo hold of the helicopter. I watched as he put his full body weight behind them to get them to fit and then slammed the door closed. The pilot started the helicopter, which coughed and snorted before roaring to life, the rotor whipping above us. It flung a fine grit off the asphalt that stung our faces. I pulled my Oakley's down onto my eyes.

Ten minutes later we were airborne. I adjusted the green headset over my ears. The headsets allowed everyone, including the pilot, to talk to each other with the built-in mic, but it was mostly just ear protection.

Psycho stared silently out the window. He hadn't spoken since I met him in the Hotel. He was like a kid at the window though, his posture straight, eyes alert. He took it all in excitedly as the beautiful land fell away below us. There was a weird childlike innocence in his eager posture, an innocence that disappeared every time I glimpsed his eyes.

Hulk looked like he was already asleep, and Mex wiped his glistening brow nervously, and when the helicopter banked or bounced unexpectedly his hands shot downwards to grip the seat.

"How long to get there?" I asked Tex. He was sitting across from me.

"Couple of hours. Shouldn't be too bad," he said.

"What did you do before?" Mex asked.

"Marines. 2nd Raider Battalion," I replied.

"I was Rangers."

"What was everyone else?" I asked.

"101st, Combat Medic," Hulk replied.

"You're big enough to carry our fat asses out," I said.

Hulk chuckled.

"Rangers," Tex said.

I looked at Nord.

"SEALs. I'm the boat driver," he responded.

I didn't bother with Mike. I already knew he was Special Forces from the plane ride together. I pointed to Psycho, but he didn't seem to notice, engrossed as he was in the window.

"He was Afghani Special Forces," Mike responded. "Doesn't speak English, but he's bright. Pulled me out of more than one tight spot."

Mike said something to him in Farsi, and Psycho responded back with his signature scowl and an even colder smile.

"His whole family was killed by the Taliban. He paid them back seventy times seven," Mike said, turning back towards me. "Now he rides with me.

He wouldn't make it a year if he had stayed in country."

I nodded to Psycho. He nodded back, his eyes ancient, set too close together. They were the eyes of a cold-blooded killer. I had only seen the look a few times before. He was a man from another time, from the rootstock of those that had stood against Alexander, beat back the British, the Soviets, and—us. At every turn, civilization had tried to drag the Afghanis out of their tribal ways and into the glaring light of the 21st century, but their roots were too deep.

"It was fucked up what we did to them," I said.

"They wanted it more than us. I think they earned it," Mike said.

"And what about him?" I asked.

"He's not the first warrior to pick the wrong side," he paused, then added, "maybe there is no wrong side for warriors."

There was about an hour's worth of sunlight left when the helicopter shot over a bunch of hills and we were quite suddenly flying over the Atlantic. We circled around to land and approached a small, sheltered cove. This was it. Where Patagonia met the Atlantic.

Two black patrol boats were anchored next to a rickety looking dock. Set a couple hundred feet back from the water were three aluminum Quonset huts. To the left of those, an earthen pad obviously meant for the helicopter. The pilot gently guided the bird towards it.

Upon landing, we piled out of the chopper and immediately took to unloading our things. I waited for the others to gather theirs. This was base camp, and the location couldn't have been more beautiful. The sun had just passed below the hills behind us, the ones that hid this place. It was a small circular bay with a narrow entrance that let out to the Atlantic beyond. Waves broke in frenzied crashes just beyond the mouth of it. The air was fresh and clean, and the water lapped doggedly at the shoreline, striking a gentle chord to the drumbeat of the waves beyond.

A small ATV trail snaked up the hills behind us and then disappeared. Where there wasn't grass, there were large gray stones, most of which were covered in bracken. Canelo trees whispered in the breeze; their branches already covered in white flowers for it was the end of spring.

"Alright, let's get you fucks set up," Mike said.

He showed us to the bunk house which was the nearest Quonset. Mike flipped a light switch and a couple fluorescents flickered to life. They hung precariously from the curved ceiling. The plywood floors creaked underfoot.

The Quonset was portioned out via flimsy plywood walls into rooms. Each room had a bed, a chair, and a giant footlocker. I picked the one at the far end and dumped my bags onto the bed.

"This is where you sleep. Mine's in the office, back of the command post. We do have electricity, because of the generators, but if you don't keep feeding them diesel then you aren't going to have lights. Or heat for that matter."

"What about water?" the Nord asked.

"Set your shit down, and I'll show you," Mike said.

Mike showed us the generators set back behind

the Quonset huts. They were sheltered by a piece of sheet metal screwed into the back of the hut to keep the water off. Then he walked us down by the boats where three elevated fuel storage tanks were set back from the water's edge. One green and two red.

"Green is potable water, but that's for drinking, so I suggest you get used to bathing in the ocean," Mike said.

"Ah fuck me," Mex said.

"And the red ones?" the Hulk asked.

"Diesel," Mike said, and turned to point at the boats. "For these."

"You did good, Mike." the Nord said. His eyes bright at the sight of the boats. He hadn't even bothered looking at the tanks.

The boats were matte black and muscular, like something out of a movie. Something Bale's Batman would use if he'd ever needed a boat. Each one about 15 yards long from stem to stern, an enclosed cabin, and an open rear deck. They were all cut in hard angles.

"Are they stealth?" I asked, only half joking.

"Designed to have a low RCS," Mike said. "They're beauties, huh?"

The Nord jumped from the rickety pier onto the deck of the nearest one and gave a sharp low whistle.

"Barracudas from Safehaven Marine," Mike continued. The Nord disappeared inside the cabin, and Mike continued, "they'll do 40kts. Got a range of over 200 nautical miles. Seat up to eight at a time."

"Power?" Tex asked.

"Pair of Caterpillar C7.1 diesel engines."

"And guns?" I asked.

Mike smiled at me and then tossed the Nord a set of keys, "show him the guns." The Nord snatched them out of the air and disappeared back inside the cabin.

The boat purred softly. Then with an electric whir, two doors lying flat on the front of the boat, slowly opened skywards, blooming like a deadly mechanical flower. A turreted gun rode its platform upward and clicked into place. The gun slowly rotated on its turret until we were all looking down its three barrels.

"A remote controlled, gyroscopically stabilized GAU-19. Electrically driven, three-barrel rotary heavy machine gun. Fires .50 BMG. And that one," Mike turned to point at the other boat, "That's our bruiser. She's got the MK 19."

Tex whistled, and the Hulk laughed with delight. The MK 19 was a 40 mm belt-fed automatic grenade launcher.

"You wanna take her out?" Mike asked.

"Fuck yeah, let's go." Tex said.

There were seats for eight. I buckled myself into the shock mitigating seat. At the front of the boat was a seat for the driver and his copilot.

Mike sat in front of the boat's yoke and gently pushed down on the throttle. The boat pulled forward gently and then hit another gear and surged forward tossing me hard into the seat. The cabin was climate controlled and fully enclosed.

"The cabin is rated BR6 for ballistic protection," Mike hollered over his shoulder.

"What's BR6 mean?" Mex asked.

"Anything over 7.62mm and you might be fucked," Mike said.

Me and Mex looked at each other and he pursed his lips as if to say not bad.

Mike tapped the large display set in the boat's carbon fiber dash and said, "It's also equipped with FLIR Thermal and night vision infrared cameras."

By this point we had reached the mouth of the bay, and the boat pierced a wave head on, water washing over the windshield and running quickly off the boat's hull. Mike flipped the wipers on, and then we were on open water.

The boat slid smoothly across the water, piercing one wave, and then riding another. Occasionally, as a wave dropped out from beneath us, we'd be suspended in the air, and my belly would drop out beneath me, and then the boat would crash into the water with a heavy thump that shook my whole skeleton despite the shock absorbent seats.

Out on the water, Mike brought the boat to a crawl and then a stop. He clicked the engines off and we unclipped our belts and walked out onto the open deck. The seas were relatively calm, and the sun had just begun to set, lighting the sky in pinks and purples. The water lapped lazily at the sides of the boat, and save for the sounds of the sea, it was completely silent. Eerily silent. Peaceful. In the distance was the shoreline, and I could just barely make out the tiny gap in the hills where our little cove was located.

"This is it boys," Mike said. "This is Mar Argentino."

Chapter Seven

The other two Quonset huts were the "command post," and "armory." The Armory mostly contained pallets of dry foodstuffs, gear, ammo, and explosives. We gathered in the command post at 2100. At the head of the room was a massive whiteboard with an equally massive map of Argentina and its sea plastered on the back.

The seating arrangement was lawn chairs.

"You know, this is the most comfortable chair I have ever gotten a briefing in," Mex said as he sat down.

The others filed in after me. Mike was already working at the desktop computer in the front corner of the Quonset. His eyes flicked back and forth between the dual monitors, a large coast guard radio going off behind him.

"We got a tip about a Chinese boat working its way back towards us," Mike said. "Been tracking it all day through its AIS. The Coast Guard says it has turned its AIS off several times in the last two weeks as it nears Argentina's territorial waters."

AIS is the automatic identification system. A

ship transmits its position through AIS so other ships are aware of its location. The signal is received and transmitted via ground station and satellite. Commercial fishing vessels, like most other large vessels, are required by international law to broadcast their position with the system.

"Nord, you and Hulk are going to work The Bruiser," Mike said. The boat carrying the MK 19 had been affectionately named The Bruiser. "Everyone else comes with me on the Ares."

"How are we running this show?" I asked.

"Quietly, if we can," Mike said. "We're going to shadow the boat just outside of visual range, but if it turns off the AIS, we have to beat feet to where it last was and hope they didn't go lights out."

"Yeah, but how are we going to take her?"

"We approach in an inflatable RIB and then climb up the sides. She should have a steel rung ladder built into her portside based off old imagery. We go up. Take the cabin before they can send any messages out."

"And that's it? They turn off their AIS and its goodnight. We don't have to confirm what they are doing?" I asked.

Mike smiled with the same wolfish grin he had given me across the ring in our boxing match. "This isn't Afghanistan. Or Iraq. We don't exist. We're God out here. We're karma. Force Majeure. We're the consequences for actions."

Mike bent over and picked up a large Pelican case. He unclipped the latches and handed out NVGs. "We leave in two hours. Make sure your rifle is on the right boat. No excuses. We go in hot and heavy and get out."

I grabbed a pair of NVGs and steadied my breathing.

I SAT in the back of the Ares directly behind Mike. Mex sat in the seat across from me, and Tex sat by Mike.

Psycho sat by himself behind all of us. I didn't like having Psycho behind me. But I was beginning to think that was the point. Psycho was Mike's dog. He heeled at his command, looked to him for direction, and only responded to Farsi. I hadn't seen it at first. I had taken things at face value. But I saw the power in it now. Or maybe it was just the fact I couldn't shake the idea of a green on blue attack. Too many had died that way.

We navigated exclusively by the boat's navigational panel for the night was moonless and both boats had all their lights off. The Barracuda plunged headlong through the black void, and where the sea met the sky was uncertain, for it was dark out and all looked like one long shuddering abyss. I pulled a pill bottle from my cargo pocket and shook two of the tiny tablets into my hand. Dramamine. Then I washed them down with a swig of water from my canteen.

Tex held a tablet with what looked like a satphone antennae plugged into the tablet's charging port. He was tracking our target on the AIS. Just a small red dot in a sea of blue. He occasionally read off coordinates to Mike, who would then punch them into the boat's nav system and adjust course.

A hand touched my elbow, it was Mex.

"Give me some," he said.

I handed him the Dramamine, and waited as he fished out the pills.

"This shit is wild," he whispered.

I gripped the side of my seat and controlled my thoughts. Sweat beaded up under my Kevlar and soaked my shirt. Somehow, I felt hot and chilled at the same time. Claustrophobic. Like I was trapped in a tin can, and someone had kicked me down a bottomless well. I concentrated on my breathing.

"Can you turn the heat down?" I asked Mike.

"It's already off, buddy." Mike responded.

Another hour came and went, before Mike pulled the boat to a crawl.

"Get some air," Mike said. "We'll wait here for a while."

Mex and I unclipped our belts and popped the little side door. I bent to get through it and still bumped my NVGs clipped on to my helmet on the top of the frame.

The boat rocked gently in the water, and I took a deep breath. The chill air feeling like a tall drink of water. I was thankful to no longer be locked in the boat.

"You ready?" Mex asked.

"Yeah," I responded slowly. Despite the sea sickness, and the cloying claustrophobia, this is what I loved. Out here, the slow suicide of a cubicle was a distant memory. Out here, my only concern was making it through the night. Out here, there was something about stakes that made life worth living. To be absent stakes was to be absent life. Man can't live on bread alone.

Mike stepped out onto the deck.

"Why'd you name her Ares?" I asked.

In the black of night, I could feel rather than see him grin.

"Scholars say that Ares wasn't particularly liked by the Greeks. That he represented rage, aggressiveness—thirst for battle. But he was esteemed in Sparta."

"And we're Spartans, eh," I asked. I dug around in my pocket for the can of Copenhagen and pulled out a pinch, shoving it in my bottom lip.

"I think Athens got sick of getting their ass beat by Sparta, and that's why they hated Ares. They loathed the patron god of Sparta. And because the Athenians had all the scholars and politicians, shit even Homer, what do we get to read now. Just a bunch of Athenians kvetching about the God of War."

My head was swimming as the nicotine and dramamine worked other. I spat into the Atlantic.

"What about Athena?" I asked. "Wasn't she the goddess of military victory?"

"Yeah, and wisdom," Mike said. "More Athenian bullshit. You know why so many guys come back fucked up?"

"PTSD?" I asked.

"Yeah, that," Mike said. "It's because they worshipped the wrong god."

I started to argue but held my tongue, curious where he was going with this.

"These guys go out there thinking they are serving truth, justice, the American way. Whatever that is. But the battlefield is owned by Ares, it's his church, always has been. There's no truth out there.

No justice. Only blood. It's a disease of the spirit. All that other shit comes later."

Tex stepped out of the cabin; his face illuminated by the low glow of the iPad he held in his hands.

"You got em?" Mike asked.

"They just went dark," Tex said.

We piled back into the Barracuda, and Mike fired the engines so that again I could hear their soft familiar purr. Tex read off the last known coordinates to him, and we pulled off in the direction of the vessel. Tex lifted his push to talk radio and let the Bruiser know it was go time.

Mike laid into the throttle and the Barracuda bolted forward throwing everyone backwards into their seats.

Tex mapped a quick search area based off of where the boat had turned off its AIS, where Argentinian waters started, and the ship's last known heading. He uploaded it from the iPad to the boat's nav system.

Over the push to talk, he gave the other boat the grids for the four corners of the box and told them to start searching the southern half while we took the North.

No less than ten minutes later, the radio crackled, and Hulk's voice came through, "We found them. Eyes on."

"Alright, give us the grids," Tex stated.

The radio crackled and went static.

"What the fuck was that?" Mike said.

"Come again?" Tex said into the radio.

There was no answer.

"Here I got it," Mike said. He flipped screens on

the boat's dash and brought up the Bruiser's position. "We'll just meet them there."

***

Our Barracuda slowed as we pulled up alongside the Bruiser. She was sitting silently in the water. Mike killed the engines. I pulled my NVGs down over my eyes and flicked them on. The inside of the boat flickered green. We all moved out onto the deck. The others looked like three-eyed aliens.

In the distance I could see the Chinese fishing vessel, all lit up like it was Christmas. She was probably no more than a mile away from us, but it was hard to tell.

"We lost you on the radio," the Hulk shouted.

"Same. We found you though," Tex shouted back. "It must have been interference."

Mike readied the inflatable RIB at the back of the boat. The little electric air pump whirred as it slowly inflated. Ten minutes later it was ready. We handed our Barracuda off to Tex.

Myself, Mex, Mike, Psycho and the Hulk would board the ship.

Mike worked the little motor at the back of the boat and floated us over to the Bruiser. The Hulk lowered himself down into our RIB. He was so heavy the boat visibly leaned on his side. Psycho moved to the other side to balance things out.

Mike gave the RIB's outboard motor a little gas and we peeled away from the others.

By this point, it had been an hour since the fishing boat had gone dark. We had found the fishing vessel 5 nautical miles inside Argentinian waters and could tell it was getting ready to start fishing.

"What if they spot us?" I asked Mike, raising my voice over the sound of the outboard motor.

"They won't. They will all be looking over the starboard side as they work the nets," Mike said. "We're looping around portside."

He turned the boat so that we were no longer headed towards the vessel but travelling parallel to it. The inflatable RIB skipped easily over the water, and I was thankful that the ocean was at least sort of calm tonight. There was no way we could do this in any rougher seas.

Having looped wide around the vessel, we made our approach on its portside. I checked my weapon by feel. It was an M4A1, equipped with a PEQ 16 laser aiming unit, an NT4 suppressor, and an Eotech SU-231A.

The inflatable RIB skipped over a wave and came down hard, sea spray washing over us. As the water soaked through my clothes, I got a sense for how cold it truly was. Something I had so far been able to ignore. I was glad for the wetsuit I'd worn as a base layer. The night air turned frosty. My hands were cold and I tried to warm them up by sticking them in my pants, afraid that they would be locked up when it came time to do work topside.

We closed on the ship quickly, and several feet away Mike eased up on the outboard motor bringing the little RIB to a crawl. He guided the boat up alongside the ship, which although anchored, still moved back and forth with the slow motion of the ocean.

The ship towered above us, and Mike secured the RIB to the side of the boat. The first rung of the portside ladder was just out of reach without jumping as it was designed to be used while the ship was in dock.

To board we had to wait until the ship creaked and dipped in the slow waves, and then at the peak of the wave, which also slammed our RIB up into the side of the ship, we had to jump to catch that very bottom rung. This was no small feat as we were all loaded with gear, and more than that, jumping from a barely stable platform and trying to catch the moving rung of the ladder.

Mike went up first, then Mex, Hulk merely grabbed the rung his height negating any need to jump. Psycho scrambled upwards, surprisingly nimble for his small frame.

And then it was my turn, I jumped, and barely caught hold of the ladder. With all my strength, I pulled myself up enough to grab the next rung. I now had both of my hands on separate rungs, and my boots planted firmly on the side of the ship.

She had so far heaved back tipping away from our side because of the ocean's movement, but now she dipped back down, even further than she had before, and I felt my boot fill with cold sea water. The rungs were slick, condensation having frozen on them, but I was wearing gloves with rubber studded palms which helped my grip. At last, I got both feet on rungs of the ladder and felt much more stable.

I barely noticed the cold, for I had already broken a sweat, and my heart pounded, sending waves of warm adrenaline through my veins.

The others worked their way up the side of the ship, and I followed behind, already dreading the fact that we would have to come back down this ladder at some point.

Had this been a full up military operation we would've perhaps inserted via helicopter. But this wasn't a special forces operation. This wasn't even a real military operation. It was piratical, we were operating in the wind.

The name of this game was adaptability.

As I climbed, I watched Mike disappear over the top edge of the boat. Then the others followed. At the top, I caught the boat's railing and pulled myself up.

Hulk grabbed me by the body armor with a powerful grip and hauled me onto the ship.

"Thanks," I said breathlessly. Suddenly, I realized just how out of shape I was. But not only that, how out of practice I was. The Marines were all practice. Every moment of every day was dedicated to training. Training for the mission. And while it required physical fitness, it mostly required the mental kind. A discipline I had forgotten about during the years of office work and my last six months of living like a hobo.

I felt the icy cold fingers of fear trace the back of my neck. The churn in my stomach as I showed up for a test I hadn't been studying for. I was second guessing myself. Second guessing my decisions. The trip up the side of the boat had rattled me, shaken my confidence.

I took a couple of deep breaths, holding a four count at the top and bottom, and then forced all these thoughts out of my head. If I didn't get my head right, I was going to get myself killed, or even worse, one of the others killed.

We had boarded near the back of the ship. It was dark, not very well lit. I flicked my NODs up as did the others because there was too much ambient lighting.

Mike moved forward, rifle held at the ready. We climbed the stairs towards the bridge. The aft deck was level with the bridge, which lay before us. This was a commercial trawler and as such the bridge was near the middle of the boat.

Down below, several Chinese fisherman worked beneath a string of bright white incandescent lanterns.

Mike crouched in a shadow, and we grouped up beside him.

"Me and Hulk take thc bridge. You three start working through the crew," he whispered.

He set off at a crouch leading us forward. The bridge was located near the midpoint of the ship. We watched Mike and the Hulk work their way to a set of bins and wait until the nearest fisherman turned their back. Then they were off.

When Mike and the Hulk disappeared into the bridge, I worked my way forward, Mex and Psycho on my flank.

I walked up behind the first fisherman, and letting go of my rifle pushed him roughly into the railing. I let him turn around and when he saw me there in full kit he panicked. Before he could scream I laid a right cross on him. Gently, I let his unconscious body slide down against the railing.

Mex zip tied his hands and placed a gag on him,

then left him on his side in case he threw up. We didn't want him drowning in it.

The next two we did in much the same way, and then a fourth working a little way up the line spotted us.

He ran off screaming something in Chinese, and Psycho took off after him.

Then it was pandemonium. Gunshots came from the direction Psycho had ran. The dull bark of his silenced rifle answered barely discernible over the noise of the ship's trawlers.

Another crackle of gunfire, and the steel bin in front of me erupted in sparks, the sharp zing of ricochets lighting up the inside of my head. I hit the deck hard and rolled to cover. It was the unmistakable sound of an AK-47.

Mex scrambled up beside me.

"What the fuck happened?" he shouted.

"He got away," I said.

"Did you know they would be armed?" Mex shouted back.

I just shrugged.

Again the barking AK and again our steel bin got thumped with a barrage of bullets. When it was done, I peeked.

A man was clumsily trying to reload. Half of him obscured behind a big blue water barrel.

"Moving," I called, and twisted around the corner.

He saw me coming and dropped the rest of the way behind the barrel.

It didn't matter though, because I mag dumped his cover and the water barrel made poor cover. About halfway through the mag the whole thing burst, water pouring out in every direction. I kept shooting until blood mixed with the water.

I kicked it over to reveal a dead Chinese man, his still unloaded AK in the bloody water next to him.

Again, came the dull bark of Psycho's rifle, more Chinese shouting and then the Kalashnikov fell silent.

Mex and I moved forward. We found that the rest of the fisherman had taken cover in a corner of the ship. We motioned for them to come out and lay on the deck which they did. None of them were armed.

Psycho came up beside us. He was smiling. He nodded to me which I took to mean that his guy had been handled.

We zip tied them and left them lying flat on the deck of the boat.

Mex and I headed towards the bridge to meet up with the others when we heard it. The silenced thwap thwap of Psycho's weapon.

I turned and ran. But it was already done, in just a couple of seconds he had strafed the prone bodies with automatic fire.

I grabbed the rifle from him and shouted, "what the absolute fuck." He fought back, stomping on my insole as we wrestled for control of the rifle.

Finally, I got it free, then I used it like a club, smashing the butt into Psycho's stomach. He doubled over, puking hard.

A huge shadow entered my peripheral. The shadow picked me up from behind. It was the Hulk, and he pinned my arms down to my side.

Mike pulled Psycho away from me and said

something calmly in Farsi. He was still doubled over.

"What the fuck was that?" I shouted at Mike.

"What needed to be done," Mike said, stepping up into me and putting a finger roughly in my chest. I squirmed beneath the Hulk's grip.

"They were un-fucking-armed," I said, fighting against the bear hug Hulk had me wrapped up in.

"Take his rifle, until he calms down," Mike said, ignoring my comment.

"He's right" Mex said. "They were unarmed."

Mike wheeled. "No shit. And we can talk about it. But it will be off this boat."

The Hulk stripped me of the rifle, and then handed my side arm to Mex. I watched as Mike dragged Psycho away back towards the bridge of the ship.

I turned an empty five-gallon bucket over and sat down on it. I stared at the bloody, mangled bodies of the dead fisherman. Blood pooled black beneath the tortured bodies. They were contorted bizarrely against their restraints. They looked almost like animals, hog-tied and slaughtered as they were.

They had all been unarmed.

In the distance, back in the direction from which we had come, I heard the dull bark of a silenced rifle. They were finishing off the fisherman we'd already zip tied.

Mex sat down beside me. He didn't say anything.

One of the fishermen groaned, blood froth on his lips as he struggled to roll over and push himself upright.

I looked up at the Hulk who watched blankly as the man struggled.

"Well," I said, "don't stop now."

My words seemed to bring him back to reality because he stepped forward silently, his giant form casting a long shadow over the struggling fisherman, and he put two between his eyes.

Chapter Eight

I SAT in the back of the Bruiser. Nord and Hulk sat in front of me. I stared out of the Barracuda's tinted windows, in the distance, against the gray sky that signaled the coming of sudden dawn, the Chinese merchant vessel erupted into bright orange flames. Our last act before we'd left had been to place shape charges inside her hull.

I pulled out the can of Copenhagen and tucked the last of my longcut into my lip. The nicotine helped soothe my already overstimulated nerves.

The Bruiser moved forward under Nord's careful hand, and I watched intently as the burning wreck slipped away behind us.

Eventually, it was gone. Swallowed by the horizon, and all that was left was a single finger of oily black smoke reaching high into the sky, like the far off sign of a burning wagon train in one of those westerns my Grandpa used to watch.

I spit into an empty plastic water bottle, and finally broke the silence.

"Did you know?" I asked.

Hulk turned. "Know what?"

"It was gonna go like that?"

"I don't think I thought about it," he said.

"It was fucked up," I said.

"You didn't do it," the Hulk said.

"We all did it. We were all there."

"Naw that's bullshit, I was with the boat," the Nord said. "All YOU motherfuckers did that." His delivery was so dry, his positioning on the subject so nonchalant that I couldn't help but laugh. With a well-timed strike, I'd been relieved of my hot air.

"It's all bullshit, Ryan," the Hulk started in. "Stop being dramatic, stop pretending you don't know what it's all about. I don't know how you haven't gotten that yet. Think Syria. Think Iraq, Afghanistan, Libya, Somalia, is any less bullshit. Where were the WMD's? We put up with Ghaddafi for fifty years, and then suddenly he had to go. Shit man, even Reagan put up with Ghaddafi. You wanna know why he disappeared. Because he was a threat to the system. That's all this shit is. We are brakes and throttle on the most powerful empire the world has ever seen. And sometimes it looks like this. It looks like collateral damage and black ops and shit they'd never put in movies. Welcome to the party."

"They were unarmed though," I said.

"They weren't that unarmed," the Hulk quipped.

"Yeah, two measly AKs," I said. "Half of them were probably slaves. You know that. At least indentured. They press gang poor people onto these things, pile them up with a bunch of fake debt and obligations, and then keep them at sea by force."

"That's the thing though. It doesn't matter and I

don't care." Hulk waved his hand around. "The only reason they weren't armed combatants was because they lacked arms. It's not your job to provide them. Imagine being a criminal and not arming yourself." He turned around and looked at me. "They are fucking the entire global ecosystem up. I mean really, let's do this. How fucking stupid do you have to be to trespass into another country's territorial waters and not arm yourself. But more than that, how disrespectful. To think you can just fish this shit dry, clear around on the other side of the fucking globe, and do it unarmed. Do it without consequences. Never in 10,000 years of human civilization has that shit been a thing. You know why everyone thinks they can just do whatever the hell they want? It's because there's no consequences." He collapsed back in his seat.

I said nothing. Instead, I stared out the window.

The Barracuda slid across the waves, splitting some, topping others.

After a few minutes the Hulk sat back up. "They can see this shit from space. Did you know that. They call it the City of Lights. It literally looks like a floating city from space. Thousands of vessels. A motherfucking flotilla of huns here to suck the oceans dry. Every summer they come. They've destroyed their own fisheries and now they are here, on our side of the globe. Oh yeah, and they might just be after the squid, but those nets don't only catch squid. They suck up sharks, whales, dolphins, turtles, a million other kinds of sea life. All dead. And you're gonna cry because a couple of indentured chinks caught it between the eyes? Fuck them."

WHEN WE GOT BACK to the bay it was already raining. I had thought about what he said, and it made sense. But it wasn't the answer I was looking for. The rain came down in torrents, waves and waves of ice-cold driving rain. Lightning flashed and thunder rattled around the rock walls of the cove, reverberating louder each time.

In the bunkhouse, I stood at the end of my bed and peeled off my soggy clothes. Everything was soaked and cold. I hung the clothes up on a two by four that crossed the Quonset in the middle of the room so they would dry.

I thought of Psycho, that Pashtun fuck. I didn't like him. Didn't like anything about him. I could see him now, after he blew those Chinamen away. He'd just stared at me with those close-set eyes, water dripping off his black wiry beard like the mongrel dog he was. Mike's mongrel dog. He'd looked surprised at my reaction.

I turned my attention back to my own gear. While standing there in my underwear, lost in my own thoughts. I heard Mike call out "Ryan," from the entrance to the Quonset. I pulled on pants and stepped to my door. Mike stood at the end of the hall. He stood in silhouette, driving rain behind him. In each of his hands was a pair of boxing gloves.

"You guys wanna fight? Then you can fight, but you won't be doing it on an op. Now get out here." Then he repeated it in Farsi, or so I assumed. Psycho's door opened.

Outside, he threw a pair of gloves at me. He tossed the other pair to Psycho, saying something in Farsi as he did so. Psycho lifted the gloves, looking confused at the hand wraps that fell out into the mud.

I slowly wrapped my own and watched as Mike helped Psycho wrap his. *Mike and his dog again.*

In the driving rain, I jumped up and down, waiting for Psycho to finish getting his gloves on. The dirt in front of the Quonset had turned to mud, and it squelched beneath my boots as I shifted my weight from one leg to another to stay limber.

Finally, Psycho was done, and I watched as Mike slapped him on the back.

We circled each other, gloved hands raised, and the others stood breathlessly underneath the Quonset's overhang, their arms crossed with amused smiles on their faces.

Psycho was all wires. Skinny boned and thin from a whole damn life of malnourishment. I had probably twenty pounds on him and I was a lean machine.

The rain ran down my forehead and into my eyes and I wiped them clear with the back of my glove. But since my gloves were soaked it did almost nothing. I threw a left jab that tickled him.

He jumped backwards looking like some weird pale pashtun monkey. He was all limbs and moved awkwardly. It was clear he thought he had dodged something, but my punch was never supposed to land, I was just measuring out the distance.

I advanced again and he met me in the middle. I popped his head back with two quick jabs.

He ducked his head and charged, grabbed me

around the waist and lifted me up and backwards into the mud.

After that he was on me, and I covered up, blocking his blows with my elbows. As the onslaught slowed, I shoved him off and scrambled to my feet. *So he wanted to brawl.* He was deceptively strong, wiry limbs all muscle and ligament. I wouldn't let him take me down again.

He charged, retrying the takedown, but I was ready for him. He ducked his head and met my knee. There was a loud violent crunch. Then he went slack and smacked the mud face down.

He rolled over dazed and barely conscious, his nose broken. The blood streaming out of it was washed away by the rain as quickly as it escaped his face, turning the mud next to his head a slick, oily red.

I bent over and stripped him of his gloves. At first, I had planned to leave him there but my business with him was done, and he looked pathetic, so much so that I felt my part in it. I grabbed him beneath the arms and walked him over to the Nord who was now standing underneath the overhang. The others started to filter away, thinking the show was over. All except Mike, who stood grinning.

He was waiting.

I returned to the place where Psycho had fallen and retrieved the gloves I'd stripped from him. I chucked them at Mike.

"Put them on," I said.

Mike snatched both out of the air and smiled, then he dropped them on the concrete pad at his feet.

"Don't need them," he said, stepping forward.

He raised bare knuckles in front of his face, and we circled. I stepped forward, throwing a double jab and then a cross, each in quick succession.

Mike faded backwards letting my punches fall short.

I reset and again we circled.

He threw a jab in my direction, but I slipped it, rotating further out.

Our feet churned the mud, carving a circle into the earth for the worship of Ares. I wiped the rain from my eyes, and Mike smiled at me. His clothes were soaked and clinging to his muscular frame. He shook his arms vigorously, like a bull shaking off an afternoon storm.

Again, I advanced, leading with another jab—which he slipped—before following it up with a heavy right cross—which he simply batted away. This made me lose my balance and I stumbled forward, slipped on the mud and barely kept myself from falling.

I was wide open then, and he could have ended it with a left jab into the side of my face or an overhand right to bury me, but he didn't.

He simply stood up straight and reset, dancing backwards, always dancing. Luring me in. Mocking me. Taunting me.

I was furious now, and although I tried to hide it, even from myself, I couldn't. And I could tell he knew, because he smiled at me, which made me even more furious.

I barreled forward throwing a barrage of sloppy punches.

He bobbed and weaved and batted my haymakers away.

I had yet to connect with a single blow, a fact that sapped most of my strength, and he had yet to throw a single punch. My shoulders burned, and my legs felt tired. I was slowing, and as I lost confidence, he gained it. Only my anger drove me now, and that fool's impulse that led a man to die on his sword.

I threw punches that shook nothing but the empty air. I was desperate to connect. And I knew what was happening, even as it happened, I felt myself losing control over my own mind, and with it my own body. And then I threw a wild haymaker, one I was so sure of...

I DIDN'T FEEL IT. The punch that was. I came to consciousness beneath the overhang of the Quonset, the Hulk kneeling over me, and it was still raining. I was cold and while I was out, I had dreams of my own funeral. I was so cold and wet from the rain and the mud.

"Did I even hit him?" I asked.

"Not even once," the Hulk said, chuckling.

MY HEAD POUNDED and I slowly lifted myself up to my elbows. There was a scattered screeching outside as Thorn-tailed Rayaditos bantered. Their high-pitched calls dumping me instantly into a faraway land, conjuring images of a jungled plain. I slipped on a pair of Levis, and a heavy long-sleeved shirt before stumbling outside.

It was late afternoon. The storm had broken, and the birds had returned from wherever they'd gone to take shelter. Collared sparrows joined the Rayaditos outside, and quibbled with each other along the shoreline.

The others were already up and sitting in lawn chairs around a little bonfire on the edge of the water, beers in hand. I walked forward and Tex asked if I wanted one. I merely nodded, still shaking the sleep from my head and probably concussed.

"You're not supposed to let people sleep if they have a concussion," I said.

Psycho lifted the white lid of a little red cooler and tossed me a beer. He had one in his hand, and the other on his broken nose.

I caught it and nodded to him. It was nearly impossible to stay mad at a man that you had fought, no matter how deeply you still disliked him. And I still disliked him. But I respected him a bit more, and ultimately that was all that mattered. That was the minimum men required to live in proximity within one another.

Tex shook out a lawn chair and set it out for me. I cracked the beer and plopped down.

"How's the head?" Mex asked.

"Not good," I said, taking a drink.

"I don't know why you thought you could fight Mike," the Nord commented.

"How is he," I said, motioning to Psycho.

"He's good. You busted his nose, but I fixed him up," the Hulk said.

I opened a new can of Copenhagen and put in a

fat lip. Mex dragged another branch to the fire and broke it apart slowly. He fed the fire its wet limbs. The fire sparked and cracked and smoked, and I finished my beer in one long gulp.

I motioned for another, and Psycho dug around in the cooler and passed it.

"So, any way I got to this woman's house right," Mex started back into whatever story I had interrupted. "Forty-three years old, but she still looked good—"

"Wait what did I miss?" I asked.

Mex smiled and said, "I'm telling them about the milf I hooked up with. I was in Phoenix right, and this cougar wouldn't leave me alone at the bar."

"How old were you?" I asked.

"Oh, dude I was like 20 years old. I used to sneak into this place with a fakc ID my cousin got me. Anyways this woman keeps buying me drinks, and she's hot. A little on the old side, but I'm like twenty and can't think straight and none of the other girls are really paying any attention to me. And she had a fat ass," Mex paused to shape it for us like he was Al Pacino. "Her tits, not so much. We'll get to her tits, but I was just trying to get laid. So anyway, she takes me home right. And I'm drunk but it's still kind of weird. Like this could be my mom's house. It's a nice house, well put together, decorated with those stupid signs that say live and laugh on them, that type of shit, right?"

"Aight, but what happened?" the Hulk asked, and then turning to me added, "he said this was the worst hook up of his life."

I laughed and leaned forward in my seat. Mex paused, searching for how to start the next act.

"I don't care about any of this though because I'm bricked up and drunk. Like I can't even think about anything but getting my rocks off. So, this lady gives me another drink and I try to make a move and she says not yet."

"Blonde or brunette?" I asked.

"Blonde," Mex said. "Anyways... You gotta warm me up first, she says. So, we move to the couch, and she puts on the TV—"

"Wait, she said that—warm her up first," the Nord cut in.

"She was weird. I told you that," Mex said. "Anyways, I don't even remember what she put on. Might have been like some dateline shit—"

"Wait, like the murder show?" Nord cut in again.

"Holy fuck," Tex said, "let him finish the story."

"So we are making out," Mex continued, "everything is cool, she's a good kisser. Then she stops me cold and says she doesn't know if she can do this.

"Chingau, she has been buying me drinks all night and whispering in my ear how she is going to blow my mind, and how older women know what they are doing. All this shit right. So, I'm totally confused at this point.

"Anyways I ask her what's wrong, you know, as nice as I can. And finally, she tells me that one of her tits has ruptured a while ago, and she never got it replaced—"

"Wait, so she only had one tit?" the Hulk asked.

"It's like a thing that can happen when you have fake tits. Sometimes they'll rupture, and the saline solution just gets absorbed by the body. I had to look it up."

"So, she had like one big, nice juicy tit, and the other is like... a flat tire, basically?" Tex asked.

"Si," Mex said slowly.

"You dog," Nord said.

"Yeah, so anyway, I'm like totally cool about it, tell her I don't care. All this shit. So then she is down again. But I am so horny and also disgusted but now I don't know how to back out."

"Did you fuck her or not?" the Hulk asked.

"This is like the longest way to tell someone that you fucked a bitch with one tit," the Nord jumped in.

"And we had to hear the first half twice because of numbnuts here," the Hulk said pointing to me.

"But yeah," Mex said, "Dios mio, I fucked her. And the whole time all I could look at was that one deflated tit. I don't even remember anything else about her. Not even the ass. Just that sad saggy titty."

"What about the big juicy one?" Tex asked.

"One rotten apple spoils the whole basket," Mex said.

"Wait, why didn't you just flip her around and do it doggy?" the Nord asked.

"She wouldn't let me!" Mex said defensively.

The rest of us lost it at that, and it was several minutes before we stopped laughing.

"So she put up all that fuss about you seeing her bad tit, and then wouldn't let you hit it doggy?" the Nord asked, between wheezing gasps.

"So did you finish?" the Hulk asked.

"Yeah, I finished and then picked up my clothes and shit and bounced. I just started walking and then called an uber. I had to get out of there."

"Did you say anything to her after?" the Nord asked.

"Yeah probably, I don't really remember," Mex responded.

"You didn't say shit, did you? You just left," the Hulk accused before breaking into another fit of laughter.

I started in on my third beer. By this time the sun had begun to set, and Tex told us stories from his childhood. My head was buzzing but the weight of the day had lifted.

Tex had grown up poor, the son of a farmer in East Texas, the part that was more like Louisiana than it was Texas. His dad had run off with another woman when he was 6. He had beat his stepdad to a pulp at 14 and ran away from home. Spent a few years couch surfing; working odd jobs where he could find them. At sixteen he had fallen in with a couple of guys that poached gators along the Louisiana and Texas border.

"We would just shoot em in the head with an ol' 22. Use to skin em out and take them down across the border. You could get a pretty penny from the Mexicans down there. Knew a guy who made alligator leather for the cartels, or at least that's what my buddies suspected," Tex said.

"Did you ever get caught?" I asked.

"Shit. Did I get caught? How do you think I ended up here. I was eighteen years old and one day we got busted. So, I was legally an adult. They tried to throw the book at me, but my lawyer came up with some half-baked plea deal for me to join the Army. This was the height of the Iraq war, when they had guys doing two, three deployments back-to-back. They'd dropped all the charges if I could pass the ASVAB." Tex took a long swig from his beer.

"So, what happened?" Mex asked.

"Less than two years later I was in Ra-ma-di," he drawled, "just in time for the troop surge. Three years after that I finally got into the 75th."

"So, you've always been doing illegal shit?" the Hulk joked.

"Yeah," Tex said staring off into the fire. "Weird when you think about it. This was the likeliest place for me to end up. This or federal prison. Could've gone either way."

"Not me. No idea how I ended up here. I was raised right. Two parents. Still together. Even sent me to a Lutheran school," the Hulk said. "I graduated with an academic scholarship to Michigan State."

"You never went?" I asked, taking a swig from my sixth beer.

"Naw, I graduated 2004. We'd just gone into Iraq," he said. "You know the funniest part, is for the longest I didn't even know that Iraq wasn't responsible for 9/11. I did like two tours over there before I realized it."

"Well, I mean it was Al Qaeda, right?" the Nord said.

"Imagine still believing a couple of donkey fuckers pulled off 9/11," Tex quipped. Which drew howls of laughter from all of us. From there the conversation quickly descended into our pet 9/11 conspiracies, and everyone had a different angle.

I couldn't tell who was serious and who was just

picking the most ridiculous hill to defend. Ultimately, it was a bit of both.

Tex thought it was to cover up the trillion dollars in the Pentagon budget that had been unannounced and unaccounted for a day earlier. The Nord kept bringing up Tower 7. Mex was convinced, or at least seemed convinced, it wasn't even a plane, and that they had just used JDAMs and then CGI'd the planes in for TV *Running Man* style.

"They had just started getting good at CGI," Mex said, "you can look it up."

I was too drunk then to realize it, but there was a clear reason why almost none of us accepted the story at face value, and that was because we had all been too close to the machine. Even if the events of the day happened exactly as the government and the news said they did, after seeing the fruits of the war up close. After realizing Haliburton had more vested interest in the war than the American people. After flying to the other side of the globe to a country where 99% of the population had never even been on a plane to prevent another attack. After killing one terrorist and then fighting his son ten years later. It didn't make sense to us, not anymore.

The truth doesn't reside in the brain, the real truth anyways, but in the gut, so in the end it didn't matter who planned 9/11 or how it was carried out, because everything that came after, everything it had been used to justify contradicted it. Conspiracy theories are the myths of the 21st century, the fine ordering of the universe by bards and skalds, a grand myth that explained away the nonsense.

At some point the others staggered back to the Quonset leaving myself and Mex by the fire. Its red coals sparking lonely. A chilly breeze blowing off the dark waters of the Atlantic. The sound of the sea melodic against the shore. Waves crashing wistfully just beyond the bay.

"You comin?" Mex asked.

I looked up from the fire, and shook the beer can slightly trying to measure how much was left by the gentle slosh within. "Yeah, I'll be there in a minute."

"You alright with what happened to the fishermen?" Mex asked.

I just stared out at the black beyond. When he started to turn away, I stopped him and said, "I don't really care all that much about what happened to them. I like the ocean. I'd trade half of Asia to keep the oceans from collapsing. It's just... one time I wanted it not to feel so dirty. I wanted a real opponent. Tired of killing farmers and fisherman. That's who always seems to get it. You read about WW2 or Korea and I think those would've been easier on the soul. At least the guy on the other side of the trench was a soldier."

"Yeah, I get it."

Chapter Nine

For the next couple of days, we did nothing much but the same. We started fires by the ocean, we drank beer, and we told stories.

Mike joined us on the second night and drank a few beers. He didn't acknowledge our scrap and treated me as he always did, which was friendly enough. He had beaten me solidly though, more solidly than when we had first fought, and now I wondered whether he had played me during that first match. The one that started all of this. Let me get some licks in. Let me think I could beat him. Led me into the wilderness as equals—only to display his true skill.

Yesterday, had been embarrassing. It's one thing to fight a man and give what for, even if you lose. Such had been the fight between me and Pscyho. But to not land even a single punch, and then to be put down with the same, well, I would be lying if I didn't admit to a certain level of resentment. My ego was bruised and the only balm possible of salvaging it seemed yet another fight. I had gotten sloppy, let my emotions get the better of me. There wouldn't be a second time.

Mike stood, beer in hand, and filled us in on the next operation.

"Any chatter about the boat?" Tex asked.

"Not much, the Argentina Coast Guard found it and reported the incident to the Chinese embassy. They offered them a place in the investigation. Haven't heard anything else yet."

"So, what happens next?" the Nord asked.

"We wait," said Mike. "They'll do an investigation. The Chinese will try to keep it quiet, so they don't draw more attention to what the boat was doing, and why it turned off its AIS. Illegal fishing is a bad look for them. When push comes to shove, they will keep doing it. But they would rather keep the pushing and shoving quiet.

"When Argentina blew up that fishing boat, China wasn't mad because their citizens died. Shit they have what a billion of them. So, twenty peasant fishermen died. They didn't care about that, not really. What they did care about though, was saving face. Argentina did it loudly. Called them out on the world stage and made them look weak, treated them like thieves. That is why the incident became such a big deal. No, this time, the Argentinians will do their dance, pretend to investigate, hand over records of where their Coast Guard was when it occurred. But back channels will head nod at what's really going on."

"And if they find bodies?" I asked. "Bodies full of bullets."

"Well, that would be ideal, Argentina will blame it on piracy or vigilantes or whatever, shit they can call it a Nancy Drew Mystery, whatever their intelligentsia comes up with. But they get a deterrent. Fear is going to win this for them. When enough of those fuckers are scared to fish because they might get ganked, then it might make a dent in the whole thing.

"A freak accident does nobody any good, because it's a freak accident. But madmen operating on the high seas. Marauders. Well, that's something. And it's all kept modestly quiet. China gets the message. They are left to wonder whether it's a special operation or vigilantes or whatever, but they don't have to send a message out to the rest of the world that they are in control. They can try to comply and never lose face; they can make the right decisions and not look weak."

I flicked the can of dip between my two fingers, packing it.

"So, when do we go out next?" Tex asked.

"Probably not for a couple weeks," said Mike. "Trying to see how this all shakes out before we poke the hornets' nest again. I have to go back up to Buenos Aires in a couple days to debrief."

After that we all drank and laughed and told more stories, and for the second night in a row got shitfaced.

THE NEXT DAY, perhaps because he sensed we were growing restless, Mike showed us the rest of what was in the third Quonset. We had been here before, mostly to attack the pallet of beer that stood in the very back, a pallet that already had a very healthy dent in it. There were of course also pallets of ammo for the boats, and boxes full of MREs, but in the front half stood overly large and unmarked cardboard boxes.

Mike pulled out his knife and cut through the plastic strapping that held the cardboard bundles together. With the straps out of the way he cut open the box to reveal another box. It was a Bench Press.

"All this here is gym equipment," Mike said, waving the knife in a circle at the rest of the unwieldy boxes. "Go ahead, get it set up."

It took the rest of the day and most of the next to get all the equipment put together. Men are easy to keep happy and a lot like working dogs in that respect, growing irritable and miserable when given no way to work out their excess energy. And while we were here to fight, we would destroy ourselves on beer within the week, and after that be even more miserable and begin to take our excess energy out on each other. When finished, the front half of the Quonset had been transformed from storage space to prison gym.

We had two bench presses, three squat racks. A large TRX station, dumbbells, and kettlebells. Olympic bars and plates. The gym was built around compound exercises and free weights, and the only machines were a couple of rowers which I imagined had been mostly an afterthought. Tex suggested we use them for target practice.

Having spent the better part of two days staring at the pallet of beer, Tex suggested we should limit our drunkenness to the weekends or celebrations,

celebrations obviously meaning the next time that we took a ship.

The group was immediately split, with Hulk fighting the hardest to not make "hard rules." But the rest of us were convinced easily enough as we were still somewhat hungover from the last few nights of drinking and knew that the current course was unsustainable. Even more terrifying was the idea that we drank through the beer in the first month, as we had no idea what Mike's plans for replacing it would be. And so, it was decided, drinking could only happen on Fridays and Saturdays, and after a successful op.

"But in all fairness, we should celebrate putting this gym together," the Hulk said. "And to say farewell to drinking whenever we want."

And so, we got drunk again, and grilled burgers by the ocean on a little charcoal grill. This was no different than most nights, of course, as our food up until this point had been two things, burgers and beans at night, and MREs during the day if you were hungry enough. There were two chest freezers at the back of the Quonset filled with nothing but frozen beef patties. Not the good kind either, but the bulk kind that turned your guts to mush. The idea of living like this for the next four months was already causing extreme dread.

And it was at this point that Mike revealed the last of his gifts, and from the back of the command post, he revealed several heavy rods and reels for sea fishing. His foresight had thus far been immaculate. He knew men. How to fight them. And how to lead them. I couldn't argue with that. The man was a master of morale. The only thing we were missing was a strip club.

THE WAVES ROCKED the Ares gently. The ocean was calm and the sun high. The rays soaked into my skin. I sat in my lawn chair, feet up on the side of the Barracuda, and watched the tip of my fishing pole for any sign of a strike. In my lap was an old western paperback, one of several I'd packed for the trip—*Desert Stake-out* by Harry Whittington.

"You like those" Tex asked. "When I was in jail, guys would pass L'Amour books around."

"Yeah," I responded. "I grew up watching westerns, riding horses, shooting guns... on my grandpa's ranch."

"Where was that?"

"Wyoming," I said.

"You miss it?" Tex asked.

"All the time," I said. "Even got into three gun competitions when I was a teen."

"Damn," Tex said. "So you can draw and all that."

"Yeah, I had a special rig for it," I said. "Would do western three gun, so it was a single action revolver, a lever-gun, and a double-barreled shotgun."

"Real cowboy shit," Tex said.

"That's your nickname then," Mex said, "Cowboy."

Tex laughed. "Explains why you got your panties in a wad over those fishermen."

"Or we can call him John Wayne," Mex said.

"Cowboy is fine," I said, knowing you gotta jump on a decent nickname before a bad one gets picked out.

Tex picked up a pole from one of the rod holders. He'd cannibalized a piece of gym equipment and fashioned rod holders out of the rings. He welded them into the side with a little arc welder we found with the rest of the tools in the back of the storage Quonset.

Tex and Mex were the only others that had wanted to come. An oversized tub sloshed with each tilt of the boat, and the small fish we had caught to use as live bait darted around their new cell.

"I would have stayed in, if every deployment had been like this," Mex said.

"Why'd you get out?" I asked.

"The money," Mex said.

I just nodded my head.

"Not like that though," he continued, "it's more complicated. I was about to re-enlist when Mike approached me. He talked me out of it."

"He give you the ol' sales job?" I asked.

"My mom has cancer. She beat it once, but it came back. The treatments from the last time almost bankrupted her, and we were poor, grew up poor, I did what I could. But shit man, even on E-6 pay that's not enough."

"I'm sorry about your mom," I said.

"It's life man. Death comes for all of us," he said slowly. "She's getting the best treatment possible now." His eyes looked misty.

"Is your Dad there to help?" I asked

"What Dad?" Mex scoffed. "She was a single

mom. Ran off before I was even born. I don't even know if she knows who he was."

"Do you have siblings?" I asked.

"Cousins," Mex replied. "They help some, but it was always me and her. Mostly her... against the world."

The bright blue waters of the Atlantic stretched out before us and I felt the sudden loneliness of the place. Like a void. Existence was a fragile thing.

"That's heavy," I said.

"What about you?" Tex asked.

"I was kicked out," I said slowly, trying to buy time, trying to decide how much of the story I wanted to divulge.

Tex raised his eyebrows. "Oh yeah? Was it bad?" he asked. Then followed up by saying, "you don't have to talk about it."

"It's fine," I said. "I punched out my commanding officer."

Mex chuckled and said, "that'll do it."

"I was a proud Marine Raider for all of a year and a half. Almost got court martialed for assault and insubordination and discharged in the middle of my first deployment."

"Why'd you, do it?" Tex asked.

"He sold out a friend," I said. "A Kurd. He saved my life in Mosul. And they just let the Turks move on them. Turks hate the Kurds but Turkey is in NATO, and the Kurds, well, they aren't no one to anybody. Wouldn't even let me give them a heads up. They had to tie me to a bedpost. I beat him half to death when they let me loose, the stupid fuck. They discharged me quietly to avoid a trial, gave me an honorable so I wouldn't push back. They just wanted the whole situation gone. And they definitely didn't want any media attention."

Tex just nodded his head. "Well, it sounds like you had good reason."

"They don't care man," I said then. "These wars, if that's what you want to call them, they're ran by bean counters." I said, my voice cracking. "That's it though. That's the story. After that, I went back to school, got my degree, worked in some gay ass office and thought about blowing my brains out every day. When that was untenable, I tended bar and surfed every day. Then Mike found me. Now I'm here."

My rod bent violently, and we all jumped up. I snatched up the cork handle of the rod and felt something lurch at the end of my line, all its movements transmitted to my hand. A monster on the other end.

Adrenaline hit my veins, and a rush of excitement sent my head spinning. The pole vibrated in my hands, and it took all my strength to hold onto it. I planted the handle in my thigh and leaned back as I fed it more line and let the thing run.

We took turns for the next thirty minutes, each one of us fighting it and at last we got it on the boat. Probably close to 60 lbs. and it was a bitch and a half to get into the boat. It was a Yellow Amberjack. When we finally did, Mex stuck a knife into the back of its head. It flopped on the floor of the boat as we tried to stay clear of its tail.

We settled back into the rhythm of things after that, and Tex revealed a cooler of beers he had smuggled out of the storage shed.

"Don't tell, Hulk," Tex said with a wink.

"Weren't you the one that suggested we keep our drinking to the weekends?" Mex asked.

"Yeah, but fishing is different," Tex said. "Fishing don't count against you. Fishing sober is sacrilegious. Shit these chinks out here fish sober and see where that gets em."

I laughed at that. It was Tex. Tex was funny. The kind of funny you couldn't take any where public.

We sat there soaking up the sun and waiting for another bite. I cracked my beer, stuck another lip in, and for the first time in a long time felt some sense of peace.

On his third beer Mex asked, "aren't we illegally fishing?"

"I think that's the last thing we have to worry about if we get caught out here," I said.

"Yeah, and who's gonna stop us," Tex said, motioning towards the black boat's gun. "Say hello to my little friend."

There was a sudden noise behind us, like a tire violently releasing all its air at once, and we all jumped up. I dropped my beer and scrambled to pick it up.

"What the fuck was that," Tex said.

When I at last had control of my beer I stood up and followed Tex's eyes. Something moved in the water, just a shadow, and then it breached the surface and forcefully blew out a stream of water and air. Black and white spots briefly shimmered above the water's bright blue surface, and the gentle breeze blew the fine mist in our direction.

"There's more," Mex said, pointing to the other side of the boat.

It was a pod of Orcas. They circled, shadows just beneath the water.

"Should we get out of here?" Mex asked, a tremor in his voice.

"Naw," Tex drawled. "They're just checking us out. Orcas are friendly to humans."

"Yeah, that's why we call them killer whales," Mex quipped.

"They aren't though. They're dolphins," Tex said defensively.

One of them breached the surface and appraised us with a single eye, its head bobbed just above the water. Rows of white jagged teeth showed where it got its name. A long scar cut across the top of its face where the once smooth skin had reknitted in knots. I wondered what had happened to it. If it had tangled with a shark or something else, something of a more mechanical nature.

"Do we have more of that bait fish?" I asked slowly.

"Yeah, why?" Tex asked.

"Give me one," I said, extending my hand behind me. My eyes remained locked on the Orca's.

Tex retrieved a fish from the bucket and slapped it into my hand. I felt it wriggle beneath my grip, its body slick, and slowly I brough it in front of me. I shook the fish at our new friend.

The orca dipped suddenly beneath the surface and breached the water just feet from the side of the boat.

I tossed the fish to it. It bobbed upwards, like a dog when you throw it snacks, and caught the fish. Its gaping jaws flashed a bright pink mouth and white teeth, then it disappeared once more under the surface. It breached again a little way off blowing forcefully in what I imagined meant thank you.

Then two more breached the surface, near where the first had, bobbing expectantly and chirping. I tossed them each a fish and they disappeared beneath the surface only to breach again, forcefully blowing their thanks.

There were three of them in total, and this continued for as long as I had fish. Their shows of gratitude growing more playful and ecstatic each round. They leaped into the air making larger and more and more impressive splashes.

The boat rocked and bobbed on the waves they created. When I at last ran out of fish, they bobbed expectantly, and I waved my empty hands at them. They blew forcefully, then disappeared beneath the surface, breached one last time a little ways off, and were gone.

"That was cool as fuck," Mex said, seemingly in shock.

I started a slow nervous chuckle that slowly became a laugh. "That was fucking awesome."

"That might be the coolest thing that's ever happened to me," Tex said.

Chapter Ten

THE NEXT DAY, the helicopter arrived. It started out as a black speck and grew larger and louder the closer it came. We watched it circle our little camp and then line up with the dirt pad next to the Quonset.

"I'll be back in three days," Mike said. "Stay out of trouble." Those were his last words to us. He was off to brief our customer.

We watched him go. The chopper's rotors thrummed and thumped the air and then it ascended, straight up, before accelerating forward, nose down and tail up. He had let the lunatics run the asylum and we were feral.

Mike had no sooner left, when I went to work out. Hulk was already in there, benching two plates as if it was a warmup. When he was done with his set, he added a third and asked me to spot him.

With brow furrowed, I said, "You probably don't want me on that unless you are trying to die."

He laughed. "Don't worry, I won't even need you." And he was right. He didn't need me. Because he pumped out six of the smoothest reps I've ever seen someone press with three plates on the bar.

"You wanna try?" he asked.

"Gonna have to drop that down a plate," I said.

I barely had the thing racked again when Tex entered, followed by the Nord and Mex. They were all looking shifty and had a certain spring in their step, the kind of look men get when they are planning something.

"Well?" I said.

"Come on, both of you. Get a bag with some decent clothes," Mex said.

"Why?" I asked.

"We are getting out of here," the Nord said.

"How?" The Hulk asked.

"And where?" I followed up.

Tex gave his signature smirk and said, "to get some real food, and maybe something else to drink besides shitty beer and water."

"There's a fishing village like two hours up the coast," Mex said. "It's a decent size too."

I wiped my brow, still confused. "Like a two hour walk?" I asked.

"Drive," the Nord said simply. "Just get your shit, cus we will still have to walk like two hours."

* * *

In front of us was a long-abandoned barn, its brown rotting and weathered plank wood long since abandoned to the elements falling free of the heavy timbers that made its frame, the rusted nails that had held them in place giving way one at a time.

Long grass grew up around the sides of it and a tree was growing through the side. The building's tin roof was full of holes, missing panels.

As we approached, we walked around a sheet of tin metal that had been shorn clean from the roof in a storm long past. It lay in the dirt, half buried, grass growing on top of the covered part.

"How do you know a vehicle is here?" I asked.

"I saw it," Tex said. "On Google Earth."

"How old was the imagery?" Hulk asked.

"A year," Tex responded.

"What the fuck," Mex muttered.

"How do you even know its operable then," I asked.

"That's why we came, to check it out," Tex said.

The Hulk snorted.

"That would have been good information to know before we started," I said. The sun hung high in the sky, and I was by this point soaked in sweat. This tiny, abandoned place was about twelve miles from our cove. I was guessing it used to be part of a larger cattle operation, or maybe the edge of a homestead, but I didn't know. It had taken us a little under 5 hours to make the hike. All of which was apparently based on a hunch and a prayer that we could get a long-abandoned vehicle going in order to make the trip to Villa del Mar. We had all came, and left Psycho to watch the place. I wondered if he minded. He didn't seem to, but then again there was no way to communicate absent Mike.

"You guys are a bunch of pussies," Tex said over his shoulder. "I'm a Navy Seal... my feet hurt, army strong... my asshole hurts." He mocked us.

"I'm Tex, and on this week of swamp creatures

I'm going to show you how to poach a gator," Hulk mocked back. "Oh shit, the feds. Guess I'm in Iraq now."

Sure, enough though, parked on the other side of the barn was a little white Toyota Hilux.

"Dude, there is no way we are going to get this started," I said. "Whatever gas was in there is evaporated."

Tex waved the two fuel cans he'd toted the entire way at me. "You forgot about these dumbass. Make you carry them next time." He dropped to one knee and pulled off his pack. He pulled out a crowbar. "It looked like there was a fuel tank on the other side of the barn." He walked off to check.

I pulled on the door of the Toyota and was surprised it opened. It wasn't even locked. The keys were inside, just tossed onto the seat. I guess when you are this rural you don't worry about people stealing your shit. That or it was already stolen. I pulled myself inside and turned the keys in the ignition. Nothing. It was completely dead. Not even a dash light. Which is about what I expected.

"I doubt they left this shit out here because it worked," the Hulk said.

"It'll work," the Nord said. "Tex can get just about anything going."

I was unsure what was driving his confidence, but he always seemed to have it.

Tex returned wiping his brow, "It's there. Pop it in neutral and we will roll you over there."

I released the parking brake and pushed in the clutch with some effort. "Alright, push," I shouted.

They rocked the old Toyota back and forth until it finally came free of its resting place. The weeds that had grown up around it added resistance. Somehow the tires were still good. As they pushed, I guided the truck around the back side of the barn to where the fuel tank was.

It looked old, its once red paint flaking to reveal a layer of rust. The old rubber hose cracked, and brittle was connected to the still shiny stainless-steel nozzle. The nozzle itself was latched down with an old padlock.

Tex took the crowbar to it, snapping it open. "Locks are really only for the lazy and disinclined," he said. "That's what pops used to say."

"Yeah, how'd that work out for him?" the Nord asked.

Tex purged whatever was left in the hose out on the ground next to us. When the diesel coming out changed from a light amber color to red, he looked up with a giant shit eating grin and said, "It'll work, she might hate us for it, but I think it'll work. They usually treat tanks like these." He stuck the nozzle in the old Hilux, and we waited for it to fill.

"So, we gonna try to push start this bitch," I said.

"Yeah, put her back in neutral until we get you out to the road," Tex said hanging the nozzle back up. He put the fuel cans in the back of the truck. "We'll save these."

Luckily the barn was at the top of a small bluff, and while it had made the hike up a bit more painful, that same incline could mean success here.

"Alright," Tex said. "Put her in second gear but keep the clutch pushed in. When you get some speed let her out slowly."

"Thanks. Not my first rodeo," I said.

I put the truck in second gear and pushed in the clutch. The others pushed and I eased my foot off the brake, letting her roll. With the help of the incline, I gained speed. Slowly, I let up on the clutch until I felt the engine start to catch, felt resistance, the engine started to chug, and the flywheel finally caught. The engine sputtered to life. I let the clutch out all the way and fed her gas until she was purring smoothly. She clunked occasionally but never died.

At the bottom of the hill, I put her in neutral and waited for the others to catch up, feeding her a little extra gas as I waited. The Toyota's engine hummed smoothly. Tex and the Nord slid onto the bench seat next to me and Hulk and Mex jumped into the bed of the pickup.

"Well, where are we going?" I asked.

"Just follow this road out, I'll direct you from there," Tex said.

Chapter Eleven

Villa del Mar was a small quaint-looking village located right on the coast. It was roughly two hours away from our cove. Our entrance drew little attention, but what little it did was only the curious kind, and not the overly concerned.

In our North Face fleeces and Patagonia wind breakers we looked like tourists, or so we thought. I hadn't shaved in a week and had a nice patch of stubble going, while the others were in different stages of beards. All except the Nord, who sported a blonde handlebar mustache and a thin goatee per usual.

A keen eye may have pegged us as a bit too lean, a bit too aware, and maybe just a bit too confident to be normal tourists. But to the simple residents of Villa del Mar we figured we looked like we were passing through.

The buildings were all old, of the kind that had been around for at least one hundred years and added on to every so often. They were well maintained for the most part, but here or there a broken shutter or flaking paint revealed the weathered old wood beneath.

From the Atlantic a soft ocean breeze brought with it the fresh scent of salt water and mixed with the scent of the yellow flowers; little patches of Scotch Broom growing wild on the hillsides.

In front of the almacén, an old man in a straw hat slept in a rocker. The OPEN sign behind him flipped to CLOSED for what I assumed was his Siesta.

The town had two restaurants and two bars, a small grocer (the almacén), and an assortment of other businesses, all revolving around boats and fishing. We stopped another man further up the street to ask if there was a mechanic in town.

He wore a blue striped button-down with pearl buttons, blue jeans, old cowboy boots, and a straw hat. The man smiled amicably, crow's feet pulling at the corner of tired eyes, and pointed us to the opposite end of the sleepy village.

The mechanic was predictably closed for siesta and had left a note that said he would be back at 4 pm. We parked the Hilux in his lot and decided to wait him out.

I sat down on the stoop and packed a lip full of Cope. The Hulk dropped the bed of the truck and reclined. The others paced, stretching their legs from the journey.

"The whole town shuts down for everyone's afternoon nap," Tex said.

"America would change overnight if it forced siestas," the Hulk said. "Could you imagine."

It was in his most earnest moments, when he talked with childlike wonder, that I realized just how big the Hulk was. It was the sort of thing that short circuits a brain. The man stood nigh 6'5" and was barrel chested. A frighteningly big man, but mostly, when you got to know him, he was just goofy. Like a child trapped in a giant's body. A bit too nice, a bit socially awkward, and a little bit too optimistic. Unless he was pissed off, which in and of itself was not an easy feat. He had never blinked twice on the op though.

"Hulk, do you think you are so nice to people because you never got bullied?" I asked.

"Wait, what?" he asked, laughing. "I never got bullied."

"I know. That's what I mean. Cus everyone was too scared to pick on you. So, you just grew up with this positive..." I paused looking for my words, "...outlook. Outlook on people?"

"I could see it," the Nord said.

"Don't you like people?" the Hulk asked.

"Not like you do," I answered.

There was silence then. Gulls squawked overhead, and little whisps of clouds swirled in possibly the bluest sky I'd ever seen.

"Never thought about it like that," the Hulk said a while later.

"Who do you think got bullied the most?" the Nord asked, looking to instigate something.

I looked around grinning, and said, "I think Tex has seen the inside of a locker a time or two."

Tex turned back from where he stood watching the road and with hands on hips said, "You'd have to assume I was ever actually in school."

"I think it was the Nord," Mex offered.

The Nord's face darkened, a flicker of anger, or

defensiveness as his own troll backfired on him. "We moved around a lot. Can't remember a time I wasn't in some type of scrap."

"Tranquilo hombre, we're just joking," Mex said. He'd seen the look too. The kind that fought at the drop of a hat.

"Fuck you guys," he replied.

I watched the Nord as he shifted. He was silent, and I realized then how little I knew about him. He played his own cards close but was aware of others.

The mechanic strolled up a little later. He was a short, squat man in overalls, their front covered in grease and the knees patched. A grease rag hung stiffly out of his back pocket.

We told him the Hilux needed a new battery and probably an oil change and if he had four tires that would fit to throw them on. Asked him to do what he could. We offered him some extra cash to move us to the top of his list since we needed it by tomorrow, but he refused by asking, "quien mas?" and motioned to the mostly empty lot.

Then he pointed us to the nearest bar, which apparently also had a kitchen, and finished by telling us to make sure we tried the empanadas.

THE BAR WAS CALLED the La Terraza, which simply means "the terrace." It was set on the very edge of the town, its back patio beneath an overhang that looked down a rocky hill covered in more Scotch broom before connecting with the ocean below.

A little old lady seated us. White hairs taken up into a black bun. She reminded me of my own grandma, with a kind smile, and a knowing face.

We asked what they had beside beers and ended up ordering Fernet and Cokes. Apparently an Argentinian classic. It was a bitter Italian liquor that tasted like liquorish or bark or maybe saffron. Hard to pinpoint the flavors.

When the drinks came, it was not the little old abuelita that delivered them, but one of the most beautiful women I had ever seen.

Fair skinned and brown eyed, her hair just shy of black. She set our drinks down one at a time, smiling at each of us without really paying attention to any of us. There was a delicate femininity that electrified the air around me. She had a dancer's body. In another life, men had dueled to the death for her. And somehow, on the edge of the world, she seemed even more attractive by just being a surprise.

The others noticed her, but didn't linger, which I was glad for, because I had already decided I was in love. The others talked and laughed, sometimes too loudly, but their conversation felt distant, a minor drone as I waited for another glance at her.

I contributed where I could, but mostly I was silent. The next time she came around, I ordered another Fernet and managed a "gracias," and she responded with a soft and knowing "you're welcome," in English, which seemed to make the whole interaction more awkward. I think I blushed then, whether at her attention or my foolishness. Who could tell?

She smiled at me and then walked off in that

hip rolling way that makes every man think a waitress is flirting with them.

Mex kicked me under the table. With raised eyebrows and a gleam in his dark eyes, he let me know I was a fool but that he understood. I am still to this day grateful he didn't rile the others at my expense, but that was Mex—always the friend.

As the night wore on, I forgot everything I had ever known about women, about flirting, about how to tease them, and how to bed them. I had walked on to that back patio as a certain man, with experiences, a well-known horrible taste in women and a knack for getting into one-night stands when the need was right, which was mostly when the rest of my life was crumbling. But with a glance, I had been made a shy 12-year-old boy who believed in true love, and hoped one day to get married, and forgot he'd sworn off chasing women or believing in romance. And once more I had not the slightest clue how to get a girl to notice me.

The fourth Fernet came with a clumsy, half-buzzed request for her name.

"Valentina."

When she left, it was the Nord that kicked me, but his eyebrows and expression were directed at the Hulk who laughed boisterously.

"Leave it alone," I said, hoping she didn't walk in on the interaction.

When she returned, I saw a smile that was meant only for herself, full pink lips turned slightly upwards at the corner of her mouth. I watched her leave, dumbstruck.

"Go talk to her," Tex said.

"You're like a 15-year-old with his first crush," Mex piled on.

I gulped my beer, suddenly self-conscious.

"Alright, but you guys have to lay off," I said. "I don't do well under pressure."

"We see that," Tex said.

I pushed myself back from the table and said, "I'm going to find the bathroom."

"Go get em Tiger," called the Nord.

The table again descended into laughter.

I shrugged it off and pushed through the double doors to the inside of the bar. Valentina was on the far end, delivering beers to another group of locals. I found the bathroom and made my way to it. When I had relieved myself and again exited, she was back behind the bar organizing the bottles.

I sucked in my breath and wiped clammy hands on my pants. I wished we had changed clothes after that truck ride. The AC was broken, and I swore at my luck.

I had zoned out for a second, deep in thought, and when I came too, she was looking at me. She held my gaze and smiled, and I approached.

"Hi," I said, leaning up against the bar.

"Hi," she said back, slightly mocking my tone.

"I uhh... you're beautiful," I said.

"Thank you," she smiled. A blazing white smile and I could tell she was enjoying herself.

"You surprised me earlier. Where'd you learn to speak English?" I asked.

"I went to university in the U.S." she said, still wiping down the bar.

"Oh, what'd you study?"

"It's silly," she giggled, color rising to her cheeks for the first time tonight.

"Why's it silly?"

"I went for an arts degree."

"Oh, in what?"

"Painting," she said, eyebrows raised. "A literal arts degree."

"Oh," I laughed. "There's nothing wrong with that."

"Until you need money," she said matter-of-factly.

"Money isn't the only thing that matters. Not in life at least," I said, over serious, the way drunks get thinking deep thoughts.

"I agree," she said firmly. "I agree. So, what do you do Mr..."

"...Ryan," I said.

"So, what do you do Ryan?" She asked.

My mind scrambled for a suitable cover story and then almost without thinking I said, "Marine Biologist." Even as the words left my mouth, I felt bad for the lie. It was simultaneously too big to be white, and too extravagant to not collapse upon me later. But mostly I felt bad that I had lied to her. Damn this job. Damn this life. Damn women.

"Oh," she said, her interest now obvious. "What are you studying?"

"Orcas," I said. "We're tagging them to watch migration patterns." The lies kept flowing, easily now, and as they did it surprised even myself.

I watched them come out of my mouth as if I was a third party. I watched myself work from up above. This is what I was trained for. Lying. Killing. Stealing. Fighting. Manipulating. Pressure and pain. Push and pull—it was all second nature now, and I was using it on her. My stomach twisted knots.

"And have you caught any yet?" she asked earnestly.

"Not yet, but we did feed a pod of them the other day. Incredible creatures."

"I know," she said. "They were my favorite animal when I was growing up. I would drag my mother..." her voice cracked, sadness flashing across her eyes. "I would drag my mother to the library, and we would get books about whales, but I only wanted to read the parts about the Orcas."

I smiled.

"She had to read those books a hundred times," she continued. "And they were always the same books, I don't even know why we returned them."

"I was a similar kid. I think all kids like 'killer whales'," I said holding up mock quotations.

"They are actually very nice to humans," she giggled. "They have been known to save sailors from shipwrecks."

"No way," I said.

"Yes way!" she said with a giggle. "I watched a whole thing about it. There are dozens of stories of sailors being dragged back to the surface by the guardians of the sea."

"That's incredible," I said, forgetting myself for a few moments.

I shifted my footing, already feeling a bit more sober than I had just ten minutes earlier.

Valentina's eyes went wide at something behind me.

I started to turn, but it was too late. I caught the

glimmer of a bottle flashing a wide arc through the air. I felt it break over my scalp. A searing pain and stars. Ringing. Then I was falling.

I WOKE WITH A START, gasping for air. Around me were four walls painted in a soft blue pastel color, a small wooden crucifix hung on the wall directly in front of me. A jar full of paintbrushes on the dresser. A lamp next to me on a simple nightstand painted a light violet pastel.

A woman's bedroom, but how did I get here?

The bed was small, not quite a queen but not a twin either. A pile of canvases leaned up against the corner of the room, whatever was painted on them facing the wall.

I swung my legs over the edge of the bed, and my head swam. I brought a hand to the pulsing in the back of my head and felt the soft texture of bandages. I sat there for a second catching my breath. I had been stripped down to my boxers.

What the fuck?

The bar. The girl. The bottle flickering towards me under bar lights. It came back to me in hungover glimpses. Or I was concussed. If I escaped this trip without CTE it would be a miracle.

I walked gingerly around the room looking for my clothes. I stopped at the canvases by the door and pulled the one on top, turning it over. It was beautiful. A landscape scene but painted in the classical style. A woman sat on a bench as two children played in the mud below her. The sky was all haze and orange, a most stunning sunset.

There was a creak on the other side of the door, and then the knob started to turn. I caught my breath as it opened, letting the painting slide back to its place on the floor.

Valentina entered and upon seeing me in my boxers gave a slight giggle.

"What are you doing up?" she asked.

"Where am I?"

"My house," she said in a whisper. "Keep your voice down or else you will wake my father."

"You live with your father?" I asked.

"Yes," she said, "he's sick, and I take care of him. But he won't like me having a man in the house."

"What happened? Where are my friends?" I asked.

"Get dressed," she said, shoving my clothes into my arms. "Your friends are outside."

I took my clothes and was overwhelmed by the smell of detergent. "You washed them?" I asked.

"They stunk!" she said.

"Oh," I said, smelling them again. She rolled her eyes and disappeared through the door.

I slipped on my pants and pulled my shirt gingerly over my wounded scalp. A sudden wash of dizziness swept through me, and I caught my balance on the dresser next to me.

Valentina reappeared with a cup of warm coffee. "Drink it," she commanded. "It will make you feel better."

"What happened last night?" I asked once more.

"Armand. He is my ex. But we have been broken up a long time. He's jealous when he gets drunk. He hit you with a bottle."

"For talking?" I asked, incredulously.

Her face dropped, "You need to leave, your friends beat him up."

"Fuck," I muttered, "bad?" I asked, running a hand through my hair and then cringing in pain as I reached the bandage.

"Not bad, just a talking to." She winked.

"Are they in trouble?" I asked. "With the law?"

"It doesn't work like that here," she said. "The law doesn't know. The nearest courthouse is one hundred miles away. But he will go get his friends and they will come back looking for a fight. They don't like gringos."

"That's fine," I said.

"No, they are just stupid boys still," Valentina said. "But they work for bad men. You must leave."

"Cartels?" I asked.

"Smugglers," she said.

"Can we come back?"

"Why would you?"

"To see you," I said, smiling.

She blushed. "Maybe, but you need to leave."

"Fine," I said.

"Good," she grabbed my hand and pulled me through the door of the bedroom. The rest of the house was small, but well put together. At the front door, she picked up my boots and handed them to me.

"Go now," she said, giving my hand a little squeeze that made this stone-cold heart flutter.

I opened the front door and slipped out of it. The others lounged on the porch. The red rising sun cast morning rays on tired but happy faces.

"There he is," Tex said.

I felt a heavy hand on my shoulder as Hulk asked, "How you feeling' buddy. You had quite the night."

"I heard you did too," I said and pointed at Tex's black eye.

"Ah yeah, had to clean up a few of your messes but at least you didn't throw up all over yourself."

"Wait, did I?" I smelled the detergent on my clothes.

The Hulk merely shrugged in response.

We piled into the Hilux parked just the other side of Valentina's picket fence. Tex turned the key, and the Hilux grumbled to life. We rolled slowly out of Villa del Mar and hit the two-lane highway that would take us most of the way back.

On either side flat plains of yellow grass waved gently in the breeze. The sun climbed the sky higher, and the distant Patagonia mountains caught its shifting light like so many stained-glass windows, a shifting cascade of blues and grays.

⁂

It was mid-morning when we parked the Hilux by the abandoned barn. "Why don't we just take the Hilux back?" the Hulk asked.

"Are you nuts?" Tex said. "Mike will lose his mind if he knew what we got up to. He'd fire it and bury us under it. Good luck ever sneaking out again."

"Yeah, dummy," Mex added, "what he said."

I swallowed hard and felt the back of my head... still pounding... ahead of me a five-hour hike.

Chapter Twelve

The boat rocked rhythmically. I strained to keep my eyes open. There was something about the ocean that put me to sleep. The gentle rocking motion, the sound of it. Granted, it was the middle of the night, but the ocean still had this effect on me even had it been the middle of the day. It was like returning to the womb; the boat's stuffy cabin was a substitute for amniotic fluid.

"You still awake?" Mike asked. He turned around in the driver's seat and flashed a grin, his pearl white teeth reflecting green from the Barracuda's dash. I pushed up in my chair. I put a lipper in and sat buzzing.

"Is she still out there?" I asked.

"Oh, she's out there," Mike said. "Just been hanging out, doing everything she's supposed to."

"How long are we going to wait for her?" I asked.

"All night if we have to," Mike said.

I stared out the window even though there was nothing to see. It was pitch black. The slight tint on the boat's glass blocked the stars.

"Like I said before, keep your eyes peeled tonight," Mike continued.

Mike had briefed us earlier: "Argentian Intelligence is feeding their double-agents and diplomats a story about a new group of "vigilantes" or "eco-terror" types that sank the missing ship.

"As our operations continue, and hopefully become more successful, they will begin leaking a "dossier" about the group to the media. Bucaneros del Eco-Venganza. It's a giant psyop. They'll organize man hunts and patrols to put a good show on, and then we'll conveniently continue to hit boats where they aren't."

It was a good plan. Fisherman loved to talk, and more than that, they loved tall tales. While the news media was still in the dark about the ship, every seaside dive bar from here to Buenos Aires would be buzzing with the "truth" about "el pirata."

Intelligence work was about information, especially the flow of it, but even more importantly, the (apparent) legitimacy of it. Legitimacy can be manufactured though, laundered like the dirtiest money. No one believes the media. Leaking it to the press immediately would draw the wrong kind of attention. But if the story was fed into the underworld first—filtered through dirty cops, sailors, and prostitutes—then it would look legitimate, organic.

For the next two hours I sat in my seat on the boat and struggled to stay awake, feeding myself tobacco, and fighting the rhythmic rock of the boat. Tex finally sat straight up in his seat and said, "She's moving now. She's moving good."

I leaned forward and watched the little red dot

that signified the ship's position on the dash. She was moving alright. And then she disappeared. Two miles away from Argentine waters. She had gone dark.

"There it is," Mike shouted. "Pull that grid."

The radio crackled as the Nord passed the grid over the radio.

"Set a search area. Just like last time," Mike said. "Let's get these bastards."

∴

An hour later we were beside it. This fishing boat was smaller than the one before. Maybe half the size. It was called the Yu Leng 190. There were half a dozen other boats, including a larger Reefer sitting just outside the EEZ, so we would have to get out quick once we sank this one.

The RIB bumped up against the side of the boat. Sea spray swept over the edge of the tiny RIB and swirled at our feet. There were no steel rungs this time so Mike hooked a rope ladder up to the topside with a painter's pole. The nervousness I had felt on the first mission was mostly gone. I was now fully in the groove. The pit in my stomach was still there, it was always there, but you learned to ignore it.

The others went up the ladder and I followed. Topside, I swung onto the deck and landed in a crouch behind the others. I scanned the deck through my NODs. This one was barely lit up. And strangely silent. My skin crawled.

"We take the bridge first," Mike said in a whisper, and then he led off, waving us forward with two fingers.

The bridge of the ship is its heart. If you control the bridge, you control the ship. Most fishing boats, well most boats in general, have their communications space co-located on the bridge, and if it isn't, it's usually in near proximity.

We cat walked to the bridge, slinking through shadows cast by the ship's yellow lamps. We all lined up behind the door to the cabin. Hulk had thus far doubled as both our breacher and our medic. Strapped to his back was a hooligan tool and a 12 gauge Mossberg Shockwave loaded with 00 buck. He was also carrying sheet explosive in case we really needed to breach anything.

I crouched next to the wall of the bridge just beneath a porthole and covered the stairway behind us. The ocean breeze was light and cool on my skin, like fresh sheets.

A sharp crackle of electricity climbed the base of my neck and my vision narrowed slightly, I felt it. That thing I felt while surfing. We were all in it now. Connected. Like a hive mind. Each one of us sharing a telepathic link. Operating as one body, with eyes that saw everything. As individuals we had blind spots, but as a group we did not. We were one organism, like an octopoid monster—each tentacle operating independently, yet perfectly coordinated with the others.

Hulk took the hooligan tool to the door and wrenched it open with a loud crack; the wooden door splintered around the handle.

Mike kicked the door in and swung his rifle up while screaming something in Mandarin.

Mex went in next; I was third.

It was dark inside.

A Chinese man shouted something in gibberish and raised a revolver. Mike put two in his chest with a muffled thunk-thunk. He dropped like a sack of rice, red blooming on the front of his white linen shirt.

A door to my left opened, and a man appeared in the frame. Less than a heartbeat, and I clocked that he was unarmed. It took me three steps to get to him—I slammed the butt of my rifle into his neck knocking him backwards.

He made a horrible choking noise and grasped at his windpipe. He dropped to his knees and I kicked him in the chest sending him sprawling backwards.

Without looking, I stepped past him, weapon and eyes trained forward. The room was empty. "Clear," I shouted.

It was small, and there was a bed in the corner with rumpled sheets. It was the captain's berthing.

I dragged the gasping Captain out by his collar and tossed him on the floor in front of the others.

Hulk zip-tied him.

The dead one was slumped against the wall, dark red pooling on the ship's rubberized floor.

"Too easy," Mike said. "Round up the rest."

He unhooked a thermite grenade, pulled the pin, and set it on top of the communications equipment. The grenade smoked before throwing bright sparks across the inside of the bridge. As it reached its white-hot crescendo, we were already leaving.

We worked our way down towards the lower

deck. Psycho was running point. Myself and Hulk behind him.

As we rounded a corner, we found two men standing guard by the entrance to the crew's berthing.

One of them started to raise a rifle. There was a brief moment where I saw his face. He looked more confused than terrified. And no doubt, considering it was dark out and we likely just looked like shadows.

But Psycho's rifle thumped and the man twisted backwards. As he spasmed, he fired off the AK and sent a loud cacophonous round into the steel grating at our feet. Green sparks flashed and the ricocheting bullet whined off into the night.

His buddy jumped, having been smoking a cigarette and looking fully the other direction.

I squeezed off two rounds into his chest and sent my third through his face as he dropped. He never even managed to unsling his rifle.

There were shouts coming from the crew's berthing below.

"I got door," Hulk called.

Immediately, I pivoted to cover the front of the ship while Tex took a position covering the passageway behind us.

From behind me, I heard the big door to the mechanical berthing open behind me, and then I heard Hulk's Mossberg bark, a cha-chunk as he racked it, a scream, and then another heavy concussion as Hulk let them have it in the staircase.

"Moving," Mike called.

I glanced back to watch him disappear down the stairway, followed by Hulk and Psycho.

Very distant and muffled, came the sound of gunfire in the berthing.

I heard yells from the other side of the ship and knew whoever else was above deck would have heard enough of our noise to move on our position. The nice thing about ships is that they are all right angles. Its rooms, and halls, and passageways, and shooting lanes through cargo containers. This makes it easy to defend and hard to advance.

"Contact," Tex called as he let his big gun rip.

I twisted right and took cover behind a steel door as a bullet snapped overhead.

The sharp crackle of an AK-47 answered Tex.

I spotted the muzzle flash and squeezed off several controlled bursts at the place where it had been.

"Moving left," Tex called.

He was circling for a flank.

"Covering," I said, and squeezed off several more rounds. The AK had yet to respond and I imagined he'd either already moved or was too scared to poke his head out. Regardless, no one was moving up the right side of the ship without me seeing them.

I felt the slide side forward with a bit extra oomph and knew I was empty. I removed the empty mag, pocketed it, and reloaded a new one. I racked the charging handle and then poured more covering fire down the passageway.

In the distance, I heard the muffled thump of Tex's rifle.

I paused my fire. And then over my headset heard Tex's voice. "I got em."

"We're coming back up," Mike said. "Crew berthing secured."

"Pretty heavy for fishermen," Tex said over comms.

"Yeah," Mike said. "This is no fishing boat."

WHEN WE'D SWEPT the top of the ship twice over, we rendezvoused at the door to the boat's cargo hold. It was chained shut and locked with a padlock. Hulk took the hooligan tool to the Masterlock. We pulled the metal door open, and I entered first, my rifle raised.

No one was there to meet me.

It was just a long stairwell, maybe twelve steps down, and then another door at the bottom. A sweaty, musty stench stung my nostrils.

The stairs were rusted and covered in water. A decomposing rat lay in the corner, and I instantly connected the sight to the overpowering sickly-sweet smell.

At the second door, Hulk made a gap with the hooligan tool, working its wedge-shaped head in-between the door and its jam. I posted up behind him, barrel over his shoulder, ready for whatever lay behind the door.

Hulk pried the tool back and forth, working it deeper into the door, and then when it was just right, he reached back and slapped my leg. I tapped his shoulder, signaling I was ready.

He gave the hooligan tool two more heavy pulls. It bent and groaned under the effort, and he slid the hooligan tool up higher. With the next pull the door popped free with a loud crack.

Before me—dozens of bodies, crouched and shivering in the damp dark of the ship's hold.

"They're... women," I said.

Then movement in the back corner—*a shoulder strap—an AK-47*.

My finger tightened around the trigger and I sent two rounds through his midsection. Hulk fired off towards the other side of the room, another bogie fell.

We moved into the room.

There were fifteen or twenty women all crouched on the floor, shivering and chattering in a mix of languages. Some sobbed hysterically, but most cowered, trembling in fear. All of them were chained to the floors.

"What the fuck is this?" the Hulk asked. The hold was small, he had to crouch slightly to keep his head from scraping the ceiling.

"I think they're prisoners?" I said slowly.

"Sex trafficking?" the Hulk asked.

"I don't know."

My man in the corner moaned. Somehow still alive, he started to crawl towards his AK.

"Grab him," Hulk said.

I slung his AK and grabbed the wounded man by the collar. Hulk grabbed his man's rifle but left the body.

At the top of the stairs, I dropped the body and set the AK off to the side.

The Chinaman squirmed around in his own blood. He was gut shot.

The wounded man reached a bloody hand out

and grasped my ankle. I kicked him off and stepped backwards.

Mike stepped up and knelt by the man. He spoke to him in Mandarin, and I could tell the man understood, because he stopped gasping and squirming. When Mike had finished his spiel, the dying Chinaman started to rant and rave, whatever story Mike had asked for he was only too happy to give.

When he was done, he looked satisfied. Then in broken English said, "You help now. Help now."

Mike stood up and pulled his 1911. He put one in the man's head.

"This is a bordello. A floating whorehouse. They use the girls to service the different fishing boats," Mike said.

"That's why they were armed," Tex said.

"Well, what the fuck are we supposed to do now?" the Hulk asked. "We can't kill them."

"Well we can," Mike said. "But we won't."

Hulk may not have had a problem with killing fisherman on the high seas, but I had a hunch his line in the sand rhymed with women and children.

Mike paced, and then asked, "how many are down there?"

"Twenty, maybe thirty," I replied. The Hulk nodded his agreement.

Mex had remained silent up to this point, but I knew where he would stand.

"We leave them..." Mike said.

Mex looked up, and started to speak, but Mike held out a hand and said, "Let me finish. We dump the dead bodies overboard, and then hit the distress beacons on the lifeboats. We drop Argentine intelligence a line. We tell them to get the Coast Guard out here. They'll have the women safe by morning."

Mike dropped to a knee and swung off his pack. A moment later he produced cans of green spray paint. He handed one to me, and the other to Mex.

"Use these on the bridge and anywhere else you want to tag. Write shit like Viva la Tierra and Green Peace and Death to Sex Traffickers. Throw in a Bucaneros del Eco-Venganza somewhere."

"Does it all need to be in Spanish?" I asked.

"No, mix it up," Mike said. "Will make us look like a mixed crew. It'll give the Argentinians something to work with when they start leaking shit to the media."

∴

THIRTY MINUTES LATER, I was tossing bodies overboard. We cut them open stem to stern so they wouldn't bloat and float.

There were 28 girls all told, well 27, because one of them was dead. She got hit with a passthrough when I shot my man in the hold. I could add her to my list of night terrors.

We unchained the women. They huddled together under blankets from the crew's berthing. All looked frightened and traumatized, but a few looked relieved. A couple, elated.

I helped Mex pull out the inflatable life rafts. We inflated them, hit the distress beacons, and tossed them overboard so the girls didn't try to do anything stupid when we left.

And then we were gone. Our RIBs plowing

through the open water, I flicked my NODs up on top of my head and looked out into the darkness. The entire milky way spun overhead, stars so close and so bright that I could reach out and touch them.

The ocean in front of us as black as darkest night, and only discernible by the other senses—the taste of sea spray, the smell of salt water, the motion of waves. Two small green lights bobbed out in the void, beckoning us—our Barracudas.

Chapter Thirteen

The sun was rising when we got back to the cove. Everyone was still buzzing from the op.

The Nord got the fire on the beach going, and we stood around it, stripped down to our wetsuits, beers in hand. The Ares and the Bruiser slumbered in our makeshift harbor.

I took a sip of my beer, savoring the flavor, and trading my stress for the alcohol's sweet release. The others were feeling good about saving the girls, I was too for that matter. I wondered what lives we had saved them from, but the cynic in me wondered if they wouldn't find their way back to it. Victims had a habit of becoming the victimized.

We settled into our beers and our jokes and tried to forget what had just happened. Four beers deep and Mike held court, talking about the Comanches, how they would tie settlers to their own wagon wheels and burn parts of them off.

"The Anglo-Saxon and the Comanche," he said. "Now that was a who's who of history's biggest bad asses. You figure just a thousand years earlier and the Anglos were the same thing, a bunch of feral pagans running around with blue painted faces and feathers weaved into their hair.

"The Spanish tried to take out the Comanche and couldn't get it done. They got beat back every time. Can you imagine. The same empire that razed the Aztecs and laid low the Inca got up to the plains and noped the fuck out. Lords of the Plains. Motherfuckers even wiped out the Apache, or tried too.

And then came the Anglos, bunch of mooks with nothin better to do, just kept throwing themselves at Texas, and you know why they got it done when the Spanish couldn't? You know why? Cus they fought em on their own terms."

"I've got some Comanche blood," Tex said.

"No shit," Mike said.

"Yeah, on my mom's side," Tex said, "couldn't evcr prove it though for college."

I sat in my lawn chair, bare feet feeling the grit of the sand, and experimenting with how close to the fire was just right for them. It was harder to gauge the right distance with bare feet than it was with boots. Which was counterintuitive.

But every part of my body cried out with relief in front of the fire, and my mind sung with endorphic release. I took the moment in, like a fly on the wall, as if a casual observer.

The others laughed over the fire, releasing the tension of the night's ordeal as we'd done for millennia.

I caught Psycho's eyes, and they were full of light, full of life, he could feel the energy too. *Why did I resent him?*

The booze was setting in, releasing my mind from "safe" delusions. For killing the fisherman? I should be thanking him. Thanking him for keeping my conscience clean. And maybe that was why? I resented myself for letting him do the dirty work. Letting him kill while I tried to pretend my hands were clean. The blood was as much mine as his, anything else was delusion.

He smirked at one of the Nord's one liners, but caught me looking, and went deadpan, and that's when I realized that Psycho could speak English.

Part Two

The Ballad of Bahrawar

March, 2001 | Bamiyan Valley, Afghanistan

Bahrawar walked through the encampment, the rough stones of an ancient and long dried riverbed underfoot. He circled an old Toyota pickup, vinyl decals ran the length of it, chipped and flaking. Mud thrown from the wheel wells had turned the white truck mostly brown. As he circled, the young boy examined the large gun in the bed of the truck with boyish wonder. It was a DShK. A large belt-fed machine gun designed for both anti-air and anti-infantry operations.

He imagined himself up there, shooting at invaders with the weapon's butterfly trigger. He picked up a rock and tossed it absently into the desert, for no real reason other than rocks were meant to be thrown, at least that's what rocks meant to little boys.

Bahrawar assessed the line of motorcycles next... with their ragged, dusty tires, and their mismatched paint schemes. Some of them were nothing but a crude mockery of a motorcycle, having been frankensteined together with parts cannibalized from even worse motorcycles.

The sun was high in the sky, and the early spring wind was warm on Bahrawar's small, dirt covered face. As long as it was no longer winter, Bahrawar was happy. Just over eight years old and he had already learned to dread the winter. Learned to dread the harsh cold winds that swept off the Hindu Kush Mountains. Learned to dread numb toes and burning fingers; the cold that crept in everywhere and never left. But he had also learned the warmth of spring. The new hope that was green buds and a yellow sun. The warm wind that thawed the snow, and the joys of birdsong. Only one that suffered in the pit of winter could know the joyous heights of a spring thermal.

The blazing Afghan summers and brutal winters had already left their mark on the young boy's soul. Hardened his spirit, just as the country had turned his naked soles to shoe leather and weather-chapped his ragged knuckles. Already, he possessed the leathern look of a shepherd, one born in the desert and raised on the mountain. Lean and ruddy.

From the tent ahead of him he could hear his elders arguing with the visitors. The same ones that belonged to the motorcycles and the truck.

The low growling voice of his Neekuh or grandfather, the tribe's patriarch, carried far, even when it was not raised, but right now, it was raised. Bahrawar had already begun to equate Jirgas with trouble—or marriage. Feuds and marriage and sheep, that was all the Kochi seemed to care about.

"Bahrawar, where have you been," the voice of his uncle came from behind.

Bahrawar turned, "I came looking for you."

"Come then," his uncle said. His uncle was a lean man, with a beaked nose and high cheekbones set below sunken eyes so brown that they often looked black. While not a mean man, he often looked more stern than he was. Barely thirty years old, lines carved into his forehead and baked in by the sun, he looked nearly ancient to Bahrawar.

In his hands he carried an old Mosin-Nagant with a stock so battered and scratched that it looked like it had seen a hundred wars. Bahrawar stared at the gun jealously as he followed along behind, excitement climbing his chest.

They followed the dry riverbed down into a narrow glen, leaving the tents that Bahrawar called home behind them. They continued like this for nearly a mile, finally stopping where the sheep were pastured.

His uncle showed him a rock.

"Here is good place. You sit," he commanded. The man watched as the boy did as he was told, and then continued, "you see how it is higher here, how you can look out over all of them."

Bahrawar nodded his head, and his uncle took a seat next to him. He leaned forward on the gun as if it were a cane or a shepherd's bow, his keen eyes scanning the flock for anything out of place. They sat in silence, merely watching the sheep.

"What do those men want?" Bahrawar asked, his curiosity finally getting the better of him.

"Aslam. He has come to restore his honor," his uncle replied, then added with a chuckle, "he thinks commanding fighters makes him a big man. He thinks he can make demands."

"So, he has come for restitution?" Bahrawar asked.

"Aslam thinks only of wealth."

"What will Neekuh do?"

"He will send him away."

"But what if he takes his revenge?" Bahrawar asked, his eyes wide.

"He won't, he is a coward," his uncle spat into the red dirt at their feet.

This answer satisfied Bahrawar. The two of them again sat in silence, and the sheep grazed.

"But tonight, you will learn bravery, so you don't become like your cousin Aslam," his uncle said.

Bahrawar gulped hard as his uncle passed him the Mosin.

"You remember what I showed you?" his uncle asked.

Bahrawar nodded excitedly.

"Good then," he said, and pulled a piece of cloth from his wool trousers and handed Bahrawar his dinner. "I will come and get you in the morning."

"Remember. Fear... is only up here," his uncle said, bouncing an outstretched finger off Bahrawar's forehead, "but here," he said, pointing to the boy's heart, "is always stronger."

Bahrawar watched his uncle go. *He would prove his bravery tonight.* But even as he thought these things, he would still pray to Allah that the wolves did not come.

As the sun sank lower in the sky, Bahrawar unwrapped the small cloth that his uncle had handed him and ate slowly of the bread and cheese within. When he had finished, he took two large gulps from the canteen slung around his shoulder. It was dented and had a faint smattering of rust along the bottom. A small chain dangled from the cap, which no longer connected to the main body of the army green container, the weld that had connected it was broken. It was an old Soviet canteen, and a gift from his father, taken off a merchant in Bamiyan. The boy traced a finger over the dented metal and wondered what battles the old canteen had seen.

When the sun finally passed below the horizon, Bahrawar felt worms of fear wriggle up his spine. It was dark out, and he prayed for the moon, even though he knew it would not come, for it had been a full moon but a week ago. The stars would be his only company tonight.

Bahrawar pulled his knees in against his body and huddled beneath the blanket his uncle had left. He clutched the Mosin across his chest, and it gave him comfort.

The temperature dropped and his breath turned frosty. His toes began to go numb. The night was overly silent, and occasionally the sheep would mill about and crunch dead leaves or grass which always plied his imagination with certain danger—*or maybe the Madar-i-Al.* She was the old hag who stole boys that wandered alone in the night.

At one point he thought he heard gunfire and screams in the distance, but he decided these too were only specters of the night.

His older brother had often told him stories about the mountains. How at night, when the wind was long, if one listened closely, he could hear the distant clang of ancient battles.

His brother had once sworn that when he was tending sheep late one night, an invading army with a Khan at its head had passed through the valley below him, their eyes blazing, bows silver in the moonlight. He had hidden himself until they passed by, the thundering hooves of their ancient army pounding thunder in his head.

The next morning, when he had inspected the valley below, he had found no sign of them. No track nor disturbance in the earth. All he had found was an iron arrowhead. He had shown it to Bahrawar and it had been enough to convince him that his brother really had seen a ghostly army.

In Afghanistan these stories were easy to believe, for the scars of long ago wars lay scattered across the land, plentiful as so many flowers in a poppy field.

Even now, several kilometers away lay the ruins of Shahr-e Zuhak, The Red City, the place where Genghis Khan's own grandson had been killed. It was said that in the still and silent moments of the night, if one snuck into the ruins of the city, he could still hear the screams from the slaughter that had followed.

A wolf howled somewhere off in the distance and Bahrawar sat up straight. He let the blanket fall from his shoulders. He clutched the rifle forward. His finger clamped around the trigger.

Bahrawar stayed like this for several minutes, fear and adrenaline turning him statue still.

After a long interminable silence, Bahrawar collapsed backwards onto his rock and rewrapped the blanket around his shoulders. The sheep milled peacefully, and sleep beckoned him. Fear and tension having done their part to wear him out, tiring him to the extent that he no longer cared about wolves or lost armies—*not even the Madar-i-Al.*

Bahrawar awoke some time later to the terrible sound of crying... and snarling.

Bahrawar leapt from his rock; the Mosin clutched tightly forward. He ran towards the sounds. Compelled forward not out of a sense of duty but a fear of failure.

Ahead of him, in the inky black Afghan night, a shadow moved across a still lump of wool, faintly luminescent in the starlight. It was a wolf.

Bahrawar's rifle found his shoulder. He fired. The animal yelped. The brilliant flash from the old rifle left him blind. He swung his head around frantically, desperate for his vision to clear, his ears ringing from the gunshot.

He dropped to one knee and pried the bolt of the Mosin back. His hands were shaking terribly and it took him several attempts to work the bolt open.

A deep low growl invaded the ringing in his ears.

The bolt slid backwards, and the clang of spent brass clattered against the rocks at his feet. He chambered another round and popped up to his feet, turning circles in the darkness. He was disoriented.

Another snarl and a whirl of movement.

Bahrawar pivoted in the direction of the noise and started forward. He glimpsed movement and heard scuffling on the rocks.

Bahrawar aimed, flinching as the rifle went off in his hands. The bullet whined off some rocks. He had missed yet again.

He was again blind, and his ears rang even louder. Again, he dropped to one knee and worked the Mosin's bolt.

The ring of spent brass.

He slammed another round forward.

More snarling.

His night sight returned and with it the wolf. Bahrawar raised the rifle slowly. He focused his breathing and took a few extra moments to steady his aim. Again, the rifle leapt beneath his touch, but this time it brought the satisfying thump of a bullet striking hide.

When the sun rose the next morning it would be upon a man, or at least that is what Bahrawar's uncle had told him. But Bahrawar felt no difference. Only worse, truth be told.

He eased himself from his perch, pinks and grays filtering in from under the horizon and made his way to examine his prize underneath the light of a new day. Bahrawar poked the dead wolf with the barrel of the Mosin, surprised that the body had already gone stiff.

His first shot had been too far back and broken the wolf's hips which is why it had neither charged him nor fled. It had only snarled and tried to drag itself off. His third shot had been true, finding the wolf's heart. Bahrawar smiled. *Maybe he felt a little bit different.*

The dead sheep laid a ways off, cold and bloody, a mangled mess. He would take it back to camp, maybe they could yet make use of it. *Per-*

haps, if I would've been awake. He shook off the thought.

It was midday and the sun had climbed almost fully overhead when Bahrawar began to get worried. His uncle had still not come to fetch him. He sat impatiently on the rock. He picked apart stems of grass and flicked the pieces on the ground. Another hour and the rumble in his stomach convinced him to look for himself.

Bahrawar slung the Mosin over his back, took a long sip of his water, and plodded purposefully over to the dead sheep. The ewe stared at him with one empty eye. A fly landed on the eye's glassy surface, now hazy with death. Bahrawar waved it away, disgustedly.

Bahrawar took the sheep by its back legs and struggled to pick it up. He tried to lift it, to carry it the way he had seen his uncle carry sheep—across his back. But it was no use. It had grown stiff and was now awkward and heavy. He couldn't even get it fully off the ground, let alone across his shoulders. He would have to leave it for now.

∴

THE ENCAMPMENT LAY IN RUIN. Tents overturned. Cooking pots and supplies scattered. The bodies lay where they had fallen. Aslam and his fighters had taken their revenge. Pashtun justice. Balal. But Bahrawar had never imagined it would like this or come to this.

The women and the children were all gone. The pack animals were also gone. All that remained were empty tents and the bodies of the men that had defended them.

Clouds of flies had already invaded the camp, twisting and twirling over the dead. He heard none of the usual sounds of early morning life. The laughter of his cousins, nor the grunt of the camels. Not even the braying of the donkeys. Instead just that terrible buzzing of the flies.

One of the tents had been set on fire, a thin trail of smoke twisted upwards having mostly burnt itself out. Smoke stung his nostrils.

The Kochi were nomadic. Moving with their herds from Pakistan to Afghanistan and back again, as they had done since the times of Alexander. Home was the mountains. Home was the green pastures. Home was the gurgling river. Home was this burning tent. Home was anywhere his people were. Home was gone.

A bit of color drew his eye and he suddenly recognized Neekuh's striped kamiz. He stumbled forward and knelt by the body of his grandfather. The earth was black where his blood had pooled.

After a bit he rose and his sandaled feet picked their own path through the mess of tents and overturned camp furniture. He felt like a ghost, left behind to wander and sorrow.

He found his uncle at the far end of camp. In death, he still gripped an old Ak-47, which Bahrawar pried from stiff fingers and set aside. A bullet had torn away the right half of his face. The face of his stern but caring uncle gone and, in its place, a mangled mash of flesh and bone.

Bahrawar waved the flies off. He cringed, covering the pulped face with his uncle's own shawl.

Tears welled in his eyes and from his uncle's midriff he removed the knife that the man kept at his hip. His pesh-kabz, with its curved blade and its bronze sheath, intricately carved with Afghan flowers and scroll. It was a ceremonial dagger, a symbol of a man's honor.

Bahrawar had thought often of the day when he would be given his own. Now he tucked it into his own trousers.

There were no bodies for the women. They had not been killed but taken. And Bahrawar wondered at that. Wondered if he would ever see them again.

Bahrawar turned around and around then. The lonely mountains on each side. The Afghan wind howling. And as far as he could see there was silence. The devastating silence of an empty land, the graveyard of empires, a land of ghosts and weeping women and orphaned children.

Bahrawar screamed.

⁂

THE MAN and his son were Hazaras. Bahrawar had frantically waved them down as their old military truck chewed through the red dirt road that skirted the ruins of his former encampment.

Upon seeing his need, they'd agreed to help him. Bahrawar wondered if they would have still helped had the truck been full of product, but it did not matter.

When the old man asked what had happened, all Bahrawar managed to say was, "Taliban," and the old man had pulled thoughtfully at his white beard, green eyes saddened. "We help."

The funeral happened quickly and according to tradition. The bodies were cleansed and covered, deposited in graves marked by large stones on the side of the mountain. The sun set an hour after they were interred, and Bahrawar felt a weight lift off his shoulders.

Afterwards, the man offered to take him back to his home in Kabul. But Bahrawar refused, saying simply that he must return to his sheep. The old man had started towards him, but Bahrawar backed away, clutching the Mosin tightly.

Bahrawar set off into the inky night then, and the old man watched thoughtfully as he went, again pulling on his long white beard.

* * *

Bahrawar found his sheep scattered and after gathering them back up stayed with them.

Another month and he was sick of mutton and sick of sheep and sick of the silence. And so, he drove them onward down the mountain until he found a village. The sheep brought a small amount of coin, and he stayed the night, and shared bread with his host.

He journeyed west then, for he did not know where to go, hitching a ride with a pair of Tajiks that got him halfway to nowhere. From nowhere, he tried to hitch again but was beaten and robbed by Uzbeks. They left him on the side of the road.

He was nursed to health by another band of

Kochi and repaid their hospitality with his skills as a shepherd. He made no money, but for a time earned a full belly. He liked this band, but they were not his family, and by the end of summer his feet again started to yearn.

The United States had by this time invaded and destroyed the Taliban. They'd driven them like rats back into their mountain strongholds where they scurried around in caves and burrows only coming out at night to steal and cause trouble.

Others were not happy about the invaders, but Bahrawar smiled to himself each time he heard of an airstrike or a tale of dead Taliban fighters. Once he waved to a convoy. Allah was punishing them. Revenge was his.

SEASONS PASSED and he drifted onward, and for a time found work in the poppy fields of Omar Sayyid, who was less a farmer than he was a warlord—controlling trade and fighters. During the day, Bahrawar worked. At night, he slept in the fields.

Late one night, one of Omar's fighters came to him, for Bahrawar had not yet grown a beard, and the man having grown tired of sheep came looking for a boy, but Bahrawar had no intention of being raped, and the practice of bacha bazi disgusted him, and so the fighter found the cold steel of Bahrawar's pesh-kabz, the one that had belonged to his uncle.

Bahrawar thrust it upward beneath the man's ribs, turned it once and spilled his blood. It was the second wolf he ever killed.

Bahrawar fled west once more.

* * *

In Herat, he took up with a shopkeeper who had no son. Again he worked for a bit of bread and a place to sleep. He stuck close to himself, and made few friends, but always remembered the ways of Pashtun honor.

It was here that he learned to read and write. He would slip away from the shopkeeper's when the day was done and go to classes taught in a new school that the invaders had set up.

He took to language easily, and in the process of learning to write his own, learned English as well. He made friends with the teacher, a man from thc United Kingdom, who said he did not believe in the war, but believed in the people.

They argued often about what was best to do with the Taliban. Then a car bomb destroyed the school and killed his teacher. Bahrawar's hate grew deeper.

* * *

He was old enough to grow a beard when he joined the Afghan Army, either fourteen or sixteen, maybe older, maybe younger, he did not know, for he had no birthday and anyone that had once known, he no longer knew.

Most recruits joined for the salary and even more joined for the bribery. Where others lacked discipline, Bahrawar made up for their failings with devotion. After a single year, he was promoted to be an officer. Another summer more, and the name Bahrawar stirred fear in the hearts of the Taliban.

HELMAND PROVINCE | *JUNE, 2007*

Mike sat on the hood of his Humvee, rifle slung across his legs. He smoked a cigarette and watched the minutes click by on his watch.

At 2130 they rolled.

The rest of his unit milled nearby. They were providing support to a platoon of Marines that had been hit especially hard over the last few months. For the last three weeks, they had gone on nightly raids. The men were tired and exhausted but morale was good. The arrival of Mike's unit had made the Marines the aggressors. No longer did they go on seemingly pointless daytime patrols designed to draw fire. No longer did they feel like targets. They were raiders now. They were the ones that stalked the night. They attacked with swift surprise.

The switch had breathed new life into the platoon. Some of them having been deployed for the better part of eighteen months. The marines had joined to stack bodies, not get shot at. Mike was helping them stack bodies.

Pablo walked back from the FOB's gate. "The Afghans are on their way," Pablo said as he approached.

"Well, aint that just great," Mike replied, ashing the cigarette on the hood of the truck.

"Helluva way to treat government property,"

Mike sighed. "You should see the way I treat strippers."

Pablo laughed, his eyebrows arching and said, "Every one's got a different way of serving."

Pablo was his breacher and built like a brick shithouse. How he'd ever made it through Special Forces training, Mike didn't know.

The man was pure muscle, and muscle was heavy. In a unit full of leopards, Pablo was a bull. He leaned against the Humvee next to where Mike sat, and they watched two Afghan nationals struggle to open the FOB's gate.

"Watch your back tonight," Mike said. "I don't trust these fucks. Been a lot of green on blue attacks down here."

"Sooner they learn to fight for themselves, the sooner we can leave."

"Eh, I don't know about that," Mike said. "I think there's a reason no one's got it done here. Not Alexander, not Genghis, not the Brits, and not the Soviets."

"You don't have faith in McChrystal?"

"Fuck meee," Mike said, laughing. "Let's get this show on the road."

Mike waved his hand in the air, giving the universal signal for mount the fuck up and fifty Humvee doors all seemed to open at once as the Marines and his team piled inside their steel war chariots. Curses, jokes, and orders all being tossed back and forth with earnest delight.

Mike smiled as a surge of adrenaline hit his

veins and nested in the small of his back. War was kundalini and this shit made him feel like motherfuck'n John Coffee Hays.

Mike didn't have a lot of regrets, almost none that many others understood, but one of them was having been born in 1980. He was doing his best for the lot he was cast, but in another life, he was on the Great Plains stacking Comanches, or in a Viking longship setting fire to Saxon villages. Ares was his god. He had thought often of having them put that shit on his dog tags. Follower of Ares. God of Strife. When he inevitably ate a bullet, he'd laugh from up above as Veteran Affairs struggled through the bureaucratic red tape of "burial by funeral pyre." Pencil pushing fucks would probably just bury his ass anyways.

The column of MRAPs and HUMVEEs slowly departed Camp Bastion and snaked their way towards the rendezvous with the Afghan National Army. At the rendezvous point, the Afghan army's vehicles took position behind the column of Marine vehicles.

Half an hour later they stopped three miles from the target location, a small compound surrounded by fields. The residence of Gulshan al Boor. A wealthy poppy farmer, who for the most part had kept his terroristic footprint small.

But signals had picked up chatter about repeated movements of HME (homemade explosives) making their way to this farm. Gulshan wasn't their primary target. He was just a sympathizer and financier. A link in the vast chain of insurgency.

They'd had Intelligence, Surveillance, and Reconnaissance (ISR) assets on the compound for the better part of three months, and then at last, yesterday, their real target had arrived—OBJ Bambi—an IED maker out of Kandahar. ISR got a positive ID on him when he arrived.

Mike slid out of the driver's seat of the lead vehicle and pushed his NODs back up onto his head.

Damned things, he'd have a migraine tomorrow. A big bright, full moon was out. The same one that we had put a man on.

Pablo shouldered up next to him as they waited for Yari to make his way forward.

Yar Mohammed finally joined them. They called him Yari for short. He was an Afghani, and a solid guy, one of the few that spoke English. Before the war he had worked as a professor, now he was the unit's interpreter. He'd worked with them for the better part of a year and was, by this point, a member of the family.

"Where you want the Afghans?" Yari asked.

"Put them up front," Mike said. "I don't trust none of these fucks."

Yari seemed to ignore the implication. He didn't trust most of his people either.

Five minutes later they were off, working a long wedge formation down the empty Afghan road. When the compound was at last in sight, Mike called a halt. They had approached from the North, the same side as the main vehicle gate to the compound.

Afghan compounds were built like mini forts, with tall mud walls and a mangled mess of mismatched buildings inside. It was safe to assume they were all connected in some manner or another. The

Afghans didn't have houses. They had WACO style compounds. When the kids grew up there was no empty nest... they moved into the room down the hall, and when they had more kids than they had house or hut, they just kept building rooms, and when the grandkids arrived, they built new rooms, and new houses, that all connected to the main house through some rat hole or tunnel or doorway. An Afghani compound was essentially a human ant hill.

On the west side of the house was a small main gate. That's where his team would go in, and just inside and to their right was the room where OBJ Bambi should be sleeping. They would be in and out, get their man, and then call for the main raid. The Afghans would take the main gate, and the Marines and EOD would roll in to clean up whatever was left of the mess.

Mike and his team split off through the field north of the compound, while Yari and the Afghans took their place by the side of the road to wait for the main assault.

When Mike and his team made it to the main gate, all was quiet. Too quiet. Mike held his hand out and Pablo passed him a large hunk of rotting meat wrapped in cloth. Intel had said there were dogs inside. Mike hated dogs.

The team was made for infiltration, made for sneaking about silently in the night, they were the Army's own lab created version of the Apache, designed for the shadows, thriving in silence. But dogs... dogs ruined all of that.

Mike hucked the meat over the wall and prayed to the gods that those dogs found it. He'd give them five minutes, that was two minutes longer than the tranquilizer took to work.

If it didn't then his team would become the main assault, and that would be bad news for everyone involved.

Five minutes later, Pablo used a small drill on the main gate's hinges. Mike watched him work. No dogs barked. Either they were asleep at the opposite end of the compound, or the meat trick had worked. So far everything was moving like butter.

Green Berets were successful because they had mastered the art of adaptability. They didn't make plans, they prepared for contingencies. They were problem solvers. There was no such thing as a perfect op. They all go sideways. There was always a dog, or someone that chose that exact moment in time to wake up and go for a piss. All you could do is show up ready for things to go loud and try to keep them silent. But if they went loud, then you better make damn sure you're even louder.

Pablo removed the door from its hinges, and Mike shouldered his rifle. Two dogs lay passed out on their sides to his left, foam at their mouths. He didn't stop to admire his work, but kept moving forward as they had practiced.

To his right was a doorway, and a beaded curtain. He felt Connor lay a hand at his back and moved forward through the curtain. The first room was empty.

He felt Connor move off to his right. Mike continued left further into the dark room, his NODs illuminating everything in green. He could hear the soft shuffle of boots as the rest of the team filtered in behind him. The air was electric. The next room was empty, and he again felt a hand on his shoulder and knew from their pre-op run-through that it was Pablo.

He reached the end of the room and found no more doors. Mike paused for a moment as his head swam and stomach dropped. Their man wasn't here. At least not in the building they had thought he would be. Fuck. They could keep clearing or call the main assault and hope to wrap him up after the chaos if he hadn't caught a bullet yet.

Mike felt a tap on his shoulder and followed Pablo's hand to a small wooden ladder fastened to the side of the building's mud wall. It went up through a small hole in the roof. Simultaneously with this revelation, he noticed the oppressive heat of the small mud building. A drop of sweat ran down the center of his back.

He was sleeping on the roof.

A small wave of relief released the knot in his stomach. Obviously, the roof. Stupid. How many raids? But why hadn't ISR called out any sleepers?

Mike motioned he was going up the ladder. Pablo acknowledged and stepped aside, ready to follow.

Mike slung the rifle and drew his sidearm. A silenced 1911, which wasn't all that silent, but at least it'd only take one shot to drop whatever he hit. He loathed the Army issue Beretta's. He loathed the 9mm. He was a fudd in his heart, and he was ok with that.

Mike started up the ladder, 1911 in one hand. He climbed up into the cool Afghan air. At the top he eased himself softly through the shaft's exit.

Two men slept no more than ten feet away from him. They snored loudly.

Mike sat in a crouch and looked down the shaft. Connor was on his way up. Mike waited in the night's silence.

While the roof was mostly uncovered, the shaft from down below came up beneath a thatched overhang, obviously designed to keep rain out, and provide shade in the summer. That's why ISR hadn't seen the sleepers.

Connor reached the top and Mike stepped away from the hole, giving him room to exit.

The sleepers were gagged and zip tied before the sleep cleared from their weary eyes.

And then everything in the NODs went white...

THE OVERPRESSURE HIT him like a brick wall, reaching him just before the tremendous boom that said all hell had just broke loose.

Mike dropped to a knee and grabbed his head, now pounding like he'd been sucker punched on a night out.

"What in the absolute fuck," Connor shouted, but to Mike it came through muted and distant, as if he was being held underwater. His ears rang. All of his senses scrambled.

He ripped the NODs off and tossed them. A dusty haze off to the north obscuring the moon and stars.

"An IED," Mike said.

"What?!" Connor shouted. It sounded like a whisper.

"IED," Mike shouted back.

Mike grabbed the HVI by the collar and gave him a rough shove towards the hole in the roof.

"Got one coming through," he shouted down the hole. He threw his man down the shaft, and hoped he didn't break an ankle at the bottom. Connor was already lowering himself back down the shaft.

Mike turned and shot the second prisoner in the face. The man crumpled beneath the loud mechanical slap of the 1911's action. "No checked bags on this trip," Mike said.

To the north of him the dust was starting to settle. The night erupted with the dull crackle of small arms fire. Pickup truck lights flicked on in the field to the east of them and barreled forward towards the ANA's position. Modern chariots on a death charge, except these chariots were pulled by a 2.4-litre turbo-diesel engine placed beneath the hood of a Taliban Hilux.

They'd been waiting for them. The Reapers had probably burnt the place months ago, stupid fucks.

The faint whoosh of an RPG. Something exploded in the midst of the Afghans. Heavy PKM fire erupted from the north. The Afghanis returned fire, their muzzle flashes sparking like so many fireflies on a summer night.

Mike threw himself at the hole in the building's roof.

Mike and his team left the way that they'd come. Leaving nobody in the compound any wiser. When Mike made it to the ground floor of the building, he found Connor who was already hauling Bambi towards the door. The others were waiting at the main gate, ready to provide cover for their exit.

Loud shouts came from the far end of the compound, and they heard women and children crying. They were waking up.

Because the main gate was located at the far corner of the compound, no one saw them. Family members piled out of their interconnected rat's nest and climbed the north wall to get a better look at the chaos happening just up the road, while behind them the team slipped their man out the back gate.

They cut a large circle south, away from the fight, before working for a flank on the Taliban position.

They set up on a small hill and took cover behind a stone retention wall. This pinched the Taliban between themselves and the Marine QRF that rolled in from the North.

The firefight lasted another hour until the Apaches rolled in.

The choppers swooped low like black angels of death, the dull thump of their rotors like an archangel's wings, and the M230 chain gun mounted beneath their chins, swords of truth. Three passes by the fire breathing machines and the battlefield was silent save for the cries of the wounded.

When it was done, they walked the battlefield. The Afghans had taken heavy casualties. All were wounded. Nearly half of them were taken out by the IED. EOD guessed it was a command line, which tracked with Mike's hunch that the compound had been burned.

Seated about two hundred feet off from the main body of the Afghans was a lone figure. Mike set off to check on him. That or put him out of his misery.

He approached the figure, a heavily bearded officer sitting on a rock and smoking a cigarette he'd copped off one of the devil dogs. Across his lap lay a wood stocked RPK. His left arm was bloody, a tourniquet at his shoulder. Around him lay the bodies of dead Taliban, one of them with a bloody rock the size of a coffee can where his head should have been.

The afghani was silhouetted by the bright yellow glow of a Hilux being consumed in its own diesel fueled inferno, the smell of burning rubber and plastic seats filling the night; inky black smoke obscured the stars.

"You need help," Mike asked in Farsi.

"No help," the man replied in heavily accented English.

"You do all this?" Mike said.

"Yeah," the man said.

"What's your name?"

"Bahrawar," the man replied.

"Means lion," Mike said, more to himself than to the man on the rock.

"Yes," the man said, obviously pleased that

Mike knew his language. "The Americans call me Psycho."

"Well Psycho, let's get you fixed up and then let's talk. I've been looking for men like you. We're gonna call them Afghan Commandos and word on the street is that my ass is gonna train 'em."

A spiral of fire shot out from the truck as it found some new fuel source, and in its glow, the man the Americans called Psycho struggled to his feet. Mike glimpsed the man's face in the firelight, and the sudden rush of recognition flooded him. Could it be him?

Chapter Fourteen

Mike choppered out the next morning to give his post-op brief. He'd told Tex that the Argentinian government was crawling with Chinese spies, and by this point I wasn't all that sure this was sanctioned by the whole of government. Which was the primary reason for the in person briefings.

I sat on the stoop of the Quonset hut and watched the chopper disappear. Then I wandered over to our little makeshift gym, where Tex was already working out.

"Villa del Mar?" I asked.

"What? You want to go back?" Tex asked.

"Come on, we might as well."

Hulk walked in behind me, and Tex said, "He wants to go back to Villa del Mar."

"Hell no, I'm not walking five hours to get to that truck," said the Hulk.

"You want to go for that girl, don't you," Tex said, more than asked.

I ran a hand over my face.

"Man, what are you going to do with that," the Hulk said, "you can't keep her."

"She's not a stray cat," I said.

"That's a long way to go even if that Fernet was delicious," Tex said.

Mex and the Nord both appeared in the little doorway.

"I'll go by myself then," I said.

"Oh no, you ain't going by yourself, that's when real trouble happens," the Hulk interjected.

"What about you?" I asked Mex.

"Fuck no, I ain't doing that trip again, besides I think we made a big enough impression last time we were there."

"Fuck it, I'll go," the Nord said.

AT LA TERRAZA, we sat outside on the patio. Abuela brought us more Fernet and cokes. I didn't see Valentina behind the bar and was starting to get concerned this was her day off. I glanced around the patio on which we were the only ones on.

"So, I'm gonna run something by you," I said.

"Shoot," the Nord said, leaning back in his chair. He took a swig from the beer in his mug.

"I think Psycho can speak English."

"I know," he said.

"What's the deal?" I asked.

The Nord shrugged, "He's with Mike. He's there to keep an eye on us."

"So, Mike knows about our trips here?" I asked.

"Yeah, that would seem likely," the Nord said unconcerned.

"Why didn't he say anything," I said.

"Look, Mike has five of us that he needs pulling in the same direction. Five of us that he has to keep happy. He doesn't care if we all sneak off together as long as we don't let it fuck things up."

I nodded. "I still don't like it."

"Ehh," the Nord said. "Just keep your head on a swivel when it comes to him."

"What you mean?"

"I mean, he's smarter than you. And meaner. And there's no way this whole thing is about illegal fishing. Something bigger is going on."

"Like what?"

"You're old enough to be cynical, so be cynical. Mike was a legend. I'd be surprised if he didn't do Agency time. You don't make it to the Agency by being Captain America, you get there because you have a screw-loose, that or you don't mind fucking people over, even friends, even lovers. They hire people that are already good at lying and make them better, guys that have no higher god than themselves, the ones that could leave the love of their life in a burning building if it came to that or the mission."

I listened intently.

The Nord continued, "They don't recruit people with hearts, that's all I'm saying."

"You ever work for the Agency?" I asked.

"Me, no, but they almost got me killed a couple times," the Nord said throwing his beer back.

"When did you know about Psycho?" I asked, feeling more than a little stupid that it had taken me this long to catch on.

"To be honest, I guessed it right off. I wasn't sure of it until later, but I guessed it."

"Why?" I asked.

"There was just no plausible way he didn't," the Nord said.

I stared into my Fernet.

"You got it before the others though," Nord said.

"You think?" I asked.

"Yeah," the Nord said.

I laughed.

"You only did one tour, right?" the Nord asked abruptly, his voice taking on a careful tone. "What's the story there?"

I glanced up, trying to decide whether I wanted to rehash ancient history. "Yeah," I said. "You don't have to tell," The Nord followed up, sensing I was hesitant.

"No, it's cool," I said. "I was in Syria. We were partnered with a bunch of Kurds. Fought all summer with them. They fought for their lives against ISIS. Real men. Only fighters worth even half a damn over there, probably the only people too.

"Well, we found out the Turks were going to roll across the border to help fuck up ISIS, at least that's what they said, but the Turks hate the Kurds. Middle East politics are complicated but it doesn't take a brain trust to know they were coming to kill Kurds first, and ISIS second. Command wouldn't let me tell the Kurds what was happening, just told us to fall back. They said they needed to protect sources and methods, some bullshit like that. In the end, the Turks are a NATO ally, and the Kurds, well..." I just shrugged my shoulders for emphasis.

"So, what did you do?" the Nord asked.

"I tried to warn them. Warn the Kurdish commander who'd saved my ass more times than I could count. They tied me down to a bunk and left a guard on me. And when it was all over and my CO called me in for a reprimand, I lost it, choke slammed him through the desk."

"Holy shit," the Nord leaned forward. "And they didn't court martial you?"

"Not at first, it was all gonna blow over, ya know. The CO was pissed and tried to get me canned but it didn't take. Someone above told him to fuck off. I think they were gonna give me a smoking I'd never forget, and then prolly throw me in the ring with him. Ship me off to another Unit. But then this Army CI caught wind of it, some new chick trying to make her bones as an investigator, a real hard charger, she started poking around. Opened an investigation, and then passed it off to NCIS."

"How'd she catch wind of it?"

"Rumor was, she was hooking up with the CO I put through the desk. Which wouldn't surprise me, he was known for his woman problem. Married with three kids too. But you know deployments..."

"But it never went to court martial?" the Nord asked.

"They wanted the whole thing to go away," I said. "A court martial would've brought too much attention to the Turks and the Kurds. Media was already having a circus about what was happening. Some Marine on trial for sticking up for the Kurds wouldn't do. So, they just cut the cord and sent me on my way."

"And now you're here?" the Nord said. "And how did you find Mike?"

"He found me," I said. "Seemed fortuitous at the time. I was itching to get back in the fight, a fight, any fight. Anything that wasn't under fluorescents."

The Nord squinted off in the direction of the ocean, white foam washing over the rocks like so many clouds on a clear day in the Rockies. Deep in thought.

"What's the matter?" I asked.

"Just thinking," the Nord said absently.

I STOOD at the picket fence in front of Valentina's house and rubbed my sweaty palms off on my pants. I wanted to go knock on the door, but a heavy anchor had formed at the bottom of my stomach.

The curtains in the front window moved. And then a voice from behind me.

"You get lost?" asked Valentina.

I turned, surprised and a little embarrassed, "Oh, yeah... hey."

"Oh, yeah... hey," she said with a giggle. Her eyes sparked and the setting sun caught wisps of auburn hair, crowning her head in gold.

The front door of the house opened with a creak and an old man on oxygen appeared in the doorway. He looked mildly concerned.

Valentina raised her hand, "It's ok, Papi."

Her father raised a withered hand in acknowledgement before shuffling inside.

"Well," Valentina said, hands on her hips, she rocked forward slightly on her toes.

"This wasn't how I envisioned it, but do you wanna grab a bite to eat?"

She pursed her lips, "But I just ate?"

"A walk then, the beach maybe?" I offered.

"Sure," she said coyly. "A walk... to the beach."

I paused.

"Well come on," she said, extending her hand, and I was grateful she was meeting me halfway.

There was a little path that ran the side of her cottage, and then dipped below the hill, leading to the ocean below. The hill was still blooming with Scotch Broom, each flower hanging like a small golden trumpet. Bees went on about their business, a healing hum you felt more than heard.

"What happened to your father?" I asked.

"Oh, he's alright if he takes his medication."

"Fisherman?" I asked.

"Yeah," she replied. "His whole life."

I felt a pang of guilt.

"The last years broke his spirit though," she continued. "The fishing got worse and worse until he could barely cover the fuel for the boat."

"How come?" I asked.

"The oceans are dying—that is what he would always tell me," she said. "The foreign fleets come here with their big trawlers and pillage our waters."

"I'm sorry," I said. "You'd think someone would do something."

"The government doesn't care. They only care about their pockets. All anyone cares about."

We continued down the path in relative silence. And after a time, she continued, "He buried himself in a bottle. Liquor was cheaper than gas, and if he couldn't afford the one, he could at least console himself with the other. When I was a child I resented him for it. I didn't understand it... but I do now."

"Understand what?"

"He was mourning her," she said.

"Your mother?"

"The sea," she said. "And my mother... but mostly the sea."

We kept walking, and I didn't press further. I hadn't meant to make the conversation sad. She led me to a pair of flat rocks set in a V and facing the ocean. We sat down on the point.

"What keeps you here?" I asked finally.

"Why leave," she said. "I grew up here, everyone I know is here."

"Yeah, but you went to University," I said cautiously. "I saw your paintings. They're good."

She laughed, embarrassed. "And what do you know about paintings?"

"I know what I like."

"Good answer," she said, nudging my arm with the point of her elbow.

We talked then of my work as a biologist, and I lied some more, and some more, until my mouth dried out and my tongue was flayed.

She laughed at my jokes a little too hard, and I missed the cues. She told me about her time in university, about the parties, and then about the depression. She said big cities made her nervous now. She bemoaned the fact that nobody had vision anymore, and that art was mostly a giant money laundering scheme.

And playing backup was the sound of gulls, and the melody of break water, and the pinks and the oranges lighting up a brooding gray sky.

Brown eyes, and half open lids. Her eyes flickered, and mine retraced the edges of perfectly formed lips. And finally, we kissed.

Chapter Fifteen

Our next raid started like all of the others. We sat on the edge of the EEZ and waited. The boat rocked gently in the great blackness. The LCD screens glowed brightly up front, populated by hundreds of AIS indicators, all swarming the digital ocean.

But we only had eyes for one: the Cai Yuan 168.

She was a commercial trawler, currently flagged to Liberia. Over the last several weeks she had stopped transmitting AIS nearly every night. Every morning, she would reappear, near the EEZ, back in international waters. If she stuck to her pattern, tonight would be no different.

I threw a dip in. "Why Liberia?"

"She's a flag of convenience," Mike replied.

I spit into a water bottle.

"Liberia doesn't have any warships," Tex added.

"Why does that matter?" I asked.

"Countries only have authority over vessels flying their own flag when in international waters," Mike said. "And a country can only pursue a foreign flagged vessel if the chase starts in their own territorial waters and only then if they maintain visual contact."

"So all anyone has to do is break contact and make it to international waters," I said.

"Exactly," Mike replied. "So if a ship is flagged to a country that doesn't have any warships, well its carte blanche... they can do whatever the fuck they want when they want."

"Liberia has the most ships in the world flagged to its name," Tex added.

"Convenient," I said.

"Almost like it was set up that way," Mike said.

"A feature not a bug," Tex added.

"This is why fish at the supermarket is so cheap," Mike said. "Why your sushi dates are forty bucks in the middle of Ohio. Half these fishing vessels are using slave labor. They don't pay on time or they take meals and medical supplies out of the men's wages. It's the wild west."

"How do these guys end up on them though?" I asked. "Surely they know."

"Some do. And for some it's still the best option. Others are shanghaied from juicy bars and dockside brothels, some are straight up kidnapped," Mike said.

"So it's one big circle jerk of misery," I said. "Cheap fish, slave labor, industrial trawling, dead oceans."

"The circle of life," Mike said. "Welcome to Samsara."

I pulled a paperback from my pocket and a pen light. Tex and Mike resumed a conversation about porn stars. The steady hum of the boat's engines and the rhythm of the boat made me tired. I yawned and reassessed whether reading would help me stay awake.

"What's that?" Mex asked, leaning over.

I flipped the book over and showed him: *The Untamed* by Max Brand.

"Is it good?"

"It's not bad," I said. "The main guy has a pet wolf dog that fucks people up, and he rides black stallion named Satan."

"Sounds corny," Mex said.

"Maybe," I said. "But it's not. It's almost mythical. It feels more alien than corny."

"What do you mean?"

"Well it's implied that he can communicate with the animals... as if he too is something animal... and the opening of the book starts with allusions to Pan... and Brand is always talking about bloodlines. There is something Homeric about it, not the boomer liberalism you see later."

"Huh," Mex said, seemingly disinterested.

I turned back to my book.

"I need to borrow one of those from you," Mex said. "I didn't know we'd do so much sitting."

I closed my book, slightly annoyed at the repeated interruption.

"I always forget," he said. "I think it's not going to be boring, but then it is boring."

"Thank God," Mike said. "They went dark."

The boat's engine rumbled as Mike throttled forward. I was thrown back in my seat. I turned the pen light off and stuck the book back in my cargo pocket.

Like the last time, what followed was a mad scramble to get to the search zone, set up a grid, and find our target. This took a bit longer than usual. Two hours for us to find her. And when we did she was sitting ten miles inside Argentina's territorial waters.

"They were probably spooked," Mike said, putting the boat into automatic anchor.

I unstrapped and shuffled out of the cabin.

"They might be armed this time," Mike said.

"Yeah, but where would they get them?" I asked.

"Shit, guns ain't hard to find out here."

"So quickly?" I asked.

"Yeah," Mike said. "So quickly. Necessity is the mother of so quickly."

∴

As we pulled the RIB up to the dark side of the Cai Yuan, Mike powered down the outboard motor. Tonight it was Myself, Mex, Mike, Psycho, and Hulk going up. The Nord would stay in the RIB as there was nowhere to tie off this time. Tex was left with both Barracudas a mile away to watch the boats and pull security and support—or a fast escape if needed.

We floated the RIB along the side of the ship until we found a good place to climb. I readied the grapple. Its heavy hooks prewrapped in towels and secured with baling wire to limit the clang when we threw it over.

I swung the hook in a circle and then let it fly.

My first throw bounced off the top and came careening back down.

"Heads up," Mike called.

It plopped into the water, and I hauled it back in. My second throw got it over, but I couldn't set it. The third try was the charm, it sailed over the railing, and three hard pulls confirmed it had grabbed onto something topside.

As I was working to get the grapple up top, Nord opened two Pelican cases and produced five Atlas Powered Rope Ascenders. They were big square bulky things about as big as a briefcase that attached to the front of our climbing harnesses. Mike hooked up first, pressed a button and with a small electric whirr quickly ascended.

"You ever use one of these?" Mex asked.

"Never," I said, hooking in. "Seemed simple enough though."

"You only live once, right," Mex said.

I grinned and pressed the button.

The ascender took me up quickly and at the top Mike pulled me over. "Watch our backs," he said. "I'll get the others."

I raised my M4 and thumbed off the safety. The Cai Yuan looked like every other fishing boat we'd yet boarded, but bigger. She was a 221 foot commercial trawler. A mass of right angles, steel walls, and grated decking. We'd boarded on the bridge deck. I heard working shouts from the main deck below as the fishermen worked the nets.

The bridge itself was set forward on the bow of the ship, which was part of the reason we needed the rope ascenders, as this point of the ship was several feet higher than the main deck that they used to fish.

I quickly appraised that there were two approaches I had to cover, fore and aft.

I'd just knelt and raised my rifle when gun shots rang out.

Heavy thunder that sounded like someone was on a big .50 towards the back of the ship. I whirled and went prone out of instinct.

"What the fuck is that?" Mike hissed.

"Aft," I said. "And not at us. No one's seen us."

Mex took position next to me. "I got fore," he said.

Mike pulled Psycho over next, and then the Hulk. The gunshots from below stopped.

"What the hell is going on," the Hulk said.

"Shhh," Mike said.

It was then that we heard the clang of the bridge door. A man rounded the corner and damn near walked right into us before he realized his mistake.

A lit cigarette fell out of his mouth as he clocked us. He was a small Chinese looking man with a heavily pockmarked face. His blue coveralls were stained with engine grease and fish blood.

Mex jumped him, slamming him against the side of the bridge.

"I got him," I said, jumping in to help. I fished zip ties out of my vest.

As we subdued our man, Mike led the others around the corner. I heard a flash bang go off, sounding muffled through the bridge's steel walls. The muted slap of actions followed as Mike and the others went to work with their rifles.

We left the man hog tied and gagged at our feet. The ship lurched to a stop as the engines died and I stutter stepped forward to catch my balance.

The others came back around the corner.

"Bridge is cleared. She's dead in the water," Mike said.

We headed down the grated stairs to the main deck then, stacked up, rifles raised. When we cleared the stairs, the main deck spread outside before us. Ten or fifteen men worked the fishing equipment.

The stench of rotten fish hit me in a wave, and nearly made me gag. I clocked the cause immediately, an enormous pile of bycatch crawled with flies at my 9 o'clock. They were out here after squid, so anything else they pulled up just got chucked. A fucking waste.

"Flashbangs out," Mike called. He tossed three out at once. They clattered and bounced across the deck before going off more or less in the epicenter of working men.

I turned my head to protect my eyes and the concussive bang sent my ears ringing. And then it was on. We charged forward, rifles raised, shouting "pā xià," which means "lie down" in Mandarin. The only Mandarin any of us besides Mike knew.

Most of the fisherman hit the deck, a few cowered in fear. I stuck my gun in the face of the nearest one and forced him flat on his belly with a well placed kick. "Pā xià!"

A flash of movement in my peripheral—I looked up: a man swinging a telescoping boat hook at my head.

I slid backwards half a step, making him whiff.

Snapping my rifle up, I put two in his chest. The slap of the silenced M4 sounding both overloud and somehow subdued at the same time.

The man dropped the boat hook and fell forward. As he settled at my feet I shot him in the head for good measure. You come at me, you aren't getting up. Ever.

Seeing this, the man I'd just gotten down scrambled to his feet. I saw a glint of steel as he produced a knife.

He lunged up and at me, too close for me to swing the rifle on him. The knife sliced down my forearm, but I felt no pain on account of the adrenaline dump.

I leapt backwards and swung my rifle hard into him in an attempt to create space. I connected and sent him sprawling. I put two into the back of his head.

At this point, the other fishermen panicked at what to them now appeared a zero sum game. Several that had went prone now scrambled back up. Fight or flight had kicked in.

Mike's rifle barked dumping one that took off towards the stern of the ship. Another hurled himself over the starboard side with a scream.

Another pole hook was swung and Hulk dumped several shots into him, center mass.

Psycho and Mex fired too but at who or what I didn't see because they were clear on the other side of the deck.

The smell of gun smoke stung my nose.

And then it was over, or at least mostly over, four men were left. They lay flat on the deck, covering their heads and trembling. Their bodies having chosen freeze rather than fight or flight.

Myself and Hulk zip tied them, hands behind backs, feet secured. Then sat them up right. They all stunk like sewage having soiled themselves. One appeared to have shit himself.

Part of me didn't even know why we went through the motions of taking prisoners. I knew they were going to die anyways. The theater made it all seem a little bit more macabre than necessary, but I knew the practical reason was Mike would want to interrogate them.

"Look at this," Hulk said, kicking chains fastened around the legs of the last man we had zip tied. Two heavy padlocks hung from his makeshift shackles.

"What the fuck did they do that for?" I said.

"I don't know, poor bastard," Hulk said.

Mike stepped forward to look. "Slave, maybe... or he did something to piss everyone off."

The men looked up at us. Fear soaked faces. Hog-tied like animals for the slaughter. I felt a pang of guilt.

Mike lit a cigarette, and the eyes of one of them widened. "Cigarette, cigarette," he said, heavily accented.

Mike stooped and stuck a new one between his lips, then lit it.

"Cowboy, you need to see this," Mex called. He was standing several feet off at the stern of the ship, up by the railing.

I trotted forward and Mike followed.

As I approached, I saw the source of the gunshots from earlier. They had mounted a big .50 caliber machine gun to the railing with some type of home-brewed welded contraption.

"The gunshots," I said.

"Look," Mex said. He took position by a spotlight mounted next to the gun and pointed it at the water.

I stepped up to the railing and peered down. Black and white forms floated in the ocean below. It took me several seconds to place what they were. Orcas. At least three of them. I could see the bullet holes and torn flesh on one as it bobbed in the water.

"They fuck with nets and steal fish," Mike said, stepping up beside me. "It's shoot and shut up out here. Happens a lot."

"Illegal isn't it," I said.

"Since when has that ever mattered."

I felt a heat in my belly then, a cold heat that flooded my mind. I turned on Mike. "Ask them who did it, I want to know which one did it."

Mike grinned at me. A wheedling grin that almost made me hit him. He liked seeing me angry. "Alright, Cowboy," Mike said. "I'll ask 'em for you."

We headed back down to the four.

Mike spoke to them in an even keel Mandarin.

They all shook their heads from side to side, all except the shackled man. He said something in Mandarin.

One of the men shouted something back at him. He was an ugly man with black eyes and a wispy mustache that made his fucked up mouth look even more fucked up. He had a cleft palate that had never gotten surgery. It was the same one that had shit himself.

Mike asked the shackled man something in Mandarin.

The shackled man nodded solemnly.

"It was him," Mike said, pointing to the man with the fucked up face.

I bent and pulled a necklace full of teeth out of his shirt. They weren't shark's teeth. But the finger length ivories from an orca.

I stepped back, and the man spat at me.

I pulled my glock, put it to his head and pulled the trigger. *Samsara motherfucker.* The smell of gun smoke mixed with the rotten odor of the bycatch pile and I was suddenly nauseous.

Behind me, I heard Mike say, "lets clean this shit up and get out of here." He sounded distant, like he was underwater or on the edge of a dream.

Chapter Sixteen

Mike flew out to debrief and no one spoke about what happened. We mostly bummed it around the cove. I worked out. Tex took everyone fishing another day.

And it was three days later when Mike returned. He called us to the team house. I sat down next to the Hulk, the Nord on my other side. Mex picked at dirt beneath his nails.

"Alright ladies, we're going out again tonight. They love us out there, and the CHICOMs..." he drawled the word in a mock Rush Limbaugh, "...are pissed. But we're going to kick the hornet's nest one last time and then we cut loose early. The Argentinians are happy but they don't want us to push anymore. They're starting to get cold feet."

"What ever happened to those girls?" the Hulk asked.

"Coast Guard picked em up," Mike responded. "Most of them are Filipino, a few Indonesian. They're being sent back to their home countries once they've finished their investigation."

"And the media?" I asked. "They caught wind yet?"

"The news is running with the eco terror story. Even American media has picked it up, which is what we all really wanted anyways. It's also all over Tik Tok. Mostly favorable.

"The Chinese Embassy is pissed. They aren't buying any of it, at least according to diplomatic back channels. They want to know what happened to the sailors. Something stinks and they know it. But they can't get too testy because its bad fucking press. Too much unwanted publicity between the girls being trafficked and the illegal fishing. They are already in hot water with the UN over a dam failure somewhere in Africa."

"So, what are we going after?" Tex asked.

"A mothership," Mike responded. He flicked on the projector and continued, "there's a reefer sitting just outside the EEZ," Mike flicked open a PowerPoint and showed us a screengrab of AIS overlaid on top of a nautical map. "For the past three days, it's been meeting smaller fishing vessels that went dark. They connect with the Reefer to drop off their catch, and then go meet a Tanker to refuel before going back in." He switched to the next slide which showed a massive Chinese reefer. "The Zhonghao 998," he said. "That's our target."

"How are we going to hit it, if it stays outside the EEZ?" Mex asked.

"The same as we would if it was inside," Mike responded. "We don't give a shit. We're ghosts. Vigilantes. Eco-terrorists. Whatever they want us to be."

"That's straight up piracy," the Nord said.

"Are we sinking it?" Tex asked.

"No, not this one. We disable it. Kill the crew. It'll be a ghost ship left to wander and float until someone tries to salvage or sink it."

"Fuck me," the Hulk said.

"Dark," Mex muttered.

"Well, we aint getting up that thing with rope ladders," the Nord said. "And Cowboy barely got grapples over the last one."

"I'm glad you asked," Mike said, and then he motioned to Psycho, saying something in Farsi.

Myself and Nord exchanged looks.

Psycho rose from his seat and made his way to a place where a bunch of black polypropylene Pelican cases sat in the corner. He lifted one and set it on the table.

We gathered around to see what's inside. Psycho flipped the case latches.

"Not sure if any of you got the chance to use these when you were in?" Mike said.

"What is it?" Mex asked.

What looked like an overly large ratchet system and the equivalent of deer stands for your feet laid on black eggshell foam.

"Ah fuck no," the Nord said. "Magnets."

"What the fuck do you care," Mike quipped, "you stay in the boat."

"So how do you use them?" I asked.

"This is a Magnetic Climbing System," Mike responded. He then demonstrated how to use each piece. Two L shaped platforms attached over the boots... a toe lever engaged and disengaged the magnet. The hand grips worked essentially the same except they had a place where you could tie into with a climbing harness and straps.

"And these things will hold all our weight, and our gear?" Mex asked.

"Double, actually," Mike said.

We all spent some time setting the system up. Mike answered questions. The magnetic climbing system wasn't overly complicated, but I wasn't thrilled with my first time using it being on a mission.

"And this will work even on wet surfaces?" the Hulk asked.

"Since when does water stop magnets," Mike said.

Everyone laughed.

WE SHUFFLED out of the team house. It had started to rain. A slow drizzly rain. I felt a weariness at it, and felt the beginnings of a headache that I tried to ascribe to the pressure change. But it was more than that. A bone weariness. CNS burnout. The kind you feel after deadlifting too many days in a row.

The others split off for the bunkhouse to start prepping gear but I made my way over to the water.

I packed my lip with a giant pinch of long cut and sat down on a drift log at the edge of the beach. The water lapped at the sandy shore. It was peaceful.

The Bruiser and the Ares rocked gently across from me, their sleek black hulls somehow still shining underneath the cloudy sky. The sun was a luminescent orb trapped behind a gray curtain. The rain slowed to a drizzle, and fogbanks hung like ghost formations just at the edge of the cove. The wind picked up, and there was a chill to it. It was more than a thunderstorm, a cold front blowing in from the south, maybe.

The walls of my cubicle had returned. They were beautiful walls, but walls, nonetheless. They looked like the ocean, and the vast Argentinian plain behind us, the Patagonias in the far distance on the rim of the world. The edge of this cove that was shaped like a box, and the fogbank its lid.

I looked around, the only vehicles, the only escape from this place were the boats—and the Hilux parked five hours away. But even if I wanted to leave now, I couldn't, because I couldn't leave the others. Not the Hulk, nor Mex, not Tex, or even Nord, who I still knew nothing about. No, we were all on this runaway train together. And if a train, then Mike was the engineer and Psycho his first mate—or whoever was second in command on trains... I bristled at my analogy falling apart.

I spat a stream of tobacco on the rocks in front of me. I tongued the chew back into place. My tongue felt raw.

The ordeal with the floating whorehouse had given me a sense of heroism. A false sense. An almost convenient sense. As if at the very edge of the world, morality was coincidental. And then there was the man that'd killed the orcas, and I didn't feel anything for him. Just a numbness. And my only regret was that I'd done it angry. I had to work on that.

My thoughts turned to Valentina then, of our

kiss, and of the lies I had told her, and then of her father. The broken fisherman. His waters. The sea he had called home, and the fish that had sustained him and his kind for generations... until they hadn't. I thought about the Orcas that we'd fed off the side of the Barracuda... about the three dead ones. About waters colonized by Chinese capital. About the whole world paved over in crumbling sub-par concrete. About walking the beach back home and finding reams of plastic washed up on shore, and feeling sick to my stomach, and angry. And about the scams it always turned into. About carbon tax credits that lined politicians pockets. About EVs that spawned a hundred hellish lithium mines.

The water in the bay got more choppy as Poseidon worked out his grief. What decisions had brought me here? Were we the good guys? Was anyone? Did good really wear a white hat or did it dress up in all black.

"Cowboy," Mex called from the Quonset. "You coming or just gonna stare at the water."

I CHECKED MY GEAR ONCE, and then went back over it. I glanced at my watch—an hour left. So I gave my M4 a quick cleaning, careful to lay out the parts such that I wouldn't lose a piece. Then I worked over my Glock 23 and rearranged its holster on my chest rig. I liked the .40, it packed more of a punch than the 9mm but was easier to handle than the .45.

"Blackhawk Down is the best," I heard Mex say down the hall.

"Bullshit," the Hulk shouted back, "Fury is better."

"Apocalypse Now," Nord said, "Colonel Kurtz was right—change my mind."

"You know, I never really got the ending of that movie. Why was Kurtz the bad guy?" Hulk asked.

"He wasn't," Nord replied. "Willard was a rat fuck."

"I mean, I think you are right, but why?" Hulk asked earnestly.

"Because he knew it was all bullshit, he just went so the brass didn't can his ass," the Nord said. "You know the part where he kills Colonel Kurtz, and they show the sacred bull being slaughtered at the same time."

"Yeah."

"Kurtz was a God. A force of nature," Nord said. "He was the bridge between the barbaric and the bureaucrats running Vietnam."

"Yeah..." the Hulk said slowly.

"You still don't get it?" the Nord asked. "That's why it's the best war movie."

"We can spray paint it on the sides of these ships instead of Green Buccaneers or whatever," Mex said.

"You people love spray paint," the Nord said.

"Red Dawn was the best," I butted in.

"The original though, right?" Tex asked.

"I didn't even know they remade it," I said. "How do you remake Milius?"

"Exactly," Tex said.

"My whole childhood was playing Red Dawn

in the woods behind our house. I prayed for the day the Soviets would invade. Sad when I found out they'd collapsed before I was born."

Mike appeared in the doorway of the Quonset.

"Let's go," he said.

WE FLEW ACROSS THE WATER. Tex plugged a small MP3 player into the boat's jack and started a heavy metal playlist that conjured images of irradiated forests and far future barbaric raves, skulls mounted on stakes, scalps strung up to dry, heavy machinery armored with tack welds and heavy plates of iron illuminated by the dancing firelight of our bonfires. Girls draped in wolf furs gyrated in my mind's eye, naked legs, heaving bosoms, long black hair and painted faces.

The seas bucked roughly, and at one point the Barracuda rolled over completely as we were struck broadside by a phantom wave. It reached out from the deep and the dark of night, and our tin can was suddenly spinning, the Comanche Moon sitting high and bright in the sky—gone and replaced by the dense black that was the ocean beneath us and above us. The centrifugal motion of the spin slammed me backwards in my seat and held me down like a night terror in a dimly lit Caribbean hotel.

The boat self-righted, bobbing like a cork, the engine sputtered, and water streamed down the windows making the moon look blurry and distant. Mike laughed as he knocked the wipers up a notch, and throttled forward. He sounded far away, hidden behind the veil that was the music and the rain.

How could we see the moon if it was storming?

Tex shouted updates over the music and my heart beat to its thrum. I was focused. I could feel the buzz, the electric connection between everyone in the boat, and it extended outward even, connecting us to the other boat with the Nord and the Hulk. We flew faster over the water, but it felt mostly like we were sitting still. Mex threw up. And we all laughed. He wiped his mouth, and grinned. The smell made me gag.

"Do you miss the office yet, cubicle man?" Mike shouted over the thrumming.

"Never," I shouted back, and I meant it. I would trade it all for this, for the adrenaline, for real life stakes, for the chance to participate in the game of life. Maybe even my soul. Maybe I already had. It was funny what an hour could do to your mood.

Mike was the Mad Hatter, and we were his delusions.

The boat slowed, and then lurched to a stop, and we sat bobbing in the choppy waters.

"We're a mile off her bow," Tex said, and he flicked off the music, "do you want us to get closer?"

"Yeah, bring her closer," Mike said. "Not trying to drown tonight."

"Can do."

Tex pushed the Barracuda's throttle forward, while Mike passed the decision over the radio.

I looked out my window and I could just see the silhouette of the other boat as it shadowed us. Mad Max of the seas. Neo-Vikings.

We moved forward in relative silence now, the music gone, and the dull hum of our diesel motors fading into the white noise of the ocean and the rain.

A bead of sweat formed on my forehead, so explicitly, that it felt like I could identify the very pore it pushed its way out of, then it traveled downward, stopped and gathered strength at my eyebrow, and fell across the gulch that held my eyes before continuing down my cheek. It's what I imagined a good cry felt like.

Tex put us a quarter of a mile out from the Reefer. Which was close. As tall as the reefer was, I imagined that had the sun been out, its shadow could still touch us. The seas were still choppy, but they had calmed, and the storm had taken everything down a notch, and left us with a cold drizzle. The sea was alive, and she was helping us.

Chapter Seventeen

THE DRIZZLE and humidity had begun to fog up my NODs so I flicked them up on top of my head. The reefer towered over us, a vertical wall of steel. The RIB bounced back and forth against the side of the ship. Mex and I attached to the side of the Reefer with our Mechanical Climbing System. Mike moved the RIB a little ways down to give the rest of them a chance to get set.

Two minutes later we all clung to the side of the Reefer like spiders. When Mike had the boat tied off and was himself attached, we started our ascent. Everyone except Tex was going up tonight.

The clouds had parted just enough to give us a moon, and the drizzle had all but stopped. The moon reflected off the ocean and lit everything in a soft light. I was taken aback by how well I could see without my NODs, the moon doing its subtle work.

I unclicked the hand lever, and released the magnet, then placed it higher up. Slowly I climbed upwards. The Climbing System felt nice and solid. I got into a groove then, one hand and foot at a time, unclick, and click, like a mechanical-man-spider.

The water fell away below me as I climbed the steel cliff upwards. About halfway up, I paused to check how the others were keeping pace, and I hung there in the middle of nowhere, in the void that was the night sky on the edge of the world. My breath came easy, and the breeze cooled my skin as quickly as I sweat, and the moon reflected all sorts of weird shapes and ghostly bodies off the waves below. Stars littered the sky, like grains of sand, and gave way to a vast night sky that was nearly incomprehensible. I hadn't seen a sky like it since Wyoming. I felt a profound sense of loneliness then, like me and the others were the only ones in the universe, and this tiny battle at the edge of earth, at the edge of the cosmos, was the only one that had ever existed, and would ever exist.

I kept climbing.

At the top we all waited, just below the edge of the ship's deck. Mike gave the hand signal, and the others passed it down. I unhooked the boots, letting my weight sit in the climbing harness attached to the hand grips. Mike passed another signal down and we all vaulted over the edge. The ship's deck was about five feet below, and further than I had expected. I smacked the deck and rolled in the interest of saving an ankle. I came up with rifle ready, and considered checking to see if my NODs were still fucked.

The night evaporated as spotlights flicked on in front of us. I was instantly left blinded, and simultaneously stunned as I raised a hand to shield my eyes.

Gunfire erupted forward and aft but I was already run-stumbling towards cover. Out of nowhere something hit me like a hammer in the chest. I was torqued so hard sideways by the impact that I lost my feet.

I lay flat on my back gasping for air, even as the deck beside my face erupted in sparks. I rolled away from the sparks towards the shadows to my left.

In the shadows, I found safety and my bearings. I heard the mechanical slap of silenced actions and knew at least some of us were getting lead down range. The sound brought me comfort. And very dimly, in the back of my mind existed the idea that I had been shot.

My chest felt tight and bruised. I pulled off one of my gloves and ran a hand over the place where I'd felt the hammer blow. A smooth edge and then jaggedness and I felt the remains of a bullet lodged into my plates.

Motherfuckers had shot me.

I pulled myself up to a crouch, caught my breath as best I could and then returned fire from behind the edge of the Reefer's cabin.

I aimed first for the blinding lights that had turned us into as many cockroaches scurrying around beneath them.

The others had evidently thought the same, as showers of sparks followed the sounds of shattering glass. There was a minute of this. Alternating shots between spotlights and muzzle fire before we were finally plunged back into darkness. Muzzle flashes erupted from further down the deck and I threw my own rounds back at them.

I slumped backwards into cover, grabbing a new mag from my vest and knocking out the old. I slammed it home and hit the charging handle, then

I picked up the old mag and shoved it into the newly empty slot on my vest.

All went eerily quiet. Having lost the element of surprise, they were no doubt regrouping.

"Chinese Special Forces," Mike came in through the earpiece. "They got to be."

There was a crunch behind me.

I spun out of the way, as muzzle flash filled the distance between myself and the man that had tried to flank me. He was no more than ten feet away, and my sudden movement had thrown him off.

I flung my rifle up and fired, magdumping as I walked him down.

He staggered backwards firing wildly into the deck before collapsing beneath the weight of my lead.

I reloaded and then nudged the dead man's face with the barrel of my rifle to make sure he was good and dead. He was.

I crept to the corner of the reefer's cabin and chanced a look around it at the aft deck. As soon as I did, two separate bursts of fire erupted from his buddies who'd been trailing behind. Bullets whined off the steel wall of the cabin and I swung back into cover.

I pulled a flashbang from my chest rig and tossed it around the corner.

It went off and I could just barely feel a bit of the over pressure from this distance. I cleared the corner, rifle raised and immediately started firing. I found the top of a man's head as he tried to duck behind a steel container. It burst like a cherry red pimple and I felt, as much as heard, the thwack of the specific bullet that lanced it.

I shifted my focus to the other. He started to step out, but I ended him just as he poked his head up to send another burst in my direction.

I worked my way back towards the cabin then, checked my six again, and then reloaded even though I had only used half the mag.

I heard gunfire from further down the ship as the team engaged the rest of the Chinese.

"I'm gonna work my way to you," I said over the mic.

Nothing came back but the gunfire continued. I started forward.

At the edge of the cabin, there was a staircase of about five steps that dropped down to a lower deck that ran the length of the ship. I could tell from the sound that the team had worked their way towards the front of the ship.

"Get your ass over here," Mike said, finally coming through over my earpiece. "We're going to exfil off the bow."

"How long?" I asked, moving down the staircase, rifle held in front of me. There was no answer, another eruption of gunfire. Something moved in front of me, and I pressed the M4's butt harder in my shoulder, ready to go to work—

"Don't," a voice I didn't recognize said.

I held off and squinted, it was Psycho. He had a tourniquet tied off on his right leg and was bleeding from the opposite shoulder.

"He speaks," I said, crouching near him. "Can you move?"

"With help," the Afghan said.

I bent over and slung his good arm over my shoulder. I lifted and he gasped, but he was good.

We moved forward slowly, and I held the M4 out in front of me with one hand, my other arm propping Psycho up.

"Are you coming?" Mike came in again over the earpiece. "We have to—"

A clatter of gunfire. Close, too close.

There was movement at the far end of the catwalk, near the steps. Two men, dressed in black started towards us. I opened fire. The one on the right dropped immediately, but the second I only hit in the leg. He returned fire and I shoved Psycho off me sideways even as I lunged towards the ship's railing. I two handed the rifle and sent several rounds back. The soldier slumped; blood pooled beneath him.

"Where are you?" Mike came over the earpiece. "You are gonna have to jump."

I walked back to Psycho and responded, "Starboard side, halfway."

"We are going to bring the boat around; you have to jump. They've got you cut off."

"I have Psycho with me, he's hurt," I said. "He can't jump."

"Leave without me," Psycho said.

I unhooked my chest rig and shrugged out of my plate carrier. Then swung it forcefully over the side of the boat.

"Naw fuck that," I said. I bent over him and unhooked his shit, roughly, I pulled his plate carrier off. He groaned in pain and clinched his teeth so hard, I thought they would break. I heard shouting in Chinese and swung my rifle up, sending preemptive rounds towards the staircase.

"I can't swim," Psycho said.

"I can," I shouted.

I hauled Psycho up onto one of my shoulders and wielding the M4 with one hand sent more rounds into the staircase as I carried him to the edge of the reefer. Then I chucked him overboard.

Movement from the stairs in my peripheral. I hit a crouch and fired. A satisfying thump of my bullets into flesh. The man crumpled and tumbled down the last few stairs.

In fairness, it was an awful place to try and push in on me from. They were trapped in a blindspot, and I got first shot every time.

I shimmied up to the railing and swung my rifle over shoulder—more shouts in Mandarin—and I jumped, not giving myself time to think about how far it was.

I hit the water feet first, and it still felt like I had slammed into concrete. My feet burned and tingled from the force, even through my boots.

I shot downward through the water like a bullet, and it was instantly cold and black. So cold, I wanted to gasp, but instinct wouldn't let me, and the competing urges congealed into a searing pain of want and need and panic.

Black. Pitch black. I blinked and the salt water stung. I moved my arms, and swam for the surface, I tried to let the buoyancy in my chest guide me upwards. I very rationally swam in the direction of my outstretched arms, even as my fear soaked half told me that was the wrong direction. And for a moment I was back in training, blindfolded, in a pool diving for bricks.

I broke the surface and gasped for air. The Ares

was already there, floating ten feet away, Mike was hauling Psycho up into the boat.

I swam over as shots pierced the water around me. Gunfire erupted from the deck of the Ares pointed upwards. I swam forward and grasped the edge of the boat. Mex pulled me up. I was barely on the boat's deck when I heard the diesel engines fire, felt them kick, and was knocked flat on my ass as the Nord got us the fuck out of dodge.

"We aren't done yet," Mike said.

I struggled to stand and looked out over the water. Two spotlights bobbed behind us, gaining fast.

"They got boats of their own," Mike called out. "Probably fast attack."

I heard the dull roar of a chopper, somewhere out in the blackness of the sky, and then I caught its silhouette as it eclipsed the stars.

"Fuck yeah," I heard Mex say, racking his rifle.

And I started laughing. I laughed maniacally as the adrenaline dump gave me a second wind.

"Give me a new mag," I shouted. Mike tossed me one. I reloaded my rifle, smashed the charging handle—

More muzzle flash from above as the Chinese sprayed and prayed over the railing.

A lucky few bullets snapped overhead, but I didn't care. I was untouchable. I had already survived too much. Fear was gone, replaced by bloodlust. The singular focus of mind and body and spirit focused on the only thing it had ever evolved to do, fight and fuck. This was the drug that made the world run—war and sex. Sativa and Indica. Methamphetamine and Adderall. Nicotine and alcohol...

I fired upwards at the muzzle flashes, holding

under as I was shooting up. Sparks where my bullets smashed the steel railing. A shadow blinked out of sight and I heard screams.

The Barracuda throttled forward and I stumbled to keep my feet. I fired the rest of the mag at the reefer and then stumbled to my seat.

Tex handed me a new mag.

I watched as Mex worked over Psycho's leg.

"Did everyone else make it?" I asked.

Mex shook his head no.

"Who?"

"The Hulk," Mex said.

My vision collapsed in on itself and my stomach dropped out from beneath me, and I leaned forward and breathlessly asked, "Where is he?"

Mex said nothing, renewing his attention on Psycho's leg.

Gunshots crackled somewhere behind us, whipping across the boat's armor like hail, but I barely noticed them. They felt distant, far away...

Mike threw the Barracuda into a turn, and we worked a large circle clockwise, the other two boats still following us.

"Where is he, goddammit," I yelled.

Mike handed the yoke to Tex and whirled like a big silverback gorilla. "He's still up there!" Mike yelled. "He's still on the fucking boat, but there's nothing we can do for him, because I saw him take one to the dome with my own two fucking eyes."

"No man left behind," I yelled. "What about that, Semper Fi motherfucker. What do you think that shit means." I leaned forward, my blood thick. A red hot rage, the all-consuming kind that overthrows governments, murders spurious lovers.

"Fuck you," I spat the words with all the venom I could muster.

"And fuck you!" Mike shouted. "Now shut the fuck up and be ready to shoot." He slid back into his seat, like a snake, the snake he'd always been, and it was at that moment I stopped cutting him slack and acknowledged what my gut had always known. He was no good and we weren't the same. Something had broken off in him a long time ago.

The sound of hail again whipped across the side of the boat. A few rounds hit the bullet-resistant polycarbonate windows, and they spider-webbed with a dull splintering sound.

Tex hit the brake, and slammed the yoke hard into a turn, which whipped us around nearly 180 degrees.

"You rcady?"

There was a loud mechanical locking sound as the 12.7 mm turret at the front of the Barracuda slid into place. Spider webs the size of baseballs whipped across our windshield in a straight line, and in front of us all was dark except the spotlight speeding towards us.

"Send it," Mike yelled.

As Tex throttled forward, I was thrown back in my seat. I pawed at the wall to try to stabilize myself. The turret on the front exploded in a burst of flame and a satisfying methodical purr. Red tracers flew towards the spotlight and there was a moment where the boat caught a wave and the tracers flew wildly out into the night sky, but then we dipped, and Mike brought the gun back on target and the spotlight disappeared and in the black vastness of the ocean something exploded in sparks. Then the gun went dry, whining loudly as it spun empty, no longer breathing fire.

I slid out of my seat, threw open the hatch that led below deck and climbed down. I pulled an ammo can from its tie down when we caught a massive wave that threw me backwards into the wall.

On my hands and knees, I scrambled up the gun's turret and fed it a belt of ammo.

The boat dipped wildly, and I smacked my face on the gun's control arm as water washed over the front deck and into the area where I was standing. I slipped as the floor beneath me turned oil slick, and on my way down water rushed over my face, and I was caught somewhere between standing and sitting, choking and gagging, and holding myself up like a half-drowned rat. I tried desperately to get a grip on the floors or the walls to stand back up. At last, I did, and finished loading the gun.

Back up top, I looked around and saw no sign of our original target. Then, maybe 500 yards off, came the second boat. They had us dead to rights, and I watched in horror as they closed the gap.

"Incoming, 9 o'clock," I shouted.

Tex cranked the Barracuda hard over as muzzle flash erupted from the Chinese craft and several rounds whipped across us broadside.

Then came a dull thump, thump, and the sound of waterlogged explosions that were hard to place.

"What was that?" I asked.

"The Bruiser," Mike shouted.

"I got you guys," Nord's voice came in over the radio.

The Bruiser, which had circled opposite us, was firing off the Mk-9. Shells exploded next to the Chinese boat, looking like a brief and bright bioluminescent underwater light show. But then the surrealism of the moment, the strange beauty of the lights, was ripped apart in apocalyptic fashion—several of the Bruiser's rounds found the boat and it exploded in a white hot ball of flame. The boat continued to slide forward across the water, fire trailing behind it, so that it was silhouetted against the starry black sky and a backwash of hellfire.

Chapter Eighteen

We returned to the cove beneath the gray sky of a new day. Dawn just on the horizon. We were ragged and exhausted, and various forms of shaken, but alive. We had walked into an ambush and survived.

A deep gloom had descended on all of us over the remains of Hulk, and our inability, or worse, Mike's decision not to try to retrieve them. My anger had not cooled towards Mike. I could no longer trust him, and maybe I never had.

Pragmatism is a virtue in a warrior, but it should never be the primary virtue. Others demand precedence, such as courage, loyalty, and faithfulness—faithfulness to something, anything... God, country, brothers in arms. Always faithful meant something. Semper Fi meant something. Otherwise what was the use. Pragmatism, uninformed by these, was psychopathy, or even worse, cowardice. Pragmatism was the perfect movements of a chess master. Logical, rational, calculating. But the world was not a chessboard, it was a living breathing thing, where pawns could jump squares when given the right inspiration and knights could attack straight on if only to save a friend.

Myself and Mex carried Psycho between us. We started towards the Quonset but Psycho refused and asked that we start the fire.

Gingerly, we sat him down in a lawn chair and he groaned in pain and gripped his leg. I checked the tourniquet, and it was still tight.

"Start the fire," Psycho asked, blood flecking his lips. I had thought his only wounds to be the leg and shoulder. Hurriedly, Mex and I cut off his gear, removed his vest, and revealed a wound in his side just beneath his right rib. A round had snuck through between his plates. How he was still breathing I could not fathom. He was a tough, tough bastard.

Tex poured lighter fluid over the logs, still wet from last night's rain, and flicked a match. The pile of driftwood ignited with a whoosh. The fire smoked and crackled as the flame heated the wet wood and it released moisture as steam.

Psycho was pale white, all the color drained from his face. Beads of sweat leaked from his brow. How he had not passed out from shock I did not know.

Mike marched past us towards the Quonset, jaw set, eyes forward. He disappeared inside the team house.

Psycho's eyes tracked his movements, and I saw what I thought was hurt in them.

"Where's he going?" I asked.

Tex shrugged, more concerned with stripping off Psycho's gear and making him comfortable.

"Calling the helicopter probably," Mex said.

Psycho reached out then and grabbed my arm. He pulled me roughly to him, even as he groaned with the pain the movement caused. Ragged breath and blood-flecked lips told me it was close.

He whispered, "Not safe. He is CIA. They plan to burn all of you when this is done. That's why they chose you."

"How," I asked.

"They will send drones," he said. "They always send the drones." And then he gasped, choking on more blood. And he was gone.

The others simply stared. No one else had heard what he told me. They had seen death before. While Psycho had never said more than two words to us, he had still been one of us.

"What did he say," Tex asked.

"Nothing," I said. "I couldn't make it out." I lied, and I don't know why I did.

Mike walked back to us ten minutes later. He said nothing. Instead he stared at the body of Psycho. I looked for sadness but saw none and I knew then that no tears would ever be shed for any of us.

"Best start tearing this place down," Mike said. "We're done here. Helicopter is coming in an hour. I have to debrief. I'll be back to help in a day or two."

An hour later the helicopter arrived. We helped Mike load the body on the chopper, and then squinted against the wind and dust kicked up by its blades.

Tex gave him a thumbs up. The helicopter pulled up and away.

I watched the unmoving body of Psycho, and my thoughts turned to Hulk. Rotting in the sun on the Reefer, or floating in the inky well of the Atlantic, dropped overboard by whatever remained of the Chinese special forces.

We returned to the fire and drank beers slowly, almost meditatively. We drank and stared at the two empty lawn chairs. We put open beers in their cup holders.

The sun rose higher in the sky, and we sat numbly under its gaze. The day was beautiful, abjectly dissonant to our moods and the events of the night before.

Life—oblivion. Happiness found in the small sadness. The sun did not mourn with us. And the birds sang happily from their nests in the Canelos. The sea lapped the shore lazily.

"Let's go back," Tex said, breaking the silence.

"Go back where?"

"Out. After them," he motioned towards the boats.

"They're gone though," Mex said. "We'd never find them."

"I know where they are," Tex said.

"Where?" I asked.

"I've spent a lot of time going over the maps. They'd need somewhere to set up a base of operations. Something in international waters. They didn't send a warship, so that's out. But there's an abandoned GOPLAT just outside of Argentina's territorial waters. That's where they came from. It's got to be."

"But what if they just came on the boat?" Mex asked. "On the reefer?"

"The helicopter," the Nord said, joining the conversation for the first time. "The helo came from somewhere."

"Did any of you see Hulk die?" I asked suddenly.

The others stared in silence.

After a minute of this, Tex responded, "He was with Mike. We'd already pushed forward. When Mike joined us, Hulk wasn't with him."

"So, he might not even be dead," I said it, and even as I did, it felt like I had spoke it into existence. It didn't matter now, whether he was or not. We had no body. And so, no proof, besides of course what Mike had told us.

"But why would Mike lie?" Tex asked.

"I'm not saying he did," I said.

"Why don't you like him, Ryan?" Tex asked.

"Why do you?" I asked.

Tex just stared.

"Why didn't he ever let on that Psycho could speak English?" I asked. "Why have him silently spying on us?"

Tex took a swig from his beer, and then tossed the aluminum can into the fire. I watched the aluminum melt over one of the logs as the fire slowly worked away at it, trying to consume the unconsumable and being mostly successful.

"Why'd you get out, Mex?" the Nord asked.

"What's that supposed to mean?" Mex responded, more defensive than I'd seen him before.

"Nothing, just wondering."

Mex eyed him, and I thought I saw a bit of anger in his eyes. A bit confusing, considering the question.

Nord got up and grabbed another beer from the cooler, as if he hadn't noticed the reaction.

What was the Nord playing at?

Beer in hand, he sat back down, melting into the lawn chair with cat-like ease. The sun caught bits of his ruffled golden hair.

"I was kicked out. Crashed my car the day before a deployment. DUI," Mex said.

The Nord cracked the top on his beer.

"My mom got... has cancer," Mex continued. "Diagnosed the week I was kicked out. She didn't have insurance. State wouldn't cover chemo. If I'd still had my job, I could've helped her. But I didn't. Flat broke, with DUI lawyers and no job. Lost my clearance. A month later, Mike showed up. Offered me this job."

Nord nodded his head slowly. "And you?" he motioned to Tex.

Tex scowled. "Weed. I pissed hot."

I took a swig from my beer, and wondered what the Nord was getting at. He was putting something together, but what I couldn't quite make out.

It was evening when I woke up. I'd caught about five hours. I rolled out of my cot and slipped on a pair of slides, then I grabbed a plastic bag from the chest at the foot of my bed with a bar of soap. The others were already up.

Outside, I had to cover my eyes because it was still bright out. I squinted against the sun, and when my eyes no longer burned, I walked out to the ocean.

The water was cold at first, but it felt good. I dunked my head and held my breath, let the water roll over me. Then I walked back out, the water up to my knees, and then soaped down before repeating the ritual. It felt good to be clean.

The salt water had only seemed to help my skin, which seemed counterintuitive. Maybe it wasn't the salt water, but the sun. The Argentina summer was mild, but I had still gotten a nice tan. And I slept like a baby out here, and I hadn't seen a cell phone in over a month.

I didn't miss it. I had never realized how annoying they were until being without one for a week. After almost a month, I realized how putrid they were.

I felt a twinge of guilt at my pleasure. The truth was this place had made me the happiest I'd ever been. The truth was I wasn't ready for any of it to end. Even with all that had happened, I felt a fire in my belly. The fire of life.

I worked my way back up to the beach, a Styrofoam cup lay in the water washed in from wherever. It rocked gently back and forth, snagged on a rock.

I picked it up and took it with me.

∴

It was 1730 when I found the others in the team house. Nord and Tex poured over a map. Mex cleaned his M4 in silence.

"Which boat we taking?" I asked. I pulled up a chair and started lacing up the rest of my boot.

"Both of them," the Nord said.

"Both?" I questioned.

"Come here, I'll show you," the Nord said.

I finished tying my boots and joined them at the table. The Quonset was lit by yellow light.

"The GOPLAT?" I asked pointing to a place circled in bright red Sharpie.

"That's her," the Nord responded.

"Little far, don't you think?" I asked.

"Exactly," the Nord said. "That's why we're taking both boats."

"Gonna drop one off halfway?" I asked.

"Yup, each boat has enough fuel to get us there and a little over halfway back. Can't carry more fuel, cus we got nothing to carry it with," Tex said, stepping back from the table.

"What do we do with the empty boat when we come back?"

"Once we switch boats, we sink her," the Nord said.

"Mike'll love that," I said.

The Nord raised an eyebrow, before saying, "You know this is over, right? Mike's out there getting this whole thing called off right now, and if he's not, someone else is."

"It went hot," Tex said. "It was never supposed to go hot."

"I guess," I said.

"This is our one chance to get the Hulk back,

whether that's alive... or just his body," the Nord continued.

"And get even," Mex said.

I smiled. Truth was, I was just happy we were finally fighting something that would shoot back.

Chapter Nineteen

It was 0300 when we arrived on target. It was dark out. The windows had fogged slightly. Tex was boat driver, and the Nord sat next to him. An hour earlier we'd anchored the Bruiser halfway between our current position and the cove.

Tex cut the motors.

We'd lashed two Klepper folding kayaks to the deck of the boat. Tex and Mex made themselves busy assembling them. They'd found them in the storage shed, no doubt one of Mike's toys he'd not yet had opportunity to deploy. I started putting together the paddles. I hadn't been in a kayak in years. At least there would be no surf to breach.

Mex looked up at me, and grinned. All I could see were the whites of his eyes and a set of teeth—all of our faces had been painted black.

The seas were calm tonight, which was the only reason we were willing to use kayaks this far out. It was that, or risk the motor on the RIB being heard.

When the kayaks were fully assembled, we loaded in our gear. I set my body armor in the center. On top of that, I set my fins. Then I loaded in my rifle.

The kayaks were two person affairs. Nord settled in the front of mine, while Mex and Tex took the other. They led off.

We paddled silently, moving like ghosts across the open ocean. We hit a bit of chop but paddled through it. The GOPLAT towered in front of us, the lights up top causing my NODs to flare a bit if I looked directly at them.

We were passive only tonight, couldn't risk active IR. If this was Afghanistan or even Iraq we'd chance using a thermal monocular to get a better idea of what we were up against, but out here, against Chinese special forces, we couldn't chance it. If they had NODs, which they most likely did, then we'd be lit up like a fucking Christmas tree.

All I wore was a wet suit, my dive knife tied off in a sheath around my calf, and my Glock, newly silenced and secured to me via a chest rig. The plan was for me to make an open swim on the GOPLAT from about 500 yards out and clear out the bottom levels so the others could infil behind me with the kayaks.

We stopped. Nord stowed his paddle. A wave rose and fell beneath us. The kayak bobbed upwards in the open water.

"Fuck me," I said. "This is 500 yards?"

"Pretty fucking close, Cowboy," Nord said over his shoulder. "Having second thoughts?"

"It's been a long time since I've had to swim this far," I said.

"You know the SAS have a motto for moments like these," Nord said.

"Yeah, and what's that?" I said, grabbing up my flippers.

"He who dares, wins," Nord said with a low chuckle.

The platform had three levels, one at water level with a concrete catwalk around the perimeter. Each side had a staircase that led to the middle platform, which appeared largely empty. The chopper was parked up top. From satellite imagery it looked like the top had a main building, and a couple of out houses or offices.

Tex and Mex drifted towards us, using their paddles to get in close enough to hear.

"It looks like at least two tangos on the bottom platform," the Nord said. "But I can't be sure at this distance."

"We'll swing around to the east," Tex said. "You let us know when you've cleared them out and we'll back you up."

There was no moon tonight, which was good. It meant that we would be covered by complete darkness.

The lights at the top of the GOPLAT gave off an orange ambient light, but most of it was caught by the GOPLAT's giant platform, turning the underbelly into a giant mass of shadow.

He leaned forward resting both elbows on his knees in front of him. Rifle forward.

"You set?" Tex asked.

"We're set," Nord answered.

"Give us ten minutes," Tex said. He paddled off into the darkness.

Nord turned to me, "I'll cover you, but no

promises. I'm not the sniper that saved Captain Phillips so you're mostly on your own."

I pushed myself up gingerly and lifted my legs so that I was straddling the kayak. I eased myself off the back and into the water. The kayak bolted forward, rocking slightly, but Nord did a good job of steadying her.

In the water, I slipped on my fins and secured them. It was easier treading after that. Then I was off, using an alternating side stroke to glide through the water.

Several times waves caught me off guard and I felt a small panic crawl my spine. It had been a long time since I'd done any open ocean swims.

Five minutes in and every muscle in my body was burning. Ten minutes longer and I felt better. Tired, but good, having pushed through the pain. My muscles had warmed and all that surfing had come in especially handy.

I was close to the GOPLAT now, maybe one hundred yards out. I stopped, flipped my NODs down, and tread water, trying to catch my breath.

There were indeed only two guards, each doing a lazy patrolmen's walk on either side of the catwalk.

I left the NODs down and continued my swim, more careful not to break water. I approached at an angle, careful to stay out of the nearest guard's line of sight.

When I was 25 yards out I stopped, just letting the top of my head and eyes bob above the water. The guard walked towards me, then past, and continued on down the cat walk. At the end he spun lazily, his movements having become rote. He may have been on guard duty, but he was no longer guarding shit.

This close it was now clear he had on night vision of his own. I'd have to be perfect, lucky, or fast. Maybe all three. But then again, who in their right mind would be expecting some madman to swim up to the GOPLAT in the middle of nowhere and start fucking up his night.

And then, almost providentially, as if to prove my theory, the man stopped, flipped his own NODs up, and dug around in his pockets. I watched him, momentarily confused. Then saw a small open flame as he lit a cigarette.

I breathed out a sigh of relief, and had to physically stop myself from laughing with joy.

I swam forward gently, angling opposite of his position. I heard his buddy say something to him in Mandarin. He spoke back harshly. I imagined to tell his buddy to fuck off.

At the base of the GOPLAT now, I reached out and touched the rough concrete at the waterline. I was well hidden, up against the platform. My mark stood twenty feet off, smoking with his back to me.

I waited silently for him to finish and come back my way. I drew the dive knife. It had a five inch full tang fixed blade and was razor sharp. I'd start with that.

Another minute and the man started to move again. He walked towards me, no longer smoking, still walking easily. As he stepped past me, I pulled myself up, and then drove the knife hard into his achilles, slashing it in one quick vicious movement. The man gasped in pain, letting out a screech and dropped hard like a sack of potatoes. He fell flat on his back. I dragged the knife hard across his throat and saw blood spurt. I grabbed him by the front of his chest rig, planted my feet on the side of the concrete and yanked his dead weight into the water with me with a splash.

I heard his buddy shout something in Mandarin. He almost sounded amused. With any luck he'd think his buddy had fallen in.

I sheathed the knife and drew the Glock, I was treading water, my head just bobbing above the water.

His buddy suddenly appeared above me, peering over the side of the catwalk to look for his friend.

I fired twice, the silenced Glock sounding overloud in the night's quiet. My first round hit him in the neck and my second drilled him through the chin. I pulled him into the water with me. The splash his body made as it entered the water was indistinguishable from the waves slapping the side of the GOPLAT.

Over comms, I said, "We're good. Bottom platform clear."

EXACTLY SIX MINUTES later both Kayaks slid up to our concrete island. Nord handed me my boots, pants, my plate carrier and my rifle.

He slithered out of his seat and gracelessly scrambled onto the catwalk.

I pulled the kayak up onto the side of the platform. Tex and Mex both did the same.

I sat and pulled on the pants, laced my boots, and then slipped into my plate carrier. I was ready to go in less than a minute.

"Did they get a warning off?" Nord asked.

"No," I said. "I don't think so."

"Good."

A rusty staircase, its yellow paint flaking, led to the middle platform. We climbed it. An unmarked speedboat sat docked next to the GO-PLAT on the opposite side. I hadn't seen it on my approach.

"That'll come in handy," I said.

"Yeah, fuck those kayaks," Mex whispered.

We found a second staircase leading up to the top platform. This time I led. I moved up the staircase slowly, testing each step and applying my weight slowly to avoid the staircase from creaking.

There were two schools of thought on infiltration, and both also applied to the age-old debate on the best way to get to the deer stand. One school of thought said that it was best to move as quickly as possible and to hell with the noise. Crashing through the woods at 4 am on your way to the deer stand was bound to sound natural to any deer bedded. This way limited your exposure time. It eliminated the awkward noises, the accidental rattle of your pack, the scent you left while leaning against a tree. For all the deer might know, you're just a big bad bear on its way to the river—best to stay bedded. The tactical application of this worked similarly, except the strategy revolved around showing up with a gun in your target's face so quickly that they didn't have a chance to react to the racket anyways.

The other school said slow and steady won the race. I liked that school, but I was ready for both.

Near the top of the staircase, the stairs groaned and, in my haste, to remove my weight I stumbled.

I cringed, frozen for a second, my ears searching for any tell-tale scramble of enemy movement. The Nord quickly moved past me. The decision had been made for me; we were going in loud. School of thought number one it was.

I shoved myself up to my feet and bounded up the last couple steps. Shouts came from across the way. Chinese shouts. And then the Nord's rifle made its muffled bark.

I took cover along the backside of a small outbuilding. I shoved the NODs up off my face just a moment before the floodlights flicked on, a sixth sense saving me from the searing pain that was having night vision flooded by blinding lights.

And I was in it then, in the zone, the place where time was fluid, where I reacted to the world as it was, reacted without thinking.

I moved quickly around the backside of the outbuilding, my rifle raised—I exited cover and dropped two soldiers working for a flank. Two shots, two kills. I left each with a hole drilled through the center of their face. Fuck center mass when everyone was wearing armor.

I saw movement behind the helo and laid down fire as I moved. I didn't stop until I was behind the heavy reel of an industrial winch. I slid downward to reload.

Movement in my peripheral. I drew the Glock at my side and put three center mass. The man opened his mouth wide, goofy looking, he lurched forward awkwardly from the impacts and dropped to a knee right in front of me. I put the Glock to his head and pulled the trigger.

Then the Glock was back in its holster and I was back on the rifle.

I shook out my mag and slammed another home. I charged the handle and leaned over to fire—nothing.

A flashbang went off behind me, and I heard Nord shout that he was moving.

I smacked the bottom of the magazine, racked the charging handle, and leaned over again. This time the rifle fired. "Covering!" I yelled.

I caught movement at the far end of the platform and in a split second identified Tex. He popped up to fire diagonal from me.

It was apparent we had full control of this half of the GOPLAT. None of the Chinese had managed a flank and now it was a game of push, push, push before they tried to shove.

"Tex at One'o clock!" I shouted loud enough for Nord to hear.

I saw Mex slide up behind Tex. They both fired towards the men taking cover by the helicopter. They would hold that spot. I knew it as I knew universal truths, because we were now a singular organism, a hive mind connected telepathically.

Muzzle flash to my left. I swung and returned fire towards the open window of the main building.

I hadn't hit him, but I'd driven him to cover.

"Frag out," the Nord shouted. He was still pushing hard up the center, using a four foot high concrete wall for cover.

I heard a metallic clang as the frag bounced around the inside of the room. He'd thrown it through the same window I'd shot into.

Then the explosion. I felt a slight rush of air and my ears rang, but the room had absorbed most of the overpressure.

All was silent then.

"Three down by the helicopter," Tex called out.

I charged forward until I was even with Nord. I tapped him on the shoulder to let him know I was there.

Nord kicked the door to the main building.

I threw in a flashbang. I saw the burst of light and heard the bang.

Nord piled in and I followed.

As we cleared the first room, I stepped over what was left of the mangled body of our attacker. The grenade had done its work.

We worked our way through the main building. A maze of thin drywall and steel desks, and concrete floors. It was an old office space the Chinese had converted into a makeshift ops center/bunk house.

It was empty.

We met Tex and Mex outside. They were already dragging bodies to the center of the GO-PLAT and leaving them in a pile.

"How many?" I asked.

"Ten by my count," Tex said.

"Any sign of Hulk?" I asked.

"None," Mex said.

"Keep looking then," I said. "We got to find something."

I had just turned to start back towards the main building, with a mind to tear it apart in search of any clues when an explosion erupted in the distance. Fire shot into the night sky. I ran to the edge of the GOPLAT. It had come from the direction of the Ares.

The others joined me, and we watched the bright orange flame about a mile out.

"What the fuck was that?" Tex asked breathlessly. I had been so focused on the explosion, I hadn't even known he was behind me. The others joined us.

"I don't know," but even as I said it, a lump had formed in the back of my throat and my heart had dropped into my belly.

"It's our boat," Mex said. "And look, there's a speedboat."

I squinted and could just see a boat like shape take off from the explosion.

"Is it the one that was docked down there?" I asked.

Mex trotted to the far end of the GOPLAT and leaned over the railing. "It's the same," he called.

"Fuck," I said. "Is there another way down? There's no way they would've gotten past."

"They must have already been inside it," the Nord said.

"They rappelled over the side," Mex said, pulling up a heavy nylon rope tied off to the GOPLATs railing.

I flicked my NODs up and rubbed my eyes. "What the fuck."

"So, we're trapped here," Mex said.

I looked out at the flaming wreck on the water, and then turned around and looked at the helicopter. The others followed my gaze.

"Ah fuck no," Tex said.

Chapter Twenty

We stood around the helicopter. Nord examined the damage. It had taken three bullets to the tail fin, and some rounds through the door. One of the windows was blown out from the flashbang that the Nord had used earlier, but other than that the damage seemed minimal.

"None of you even know how to fly this," Mex said.

"Well, we can't very well call for help, can we?" I shot back.

"I can try," the Nord said.

We all turned and stared.

"Before I joined, I was taking lessons to be a pilot," he continued. "Switched to planes cus helos never quite connected with me," the Nord continued.

"Oh great, that's good, they never connected with you," Mex said.

"Chill," Nord said. "I still remember how to fly. I just never learned autorotation."

"Autorotation?" Mex asked.

"It's like gliding a plane, but for helicopters...

you know if you lose power to the main rotor," the Nord said.

"So, you do know how to fly it?" Mex asked. "But if something goes wrong, we're fucked."

"Probably," the Nord responded.

"Dios Mio," Mex said.

"But if something goes wrong, we were probably fucked anyways."

The helo was a Z-20, the Chinese rip-off of the Black Hawk. Nord worked his way around it, as if he was doing a pre-flight check.

The knot in my stomach got tighter. *We were all going to die.* I didn't voice this opinion though, since Mex seemed to have enough doubts for everyone, and I had already decided that this was the only way out. It was now time to be a true believer.

"Have a little faith," I told Mex. If Nord was gonna fly, or even crash, I'd prefer it be with balls to the wall confidence. Confidence could make up for a lot. I had no idea how it matched up against physics, but we needed any edge we could get.

"Let's at least wait for morning," Mex said.

"Why?" the Nord asked.

"Because I'd imagine it's easier to fly when you can see how fucking close you are to the ocean," he said, walking all over my true believer sentiment.

The Nord laughed. "That's what instruments are for."

"Yeah, but none of us can read those," Mex said.

"I can," the Nord said.

"Well, I wanna see the crash coming if it turns out you forgot a lesson," Mex hit back.

The Nord laughed. "Fine. We wait until dawn so you can backseat drive."

WE SAT and waited for dawn to break. Mostly it was silent. Nord fell asleep, as did Mex.

The plan was to try to find our boat, the Bruiser that we had left anchored halfway. We would then put the helo down in the water, kill the engine, and swim to our boat. It was that or try to get the helo all the way back to the cove, but it had only half tank of fuel, and the Nord had no idea how to refill it or even if it would make it all the way. There was also the problem of leaving the boat out there, to be found, and the problem of what to do with the helo if we brought it back mainland. Keeping the boat with us and ditching the helo to a watery grave seemed the least bad option.

There had been no sign of Hulk up unto this point... or his remains. But that now seemed to be the least of our worries. And the others seemed to think he was gone. Killed on the ship just like Mike had said. But I wasn't so sure, and as it looked now, maybe I never would be. I was still kicking myself for not having anyone disable the speedboat when we first infiltrated. In hindsight, it seemed like a massive misstep.

My thoughts drifted then to Valentina. I missed her. Part of me wished for this whole thing to be over, maybe I'd forget the ranch and make a home in Del Mar. Wile away my days in that girl's sweet embrace. Go deep sea fishing every day. There was a million dollars waiting for me in that crypto account, enough to do just about anything I wanted. Or maybe the ranch was still on the table. I could convince her to move to Montana or Wyoming or maybe even Colorado. She could paint rocky mountain sunsets. I'd build a big ass ranch house, with a big ass porch, and we could sit out there and talk. She could paint, and I'd smoke a pipe. We could take her father with us. Get him proper care.

The thought brought a smile to my face. I chuckled to myself and stared out at the stars slowly disappearing to the gray light of morning.

Instead, here I was, trapped on a GOPLAT in the middle of the Atlantic, and our only hope was a guy that had taken helicopter lessons once, but quit because he wasn't really feeling it. The truth of it was, I loved this shit. How I had ever thought I could make it in a normal life and not blow my brains out, I didn't know. The lack of self-awareness seemed ridiculous in hindsight. But still I grappled with it. Grappled with the idea of a normal, picturesque life, whatever that is. Even now I deluded myself with dreams of Valentina. There seemed no end to my delulu.

Live by the sword, die by the sword, came back to me, from some distant Sunday service deep in my childhood. In my adolescence, I had always assumed it was a warning more than a prediction, as if one could choose to live by the sword a little while, but he could get out while the getting was good—if he wanted. Time the market so to speak. It was the investor's fallacy.

But it wasn't that at all. It was a contract. A deal with destiny. I wouldn't even go so far as to say it had a moral weight assigned. It just was—a fact, a law of physics, a deal one made with the devil. Everyone that picked up the sword for the first time wrote this fate into stone. Wasn't this the archetype from gramp's old westerns. The aging gunfighter, the one who gave it all up, and the ghost of his past back to haunt him for the last time.

These thoughts intercut over my fantasy of a life with Valentina. Our idyllic ranch in Montana stormed by masked figures. Her body bloody, stretched across the threshold that I'd once carried her over. A bit dramatic, maybe even Hollywood.

Mex snored himself awake and popped up in a panic. When he saw me sitting there next to him, he paused, and gathered his bearings. The sky had turned from gray to a light pink, and the clouds were cirrus.

"You ever wonder why we do it?" Mex asked groggily.

"Do what?" I asked.

"This. Out here on the edge of the world. Who are we fighting for. What are we fighting for."

"Well, it's money now," I said dryly. "Which in a lot of ways, seems a more honest reason than God, and country... or even worse freedom."

"Money's just another word for freedom," Mex said.

I considered his point and then said, "when I was out, you know, I was working a 9 to 5, and I swear I considered suicide nearly every day. It's an open air prison, civi life. It's all debt and inflation, and mortgages. All designed to make you think you're moving forward. It's walls, and suffocation, and endless loops. It's not living."

"That's what I'm talking about," Mex said.

"You make enough of it, all at once, and you can buy yourself out," I said. "I'm starting to think that slavery is just the way it always is. Whether you're shackled to a boat, or made to fuck fishermen, or even just trapped in a world of excel sheets. Not that it's right or anything. It just is. Every economic system that ever was and ever is has slaves at the bottom. Maybe well fed and well housed slaves, but slaves nonetheless, and hardly what you could call men."

"What you mean?"

"I mean the Greeks and Romans, right... the slaves were quite often rich men, they often ran the business side of things, or handled trade for the nobleman while the noble was off fighting wars and shit. The warriors were all aristocrats. Now our warriors get podcasts. They can't wait to break into the merchant class. Sell one hundred dollar boots and protein powders. It's all ass backwards now. America is an entire country of merchants. Slaves with white collars... some with blue.

"And I figure, well who was above the slaves? Well, it was the warrior caste, and above them, or part of them maybe, was the aristocracy.

"But me'n'you buddy, we aint no aristocrats," I said and thumbed my chest. "We may be the warrior caste, but we aint really. There's no land grant waiting for us back home. Nothing but a colored collar and a thank you for your service."

"So who are the aristocrats?" Mex said.

"A global neo-feudal empire," I continued. "The aristocrats are just banks and private capital now. You're either a slave or an enforcer for the protection racket. No nobles to be found."

"At least there's Congress," Mex said glibly.

We sat silently for a little while, both deep in

thought. The day's new light making strange shadows out of the pile of bodies in front of us. Blood had pooled beneath them, and in places rippled with coagulation, but in other places it had dried to a mirror finish. I didn't really feel anything for them. They were merely fuel for the fire that the loss of Hulk had lit. They'd made it personal. All war was personal. That's what those bow tie fags in Washington never understood.

THE NORD WOKE ready to go. We loaded our shit onto the back of the chopper. I climbed into the copilot's seat and watched the Nord as he tried to decipher the control panel. Chinese symbols where very helpful English words should've been.

The Nord glanced at me, a wry smile on his lips. "You know what the SAS say, right?"

"He who dares wins," I said.

"That's right." He chuckled and said, "if it was easy, we wouldn't do it."

He flicked a couple switches, and the helo fired up, the rotors started turning slowly. Nord checked the chopper's gauges. I watched him intently, and he caught me staring.

"Looks good to me." He shrugged.

He gave the chopper some juice and the rotors spun into a dull powerful thump.

And then we were floating, awkwardly at first, as the helo seemed to stumble upwards into the air —its nose dipping first, and then its tail as Nord overcorrected. But he found it, the sweet spot.

I watched his feet pump the pedals gently as the helicopter reacted to his commands. And then we were gliding smoothly forward, gaining altitude. The GOPLAT fell away behind us.

Tex had brought up the maps on his tablet in the back. He passed an azimuth to Nord.

The early morning sun was our only companion, lighting up the sky in pinks and grays that reflected off the water below in a purple, pink iridescent shimmer. They were bloody waters, but beautiful.

Below us, a pod of orcas breached the ocean's surface and played a game of tag. I was happy to see them. I wondered if it was the same pod we'd ran into while fishing. They were strange creatures, hard to even call them animals when you learned what they were capable of. Wolves of the sea, they were called, because they hunted in packs. They passed hunting techniques down from generation to generation. Invented new ones even and practiced them as games. They were one of the only animals besides humans whose cultures, different to every pod, helped shape their evolution. Just hundreds of different tribes roaming the seas. Should be called Warlords of the Seas.

The trip was short, less than an hour to make it to the halfway point where we'd left the Bruiser. There was an argument to be made for leaving it, and just flying the helicopter back to the cove. A good one, too. Starting with not taking the risk of something going wrong when we ditched the chopper. But I was glad we weren't gonna lose her, there was a strange question of loyalty involved.

Ships, like rifles, take hold of a man in a weird

way. You form a connection to them, a relationship even, maybe because your life depended on them. Men had named their rifles since forever. I'd heard everything from Betsy to Ol' Painless. And before rifles, men had named their swords and spears—Excalibur, Curtana, or Tizona. There was something to a name. It was bad luck to sail a ship without a name. A name was a mark of dependability.

Mex spotted the Bruiser first, floating lonely in an ocean so big that it made the boat look like just a bit of driftwood.

Nord sent the chopper into a bank, circling back towards the boat. He hovered above it, hands and feet working in unison.

"We probably have enough fuel to make it all the way back," he said over the headset. "Still want me to put it down?"

"Yeah, put her down," I said. "We can't take this thing back to the mainland,"

"Copy that," Nord said dryly.

The helicopter descended slowly, in circles at first and then Nord brought it back to a hover.

"I'm going to put her five or ten feet off the surface, you guys jump. When you are clear, I'll set her down and bail. This could still go wrong."

He brought us close, right up next to the Bruiser and I unbuckled from my seat and walked to the back of the helo. Mex and Tex opened both doors so that the Nord could escape easily when it came time to ditch.

Then they lowered themselves to the edge so that their feet were dangling outside. We'd tied our packs and gear off to a couple of inflatable life jackets and these, they shoved out first. Tex jumped, then Mex, and I followed.

The water was cold, and my clothes wanted to drag me down, mostly my boots, but I kicked into a swim. It was less than ten yards to the Bruiser.

When we had scrambled onto the boat, we hauled our floating packs up with paracord we'd attached to our wrists and packs like a surfer's strap.

The Nord nodded to us and then pulled the chopper further away. Tex fired up the Bruiser's engines.

I watched from the boat, Mex standing beside me.

"Has he done this before?" Mex asked.

"Have a little faith," I replied.

We watched as the Nord unbuckled himself and pulled off his helmet, keeping the chopper steady no more than ten yards above the ocean's surface.

Slowly, he lowered the mechanical beast into the water. I heard the dull womp of the rotor slow as he decreased the RPMs.

The chopper touched the water and then breached the surface, and as it did Nord rolled it over onto its side. The Rotors slapped the water loudly but then came to an almost immediate stop, and then it just lay there for several seconds, laying on its side like a dead whale.

As it started to sink, I saw the Nord appear. He clambered over the belly of the mechanical beast and swam towards us.

Tex pulled the Bruiser up beside him, and I leaned over the railing of the boat and offered an arm. When I hauled him up out of the water, he was laughing. Damn near giggling like a teenage girl that had just suffered her first kiss.

"Crazy shit," he said with a giant shit eating grin. "That is some crazy fucking shit."

I looked at him confused.

And then he said, "I failed out of helicopters!" He burst into laughter. "I joined the Army to fly Apaches and they failed me out."

There was a moment of silence as I processed. Then Mex burst out laughing, the same deep laugh that had caught hold of Nord. And when I'd finally recovered from the shock, I did too. Deep belly laughs, that I couldn't control, that I couldn't stop. It was contagious.

"You son of a bitch," I said. "You motherfucker."

Part Three

Chapter Twenty-One

6 MONTHS EARLIER…

THE VILLA WAS NESTLED in the mountains of Sinaloa, Mexico. The house was nothing short of a Mexican mansion, with its white stucco walls, mahogany paneling, marble floors, and bronze hardware. In a corner of the drawing room, sat a statue of a tiger, a life size tiger, plated in 24k gold. It had been left behind by its previous owner, in fact, most of the place had been left over from the original owner. And now it was his. Mike retrieved his cigar and his drink from the foyer and crossed the drawing room to the back door.

On the back porch of the villa, he lit the ACID cigar with a torch and puffed it to life. He could afford better cigars, Cohibas or Padróns, if he wanted too. And he had a whole humidor of them for guests. But he was partial to the ACIDs. Familiarity had bred a certain nostalgia. He had a taste for low-end, in both cigars and women.

He sipped the agave martini. In front of him

was the pool, which reflected the sun back at him through blue, crystalline water. The buzz hit him like a freightliner, and he sat down in the pool chair.

He was a king, and this his domicile, a cabana chair his throne. His ranch was 2,000 acres of mountain country. All of it his, compliments of the last owner, a high-level mafioso for the Sinaloa Cartel. His new kingdom was ensured by a delicate agreement between the Sinaloa Cartel and the Tijuana Cartel. He could live here, and they could stay in business, but only as long as everyone played by the rules. His rules... the Company's rules.

When the Sinaloa and Tijuana Cartels started their all-out war on each other it had sent the region into chaos, and more than that the border into chaos. When a Company safehouse was accidentally identified as a Sinaloa safehouse, and all its personnel killed, he had been sent down here to keep the peace.

There were rules in the underworld, and The Company made them. Crime, mafias, black-markets would always be a thing. Had always been a thing, and would forever be a thing. They would never be rid of them, and the Company knew it. So, they'd asked themselves who would navigate it? Who would corral it and keep it from spilling into the overworld. This was its mission. And the number one rule of the underworld was that you never picked a fight with The Company, not unless you wanted the world's largest, most technologically advanced, and well-armed mafia—the United States of America—to fuck you up.

But accidents happen.

And when the Safehouse massacre happened,

both sides discovered that they had made a mistake of monumental proportions. The Company had hit back hard and brought the region to its knees in a matter of days. Two kidnappings, three assassinations, and two cartels were a hairs breadth away from destroying each other. But the Company didn't want them gone. That would leave a vacuum, and vacuums were bad. Both nature and the CIA abhors a vacuum.

So Mike had called a meeting. Right here, in this backyard, he had held a dinner party. And the only reason they had complied, instead of unloading on him and his men, was because projected on the far wall of the garden was a video of their missing leaders. The head of each respective Cartel tied hand and foot to a chair, their heads black bagged. And on the opposite wall was a second projection, drone feed of the dinner party itself. The message was clear. They were all going to die, or they were going to work something out.

Mike had then laid out how things would operate south of the border, south of *his* border. The successors to his two prisoners had been picked long in advance using detailed psychological profiles worked up back at Langley. They needed someone on each side just shy of being fit for the job. They needed men capable of running an organization but scared of fighting a war. They needed the cartel versions of bureaucrats, which wasn't all that hard to find.

The evening had ended with a special showcase. The execution of the two leaders, one from each organization. And for his part of the deal, Mike got the ranch. The fact he lived here was a way of ensuring security, and if anything happened to him there would be hell to pay.

He took another puff on the cigar and watched as the smoke floated up and out. The Company had been good to him. It treated its generals well. It had to for time served in the belly of hell. He called it hell and meant it. The Company was king of the underworld, which meant most of the overworld hated it. It meant no one ever knew just what exactly they did. Most Americans even hated The Company, but that was mostly because they only ever heard about the mistakes. The truth was, if someone, or something didn't trim the hedges and prune the chaos, then it was only a matter of time before it bubbled up into the civilized world. Only a matter of time before global trade became untenable. To rule the underworld, one had to be cruel, they had to be a deceiver and a manipulator. When Satan offered Jesus all the kingdoms of the world, surely it was because they were something he was in a position to offer.

Mike took a deep drag on the cigar and let the smoke settle in his mouth.

It was what it was. It wasn't for the faint of heart or for the righteous, but it was the job. He didn't make the rules of empire, and they damn sure hadn't changed in the last few millennia. Sure, the set dressing changed, the titles and the terms, but it was still a question of power, hard power. In the end, one empire operated as much as the next, and even more like the one before it.

In the distance, the dull thump of rotors broke his reverie. *A Blackhawk.* He could identify that sound anywhere. Its gentle hum rose and fell as it passed over the mountains behind the villa. Then it was close. Very close, and he glanced up as the black bug looking machine buzzed his house. The rotor wash plastered his shirt against his heavy barrel chest and blew the straw fedora off the top of his head. The helo landed with a thump just out of view, in the gravel drive out front.

Mike shimmied out of the chair, weighed down by his buzz, and slipped on his sandals. He crossed by the pool, worked his way through 100 feet of lawn and shrub, and opened the cast iron gate that led to the driveway.

The Tall Man was already standing outside. He was dressed to the tens, in a wool suit ill-made for the Mexican sun. His face was right angles, and Mike had never seen his eyes before, as they were perpetually hidden behind the black lenses of a pair of tacky looking Raybans.

"Mike," the Tall Man said.

"Administrator," Mike said. "What can I do for you?"

He waved the Tall Man in. He'd never been given a name either. Others referred to him as Mr. X, but Mike preferred the Tall Man, but to his face, he called him by his title, Administrator.

The man stepped inside and made a straight line for the patio table where Mike had been lounging. He sat the black briefcase down on the table and pulled his own chair out.

Mike pulled his pool chair to the table. He didn't like the Tall Man, and he went out of his way to play games with him. Today's head game saw Mike reclining while the Tall Man sat board straight at the patio table.

"We have a job for you," the Tall Man said.

"I thought I was out?" Mike said, bristling.

"You are never out, Mr. Allred. Not when we need you."

"What's the gig?"

"Argentina," the Tall Man replied. "We need you to make some noise."

"What kind of noise?"

"The kind you like," the Tall Man said. "As I'm sure you are aware, we have a new cold war on our hands. One that happens to be with our biggest trade partner."

"Who's idea was that?" Mike asked.

The Tall Man ignored him. "We have been in communication with the Argentinian government. They have a problem they need to take care of."

"And?"

"And if we help them with this problem, they may let us take care of more of their problems."

"So, what's the problem?"

"Illegal Fishing," the Tall Man replied. "China runs illegal fishing operations off their coast. They are bleeding the country's fisheries dry. In fact, current estimates give it about ten more years before the ecosystem in the area collapses. It's becoming a political minefield domestically."

"So why don't they push back?"

"Because they are in too deep, they need China for infrastructure and trade. Debt diplomacy that's the Chinese idea of geopolitics."

"They made their deal with the devil, why do we care?"

"Because we believe that devils need competition," the Tall Man replied.

Mike pondered this for a moment, considering his options, and said, "I want retirement rates then. And I'm still out."

"Done."

"When do I leave?"

"You have time," the Tall Man said. "We picked your team though. They'll be a bit different than the usual."

"Different how?"

"This has a high risk of failure," the Tall Man said. "And its sensitive. We won't be using Company men for this."

"So the plan is to burn it," Mike said. "And how do I know I won't get caught in the backdraft?"

"Have we ever let you down?" the Tall Man asked, his manner cloying. "Just don't get too attached."

Mike waved a dismissive hand and refocused on his cigar.

"This is who we have identified so far," the Tall Man continued. "All good operators, and all recently discharged for one reason or another. Mostly legal bullshit. DUIs, Weed infractions. Shit that wouldn't have even made it into a performance report thirty years ago."

"How many do we need?"

"Six including yourself."

"For how long?" Mike asked.

"Likely a summer, but if you make enough waves, well then, we might pull the plug on the op sooner."

"Cool," Mike said. "And the cover?"

"None. This is straight up wetwork." the Tall

Man replied. "We already set up a shell company, Ares Consulting."

"That's a stupid name,"

"It's supposed to be," the Tall Man said. "Only the Argentinian President knows about the Company's involvement, Parliament is being told that their own military intelligence is running the op. If this ever goes tits up, it needs to sound like it was ran by fly-by-night PMC retards. In fact, it's supposed to be ran like it's by fly-by-night PMC retards."

"So it doesn't matter if it goes sideways or not," Mike said. "If it goes well, the President owes us a favor, and if it goes sideways, it weakens their relationship with China."

"The devil always wins," the Tall Man said. He stood up and gathered his things. Mike kept flipping through the profiles.

"Oh, and we want you to keep an eye out for that McGowan. He's got Company potential, but he's naive."

"True believer type?" Mike said. Aware of what the Company considered potential.

"Yeah, but he doesn't know it." the Tall Man said.

"What about the others?"

The Tall man simply shrugged, and said, "They're good."

He flipped to Ryan McGowan's three-page file. So, this was who they wanted. He was discharged for assaulting his commanding officer. A good operator. He scanned the psychological assessment–he was analytical, introverted, and scored high on pattern recognition. He also scored high on both conscientiousness and openness but was also highly disagreeable. A double edged sword that made him high-risk for neuroticism. Strengths included above average improvisation skills, extreme loyalty, and conceptual thinking. Weaknesses were a disregard for authority, emotional detachment, and total disinterest in mundane tasks.

It wasn't a particularly rare profile for an operator. Most were free thinkers and fiercely independent. Special Forces and CIA was a who's who of problem solvers.

The Company liked to recruit from the broken and the damned, but it preferred the damned, because the damned were always looking for a new home. And it liked extremes. It liked fanatics. The religious did well in the Company, Mormons especially. But so did psychopaths. The Company didn't care how you were motivated as long as you were highly motivated, after that it was just a question of making itself and the mission the motivation. Like German Shepherds, some dogs were made to work.

Mike tossed the manila folder on the stack of others, leaned back and puffed the dying cigar back to life. The Black Hawk roared back to life with a steady thump somewhere off behind him. He downed the Agave martini and ashed what was left of the cigar.

"I want Psycho to go along," Mike said. "I need someone I know."

"Done," the Tall Man said.

"So that makes it seven," Mike said.

"It's a better number," the Tall Man said.

"Lucky even," Mike said.

"Unless you're playing Craps," the Tall Man said, standing brusquely.

"It says Ryan has been out for four years?" Mike said. "Is he even in fighting shape?"

"He's lost," the Tall Man said. "But he had skills, the kind that don't atrophy. Fighting shape is the easy part. Graduated top of his class at MRC. He's an expert marksman, came to the Marines that way, won a three-gun championship in high school. We've kept tabs on him, and we believe he's ready for a change. Done licking his old wounds. Sick of his job. Girlfriend is cheating on him. Last week he ordered a hormone test online. He should be an easy recruit. Getting kicked out took the wind out of his sails. The Company would've blocked it and drafted him at the time but we heard about him too late."

"Fine," Mike said. "But if you want him why burn him on the first op?"

"We'll burn him if we have to," the Tall Man said, "we'd prefer that you take him with you on the way out."

"Fair enough," Mike said.

Chapter Twenty-Two

Current Day

Mike was already there when we pulled the Bruiser up to its place by the fuel tanks. I watched him move back and forth on the rocky beach. He paced like a caged tiger. Not necessarily upset but calculating.

"How pissed is he gonna be?" Tex asked. He tossed a backwards glance to where I stood as he guided the boat to its resting place.

"Very," Mex replied.

"Fuck him," I said. "He shouldn't have left Hulk."

Tex cut the engines. I slung my gear, and followed the others as they piled out of the Bruiser.

We stood on the beach. Our feet finally back on firm ground, and it felt good, especially after being everywhere but in the last 24 hours.

"You missed the fun," I said. I was being openly antagonistic. It was better to hit him head on than let him play his games.

Mike scowled at me, jaw set, and his eyes briefly folded into a calculating squint. But then out of nowhere his posture relaxed, and he asked, "Did you find him?"

The sudden reversal caught me off guard.

"No," I said. "We hit 'em back though."

Mike pursed his lips and nodded. Then asked, "What about the Ares?"

"We lost it," Tex offered. "They blew it up."

Mike shrugged. "Sounds like you guys had a night."

He sounded almost sad that he'd missed it. But there was something there, just under the surface. A rage that I could smell but couldn't see.

"Start breaking down, we're leaving in three days," he continued. "Op is over."

The Nord glanced sideways at me.

"What about Hulk?" I asked.

"What about him?" Mike set his stance and faced me.

"Did you see him die?" I asked.

"He took a bullet to the head."

"Why should we believe you?"

"Why shouldn't you?" Mike retorted. His pupils shrank, and his eyes locked onto mine. His eyes were no longer windows to the soul, rather one-way sensors, searching, always searching for weakness.

"Why didn't you tell us about Psycho?" I took a step forward, and he held his ground.

"What about him?"

"He knew English," I said.

"You were using him to keep an eye on us," I said. "You used him to do the killing on that fishing boat the first time. How come you let us think we were only gonna capture those fishermen."

"You assumed," Mike said. "What'd you expect?"

"I expected combatants."

Mike shrugged but kept his stance. "I didn't see you do nothin to stop it. You seemed awfully pleased when you shot Mr. Ugly in his fucked up face."

Hot bile edged up the back of my throat. I swallowed my anger. "Who are we really working for?" I continued. "Why did Psycho tell me you're CIA?" I took another step forward. The others said nothing, but I felt their shock even without looking. It was in the air.

Mike was quick. Lightning quick and his green eyes never once transmitted his intentions. His fist slammed into my jaw, and in the next second, I felt his Colt 1911 pressed up against my temple. His other arm around my throat as he slid behind me, and then I was being dragged backwards towards the Bruiser.

"Don't even try it," he said to the others. "I will end all of it here."

They knew he meant it. Anything besides a perfectly timed shot to the dome from the draw position and I would be dead. It was a shot I could make, but could any of them?

We stumbled backwards down the rickety plank dock, and he dragged me into the boat, using my body to shield his the whole time. He'd placed some distance between us and them. When he had us backed up to the Bruisers door, I felt him release his grip around my neck while the Colt's barrel slid down the back of my head and burrowed into my back. I heard the door to the cabin unlatch. He drew my pistol from its holster and tossed it into the water. Then he dragged me inside.

He shoved me to the back of the boat and zip tied me to one of the chairs, making sure the position was impossible to find leverage, while using several so I couldn't break them or find slack. He knew everything I knew. We'd both been through SERE. He knew the tricks, and he cut me off at each potential pass. I was looking fucked.

I glanced out the windows. I watched as my friends retreated for cover. It was no use and they didn't trust Mike or the MK-12 on the Bruiser.

Mike started the engines and roared off, accelerating through the turn. He made a straight line for the mouth of the cove.

The Bruiser nosed through the surf and then bounced roughly as it took the next two waves head on. The movement bounced me in the seat, and the zip ties cut deep into my wrists.

My whole body hurt from trying to steady myself with only my core, and my wrists were bruised and cut, and starting to swell.

He had me dead to rights now. I was quite confident that this would be it. Death, and its sweet release. I found it ironic.

A few months ago, I had flirted with the idea of doing it myself, but now I had no desire to die. The urge to live, to survive, to fight was stronger than it'd ever been. I wondered if most of suicide, the kind that sometimes found a fighting man, wasn't just an attempt at a last stand. A revolt against ennui. One last charge towards oblivion. A chance to escape the spiritual death of a stagnant life through the cold steel of a gun stuffed in one's own mouth.

I tested the zip ties, and they only cut deeper into my already raw flesh. I kicked myself for pushing him. I should've waited, should've angled for an advantage and looped the others in. The others. What would happen to them now. We were all burnt as fuck now. If he was CIA, and his reaction had confirmed as much, then the agency had no use for us.

"I was supposed to recruit you," Mike said over his shoulder.

He cut the engines. We couldn't be more than a few miles off the coast now. I tensed.

"Yeah, what made them think that'd go over," I said.

"I have no fucking clue. Bean counters read a psychological profile and think they know a man." He sat down on a seat across from me. "What the fuck is your deal?"

"I was born disagreeable," I said. "I've always been like this."

"I tried to keep you guys alive," Mike said. "They picked you for this so they could burn you if it went south."

"South's the only direction I know."

Mike chuckled.

"What about the others?" I asked.

"They've already called in a strike."

"A strike?" I said, my heart dropping. I took solace in the fact that they were a hard lot to kill. A strike team would have their hands full.

"Not that," Mike said, as if reading my mind.

"Drone. Agency's not gonna waste any men on them."

I felt my whole body go cold at the thought. They had to get out of there. Surely, they would leave.

"We already took care of the Hilux, if that's what you were thinking."

I hadn't thought of it, but I was pissed now. We'd all just bumble fucked our way into it. It had been clear enough from the beginning.

"It wasn't about the fishing," I said.

"This is how we fight now. By proxy and by moxy. A thousand tiny wars a year so the big one never comes. Sure it was about the fishing, but also making allies, about testing boundaries. It was about making China sweat."

"We thought you were one of us," I said.

"You think brotherhood is real. You think honor wins. That right is just right, and might ain't got nothing to do with it?"

"What else is there?"

"Hard power. Fire power. Will power," Mike said. "And it looks like I got it and you don't." He bent over and cut the zip ties holding me to the chair but left the ones that kept my fists bound together. "Now stand up," he said, motioning me towards the cabin door with the gun.

I started to get up, a little too quick.

He stepped back and cocked the pistol. "You won't get it done, so don't try."

I moved to the cabin door and opened it, then stepped out into the bright golden light of a noonday sun. Mike followed behind me.

As he passed through the door, I took a stutter

step back and slammed my heel down on his insole, lowered my shoulder and spun into him as hard as I could, slamming him into the side of the Bruiser.

I heard him grunt. He shoved me off hard, and I caught myself on the railing of the boat.

I reeled around, ready to swing both tied fists at his head with all my might, when I caught the glint of the pistol's barrel.

He'd already recovered, and the gun was trained on me.

I stopped mid-swing.

"You know, I was gonna make this easy on ya," he said. Shifting his weight off his wounded foot. I'd cracked him good, and wondered if it was broken. He was bleeding from the corner of his mouth. I'd split his lip when I'd slammed him into the door frame.

"I'm sure you were," I said dryly.

"I was. I was gonna cap you in the back of the head and send you on your way. But you wanna go out with a fight. Well, we're 10 miles away from shore. At least. So, I hope you've been swimming."

Fuck. A few miles out my ass.

He lunged forward, quick and agile, so agile that I no longer believed anything had happened to his foot. And he spartan kicked me straight in the chest. I flipped backwards off the boat.

I plunged into the water and came up gasping, using my feet to kick to the surface.

Mike was there leaning over the edge. He smiled at me. It was a sadist's smile.

"They did a study with rats," Mike said. "They dropped them in buckets of water, only one at a time, and after about an hour, maybe two hours, the rats were so tired from treading that they..."

A wave washed over me, drowning out Mike's words.

"... then they dropped another set of rats in a bucket of water, but these rats, after about an hour, they offered them a piece of wood to climb up on and rest. Then after a few minutes..."

Another wave. I kicked hard in the water, my boots waterlogged now and my legs burning. The sickening fact that I'd just swam half a mile less than ten hours ago was not lost on me.

"... they took the wood away. And do you know how long the rats could tread water after that?"

I bobbed under again, as the ocean baptized me.

"... 24 hours," Mike said. "That Cowboy, is the power of hope."

A wave picked me up and carried me several feet further from the boat, and I let it, because I couldn't do anything. My legs were already tired, and my lungs blistered. I slipped beneath the water as a shallow wave topped me, before coming up gasping again.

I needed to get these boots off. I filled my lungs with air and then curled into a fetal position, letting my body sink as I drifted beneath the surface. I worked at my laces, cursing myself for taking them so seriously. Both my hands were zip tied in front of me, and so I picked awkwardly at the laces. I got the knot on my right boot done.

More air.

I kicked upward and gasped like a banked fish.

The Bruiser was leaving and the wake it created plunged me back beneath the surface.

I curled up again, and this time concentrated. I got my right boot off and half of the other untied.

A few minutes more I had both boots off, and I lay on my back, floating as best I could to conserve my energy.

The boat disappeared in the distance.

Off came my pants.

Next it was time for the zip ties. If it had only been one zip tie I probably could've just broken it on my body. But Mike, the bastard, had used three, so the knife was the only way.

My dive knife was still strapped to my calf, so I reached down and pulled it. I floated on my back and worked at the zip ties, the way an otter cracks clams on its chest. And then finally free of my bindings I stripped down to my wetsuit, and lay floating on my back. I wondered if Mike had realized I was wearing one. It was an advantage against the cold for sure. Maybe my only one.

The sun smiled at me.

Chapter Twenty-Three

MIKE SCANNED the GPS on the boat's dashboard and pulled it to a stop. This was it. He cut the engines and then threw the doors to the lower deck open. Carefully, he retrieved a time det and placed the C4 carefully on the boat's control panel. He'd start the timer when the helicopter showed up.

Mike then walked out onto the deck of the boat and waited. He heard the Black Hawk before he spotted it. The noise of its engines rising in the distance. He went back inside and set the timer for 30 minutes.

The helicopter hovered above the boat, its door slid open, and a man in a black flight suit shoved a rope ladder out of the side.

Mike reached for the ladder, but it wasn't long enough. The chopper readjusted, and this time Mike caught hold of it as it whipped towards him.

As he neared the top of the ladder, the man inside dragged him into the giant beast's belly. Mike scrambled inside and sat down next to the chopper's other passenger—the Tall Man.

The crewman handed him a headset.

Mike slipped the aquamarine headphones over his ears and adjusted the mic.

"Welcome back," the Tall Man said.

"How long before they are on station?" Mike asked. He was referring to the MQ-9 Reaper. The drones were not fast, and they'd needed about 11 hours to get on station from where they were launching.

"About three more hours," the Tall Man said.

"Well, hopefully they stick around."

The Tall Man merely waved his hands and shrugged. Mike wondered if he should tell them that the team knew they were burnt but decided against it. Best not to bring any attention to it. With any luck the loose ends would be tied and he'd be home free.

The chopper pulled forward and Mike watched as the Bruiser slipped away behind them. Dead in the water.

MIKE FOLLOWED behind the Tall Man as they descended the stairs into the safe house basement. The safe house was buried in a Buenos Aires ghetto. At the bottom, they exited to heavy cinderblock walls painted white. The bottom of the house had been converted into a makeshift ops center.

Jerome was set up at an old looking desk that looked like it had been around since the '70s, a small briefcase size pelican case designed to hold an Agency laptop sat in front of him. On the far wall hung a big screen tv, and on it was the drone feed.

Mike recognized the cove. An aerial view of the Quonset huts and the beach. The dirt pad where the helicopter had landed. The feed was in IR as it was already night time.

"They just got on station," Jerome said.

"Are they still there?" Mike asked.

"Appears so, just sitting around the fire."

Mike saw the blaze where they'd sat by the fire every night. He saw hotspots that were their bodies. Three of them, all sitting in lawn chairs around the fire. The heat signature from the fire at times threatening to wash them out.

"That's them," Mike said.

"Good to go then?" Jerome asked.

The Tall Man merely nodded.

Jerome dialed the secure phone on his desk and picked up the receiver. "It's the customer," he said. "You're cleared hot." Jerome set the phone back in its plastic cradle.

They watched as the feed momentarily pixelated, the universal sign that the Reaper had just launched a missile. Seconds later the IR picture washed out as the brilliant bright white light of the explosion overwhelmed the sensor.

The feed zoomed out several times, revealing a cloud of smoke and the rest of the peaceful cove around it. They waited for the smoke to clear. Two impact points from the missiles glowed red hot. And then several other bits of wreckage glowed, scattered on the ground, presumably bits of the bodies and red-hot coals from the bonfire.

Jerome typed something into the laptop. The Reaper stayed on target for another half an hour doing a damage assessment and then called in for fuel.

"I'm headed out," Mike said.

The Tall Man nodded. Mike climbed the stairs and stood listlessly at the top.

If he was lucky, he'd be back at his ranch by tomorrow night. He left the safehouse through the front door and walked quickly down the cobblestone street. The night was clear, and the stars were out. He walked the mile to his hotel, and then climbed the stairs to his room.

Back in his room, he opened the battery compartment of his laptop and took out the sticky note he'd hidden inside. He'd had the idea on the helicopter ride back and wondered if they'd been so stupid.

The sticky had 10 rows of figures. An account number, and beneath it a subsequent string of letters and numbers. It was the account information and passwords to the crypto accounts he'd set up for them.

Mike opened his laptop and attempted to log into each account; none of them had bothered to change their password or move the crypto to a new account. Dumbasses. He then transferred the funds from each account to one of his burner accounts, and from there he sent it to a new wallet he just opened, all five million dollars.

Cryptocurrency wasn't exactly straightforward if you'd never used it before. You also had to be a tiny bit paranoid to assume your employer would turn around and rob you, or even could rob you.

It didn't matter. The loose ends were officially tied, and he was five million dollars richer for his efforts. How was that for retirement rates.

Mike bent forward and flicked the lamp off, slipped out of his clothes, and laid down. He was out nearly as soon as his head hit the pillow.

Chapter Twenty-Four

One Month Later

Mike led the Tall Man to his den in the back of the house. He caught the Tall Man's gaze as it landed on the Gold Tiger that sat in the corner of the drawing room and wondered what he thought.

In the den, Mike pulled up a chair for the Tall Man, and then retrieved two cigars from the humidor on his mantle. This time he chose Cohibas. He poured two fingers of Johnny Walker from the crystal decanter that sat on his liquor cabinet.

He clipped his cigar, and then handed the cutter to the Tall Man, who declined, and instead bit the end off of his.

The Tall Man was a paradox, Mike thought, simultaneously holding himself with an air of high-class indifference, and speaking always with a calm, intellectual tone, yet he bit through his cigars like a dayworker on a barge. A façade of elite superiority hiding brute savagery.

The Tall Man lifted the torch to his cigar and flamed the end, turning it patiently, and evenly. When it was red hot, he puffed it to life.

Mike reclined in the leather swivel chair, bare feet on the mahogany desk in front of him. He blew rings at the wooden beams of his vaulted ceilings. Both smoked in silence, for there was little to say.

The Tall Man had been his handler for a little over a decade, and this was goodbye. He'd recruited him on a deployment to Afghanistan. The Company then worked out a deal with the Army to loan him out to them. When his Army contract was up, he'd started full time for the Company.

The Tall Man had guided him through it all, from their first meeting to his days at the farm, to his first op, but not once had a shred of personal information been exchanged. The man was easily pushing 70, maybe older, but he was still in great shape. Mike guessed Vietnam was where he had gotten his start. He had a meanness to him. The look and manner of one who'd made the nihilistic void of proxy wars and psychological operations his life's work.

"You know it's something." The Tall Man motioned to the beautiful room around him. "Not many get this far."

"They don't exactly make it easy," Mike said.

"No, they do not. It's a friendless, thankless occupation. You could do everything right, and still get burnt, or piss off some suit with a corner desk and there goes the last twenty years." The Tall Man bent forward and tapped his ash into the crystal tray between them.

"So, they approved it?" Mike asked.

The Tall Man balanced his cigar in the notch of the ash tray and brought his briefcase to his lap. He methodically worked his way through the latches and pulled out a piece of heavy eggshell textured cardstock. "Wasn't a hard ask." The Tall Man handed the paper to Mike, and he took it.

It was the deed to the ranch. One with his name on it.

"What about check-ins?" Mike asked.

"Weekly, use encrypted, so we know you're still kicking. The panic buttons will still work."

Mike nodded that he understood. A panic button had been installed in every room. In fact, there was one underneath the desk right now. Hit any one of them, and it sent a distress call to a Company safe house in Chihuahua.

The Tall Man stood up then, downed what was left of his Scotch, and reached his hand out across the Mahoganey desk. Mike took it.

"So long Mike," the Tall Man said.

"So long, Administrator."

WHEN THE TALL MAN had left, Mike walked to the stables. The ranch was a working one and employed about 30 people, half of them cowboys and hands, and the other half security. Most of them were former cops, every one of them formerly corrupt. Not that that was a knock on their loyalty. Loyalty was either bought or enforced. If the last 30 years had taught him anything, it had taught him that. For these men, he'd done both. Secured their families for life, but also painted a target on them if they ever betrayed him. They'd die on this ranch before running. He knew that in his bones.

The stable was almost 10,000 square feet. Its gabled roof was black sheet metal. Its walls brick. He'd converted a corner of it into a makeshift garage to hold a few of his toys, a few dirt bikes and a Polaris UTV. The back of the stable connected to an outdoor arena of steel pipe fence.

He stopped at the arena and watched Juanito as he worked out one of the stallions. His name was Charisma, and he was a beautiful dapple gray. A prize stud, and the best horse they had on the place.

Mike watched as horse and rider went through their paces. Both working in perfect synchrony with the other. After a few minutes of this, Mike continued his path to the stable. He found the UTV where he'd left it a little over three months ago.

It was a Polaris Ranger with a desert tan paint job. He rolled easily out of his stable and then slammed the accelerator, letting the small beast spin out in the gravel before its all-terrain tires caught and sent him jolting forward. He tore up the gravel road that led towards the backside of the ranch.

There was a spot he liked. One he had visited nearly every day when he first moved in. It was at the top of a small foothill, most of it rock, but the top evened out and was covered in grass. The last owner had planted several citrus trees along its ridge line, lemons, oranges, and limes all watered by a creek fed by a spring further up in the mountains.

Mike guided the UTV up the dirt road and

made the climb up the hill until it eventually leveled out; he then guided it down the road that curved through the tiny orchard. The fruit trees were just beginning to blossom and the air hummed with the sound of bugs. Palm trees shaded the road in fits and starts, and the air smelled fresh and good. He drove to the very end, where the hill dropped off suddenly.

He parked and took his spot in an old heavy wooden chair that he'd brought up top. Mike sat in the shade of fruit trees and looked out over the whole ranch. He pushed his sunglasses up to the top of his head and drank in the view through heavy eyes.

It stunned him now, just as it did every day, and he was filled with a sudden sadness. The kind that had started invading more and more of his headspace.

Not working the last six months had been nice, but it was starting to gnaw at him. The lack of purpose, of direction—the lack of distraction. He was all alone. There was something melancholy in the realization that scared him, and he tried to brush the thought aside.

His thoughts turned to Psycho then. The old boy was dead. Perhaps the only man that had really ever known him. It was a son of a bitch that he'd talked. Warned Ryan there at the end.

And then for several seconds Mike was back in Afghanistan. He stood outside the small red and white striped wool tent. He ran fingers through his beard and watched the small Kochi encampment intently. He readjusted his Shemagh, the traditional Afghan scarf, up over his face so only a strip of sun-baked olive skin and his green catlike eyes were showing. He'd looked every part of a Mujahideen fighter back then.

Behind him, inside the tent were the rest of his team, three of them, and the Afghan fighters that acted as their guides.

His finger traced the hard lines of the AK47 slung at low ready. He had missed his M-16, but the AK had eventually grown on him. At the end of the day any rifle was a comfort. There was almost nothing he feared if he had easy access to a rifle.

Aslam's voice carried from inside, and Mike could just barely catch the jist of the conversation. He wanted repayment, tribute, for the way he had been dishonored. He said he'd been cheated out of a wife, that she'd been unfaithful, and so demanded that the tribe provide another. They were stone age monkeys, the lot of them. It was surreal. Taking a plane, making the journey through airport to airport, and then landing in 3,000 B.C.

Mike didn't like Aslam, and he liked even less that they were helping him, but Aslam commanded many fighters, and had yet to pick a side. Intel at the time had reported that he fought for the highest bidder.

It was his team's job to fold them into the Northern Alliance. After the Soviets had left, the Mujadeen had nobody to fight, and a country they were ill equipped to run. They returned to their tribal warfare, their blood feuds, and honor killings, but this time armed with Soviet surplus.

Mike watched as a small boy ran towards the tent. Mike's finger traced the trigger of the AK. The boy was a young shepherd and had a look of virginal innocence. He was ruddy cheeked and had bright chocolate eyes. Not a mean bone in his body.

A man called for the boy from behind, and he turned on his heel and went to him. Mike watched as they conversed and then walked off, the man putting his hand on the boy's shoulder.

Mike peered out at the Sinaloa sun, anxious to stop the flood of memory. But still, they came. Night had fallen and the encampment was in flames, and he heard the screams of women as Aslam and his men dragged them off and loaded them into their trucks. He tried to raise his rifle. Tried to change the course of events where he'd last stood by, but his muscles refused to move, and he realized that what had happened here, had already happened and would forever happen, on into continuum, and he was on tracks, and powerless, as if he was watching a movie.

Mike watched the fire as it licked the sides of the wool tents, and he wondered briefly if that had been his first taste of hell. The memories came back to him now, disjointed and out of order. The crackling fire was no longer a burning Kochi tent but a vehicle.

A figure sat in front of him. A silhouette. This was the next time he'd seen the boy. But the boy was now a man, and he'd recognized him as soon as he had gotten a clear look—for the boy had often visited him in the small hours of the night. Invaded his dreams and asked him where his family had gone. He knew that massacre had been a turning point, because it was the only nightmare he ever had.

"What's your name?" he asked. Mike heard his own voice, distant and fuzzy from time.

"Bahrawar," the man had replied.

"Means lion."

"The Americans call me Psycho."

"Been looking for men like you. We're gonna call them Afghan Commandos, and my ass is gonna train 'em."

A spiral of fire shot out from the truck as it found some new fuel source, and Mike recognized the moment. Mike had never told him. But he'd felt the urge to make things right, to take him under his wing.

He shook the memories off and slowly pushed himself up in the wooden chair. The Polaris sat a few feet away from him. It was over now. Psycho was dead. Everyone was dead. And he was here, still alive. That's what mattered in the end. Gaining the whole world. That was the game.

The Company had given him purpose. Had given him a thing to do—to be. And before that so had the Army. He hadn't any idea how important that was until it was no longer there. He'd always scoffed at the older guys that couldn't turn it off, the ones who refused to retire. But it was harder than it looked.

Cicadas started to chirp around him.

Then from behind him, a twig snapped. Instinctively, his hand went to his waist, but the 1911 was no longer there. He'd left it behind today. He'd finally felt safe.

He rose slowly and turned. His eyes finding a figure standing in the shade of an orange tree. He couldn't make out a face. Just a frame. Two more figures stepped up, flanking the man. He could see the silhouettes of rifles, slung over shoulders.

"Hi Mike," a voice said. It was a voice that had been long dead.

"Cowboy?" Mike said, not believing the name even as it left his mouth.

Chapter Twenty-Five

One month earlier

If there was a hell, I was sure it was not made of fire, but of open water. A placid void seasoned with lost souls that stretched from one horizon to another.

In SERE training they had told us that the average human could only tread water for two to three hours before they became so utterly exhausted that their body gave out. Because of this it was better to make a flotation device by knotting the legs of a cotton flight suit or jacket or shirt and blowing air into it. The only problem was I had no clothing left save the T-shirt wet and clinging to my back.

The next best option was floating. Either on your back or face down. I alternated between the two, choosing face down when the water got choppier. I would turn my head to the side, take a sharp breath in and then hold my breath for several seconds before doing this again.

My throat burned, and I wanted more than anything in the world a drink of water. The saltwater dried me out and sucked my own moisture out through my pores. Hell was floating in endless amounts of the very thing you wanted the most, but being unable to partake of it lest you hurry death along.

I had a few immediate concerns. The first was drowning, but the cold was also high on the list. The water wasn't exactly warm. And while the day had been hot, it would start to cool once night fell.

I guessed the water temperature was somewhere around 75 degrees Fahrenheit right now, so I had time, but if it dropped to anything below 70, I'd be playing Russian roulette with hypothermia.

In ten hours, I would be a goner.

I floated like this for a couple hours, exhausted by my own breathing. The impossibility of surviving, of being stumbled upon or rescued plagued my mind, but I ignored the thoughts, and focused on the glimmer of hope that was a passing ship, or a lone fisherman, or a happenstance meeting with a coast guard vessel. I ignored the fact that I had nothing to signal with. No mirror, or sunglasses, no flare gun.

I visualized the rescue. As Mike had said, hope was my only chance. But for the rats it had only postponed the inevitable.

Eventually my thoughts turned to that of Mike. And a need for revenge replaced hope as my driving force. I'd find him in some dusty Cantina. Or downrange in Africa somewhere. In my mind's eye, I stalked out of the night and ambushed him.

The ocean was not a test of physicality, because physicality could do nothing. Nor was she a test of character for good and bad alike could drown just as simply within her embrace. No, the ocean was a test of the dark, hidden parts of man, of iron will and hardness of spirit. Grit was what she tested, and nothing else.

The sun limped lower in the sky, and I dreaded her departure.

My sharp breathing had filled my brain with oxygen, and the intense visualization had produced a hypnotic kaleidoscope of dream logic and sensation. I was losing it. Probably hyperventilating.

The sky was rent in two and the sun appeared simultaneously in each of its halves. The sunset on the face of the waters turned all around me into one giant pool of gold and iridescent fulgurate.

Life was fucking beautiful, and conflict was life. It was the product of struggle. Beauty was conflict—a war between between songbirds and the insects they preyed upon, between the snakes that hunted the birds, and the bigger birds that hunted the snakes, and all that was in competition with the other, and the results of that competition produced beautiful flowers and green leaves, creeping vines, the melancholic chitter of bugs at sundown, and the flitter of red-feathered wings. It was no accident that the things most ugly, were things decaying, the malformed, the decrepit. Degeneration was the sickness all of nature fought against, was revolted by, and so the greatest sins were never borne of action, but inaction, of allowance, of tolerance, and sloth. Giving up was the great sin.

I had watched the path of the sun throughout the day and knew in what direction land lay.

I decided then in my sun soaked haze that I

would no longer float, no longer wait for the cold or the dehydration to take me.

I would not wait for the rescue ship that would not come. I would not flounder.

No. I would end this fighting. I would swim towards shore and when I had no energy left, I would keep swimming, and when my muscles grew weak, I would still swim, and should the ocean still swallow me, I hoped upon her a sour belly. And so against my better judgement and all my training I stopped floating and I started swimming.

Night fell.

And I floundered forward.

Stars spun overhead.

And my vision tunneled.

I swam some more. My muscles ached and cramped and several times I swallowed sea water. It invaded my mouth, it sought my lungs, but I blew it back out. The void called to me. Its song was beautiful, and I knew then that sirens were real, they called out from the void, but they were not of this world, instead living yonder on the other side of the veil.

And then the moon rose and the temperature started to plummet. Still I swam, and several times ships passed me in the night, but they were not real either, only apparitions sailing across the river Styx.

Then a flash of black and white came to me and I heard the familiar chitter of an old friend. He brushed up against me, and was smooth to the touch. Like slick rubber. An Orca.

And another breached the water right next to me, and I clung onto his back like he was a piece of driftwood and me a drowning rat. My body was limp, exhausted, and I gasped for air.

Several others were all around me then. And somewhere in the back of my mind I heard Valentina talking about the Orcas that pulled sailors from shipwrecks.

I DRAGGED myself through the surf. The whales having deposited me on sandy shores. Cold had invaded my bones, and I shivered uncontrollably against the dread of night. The sun had not yet risen. I dragged myself to my knees.

I stumbled up to the rocks that lined the shore. I needed fire. I knew somewhere in the back of my mind that I was almost hypothermic. I found a rock out cropping that was sheltered from the wind, at the far end of it was a pile of driftwood and dried seaweed that had washed up and been trapped in the rocks from a tropical storm.

I found a sack of garbage on the beach that someone had left, full of cans and paper towels, and I'd never been so thankful for litter.

I unscrewed the fire starter from the handle of my dive knife and dug through the litter. Taking a piece of used toilet paper I scrambled back to my rock shelter. The mass of wood in front of me looked like the carcass of some hideous beast, dried seaweed stretched across its wooden bones like strips of long decayed flesh and hide. I used the flint and struck it against steel. My hands were still shaking even though I felt flushed.

Hypothermia. It was here. I recognized the signs. I'd been here before, in training, I recognized the feeling, the forgetfulness, the confusion, the shivers as white heat radiated through my bones.

I needed fire.

I worked on the flint and steel, and sparks caught. I blew softly. A flame. I nursed it to life with dried seaweed. Then splinters of driftwood. It was going good, and I crouched by it like one of my long lost ape ancestors.

I laughed at the fire, a hoarse thirsty laugh, that hurt the dried-up corners of my mouth, and split my lips. I could taste the copper of my own blood.

I rocked back and forth, laughing at the fire, drunk on its heat and smoke.

I AWOKE next to a bed of warm coals and the hot Argentina sun above. My consciousness had returned, and I was not quite sure of all that had happened the night before. Most of it was a blur. I remembered drowning. I remembered the beauty of the sunset. I remembered the pod of orcas. I wondered if they were even real, for the implications seemed too surreal for my rational mind to grasp. Yet I was here. Alive, beside a bed of hot coals.

I had no idea how I had started that fire. No idea how I had survived any of it. But I had, and the sun above was the most beautiful sun I had ever seen, and the day the most beautiful day, and the air the freshest air, and the crash of the ocean on the rocks behind me no longer something to be feared, but an ally, the music of gods.

I stood up slowly, my whole-body aching, but the ache felt good. It felt like I was the first and last man born on to the face of the earth, and everything that had come before, had been wiped away, and only the future, a sea of potential lay in front of me. I was six years old again and all that I could imagine was once again possible.

I was a new man. The old one had died, and with him all of his doubts and fears, and misgivings. Ryan had died in the ocean, or he had died on the beach by the fire. He was no longer here. I was renewed.

Then my thoughts turned to Mike. He would die and I would kill him. He had betrayed us. The others were dead probably. And when I killed him it would not be murder. It would not be revenge. It would be justice. For it was right, and right began in the heart of a man. It started in the depth of his soul and in the iron of his will. Man was law. He was right and wrong. States and governments were only a reflection of the law, a crystalline refraction of the natural order in my heart.

Chapter Twenty-Six

Twelve hours earlier

The Nord ran his fingers through blond shocks of hair, his mind reeling at what had just went down. The Bruiser disappeared just beyond the mouth of the cove, and with-it Ryan and Mike.

"He was CIA the whole time," Tex said.

"So, we were CIA?" Mex said.

"Fucking CIA," Tex said. "Just my fucking luck."

"Well now what?" Mex asked.

"They'll come for us," the Nord said.

"Who will?" Mex asked.

"The CIA, dumbass," Tex said.

"We need to start moving then," Mex said.

"No. They'll find us," the Nord said. "We have to end it." He started pacing and ran his fingers through his hair again. His mind raced, playing out the different scenarios. "They'll know we are on foot. They'll expect us to run."

"Then what the fuck do we do?" Tex said.

"Shut up and let me think," the Nord said. "Strike team is out because it'll take them too long to get here. Unless they were already on their way. But I don't think so, because I don't think Mike was planning to have his cover blown like that. Mike said three days. So they'll be scrambling now. They'll send a drone."

"We can take the Hilux." Mex said.

"That's good," the Nord said. "But Psycho was reporting back to Mike the whole time. Consider it already gone."

"We'll never know unless we try," Tex said.

"But even if we get away, then what?" the Nord said. "We'll be in the wind, and they'll find us eventually."

"We can change our names, get new documents, new identities." Mex said. "This is South America."

"Yeah, we'll have to do that regardless," the Nord said. "You think the Chinese are still looking for us?"

"I would be," the Mex said.

"If they send a drone, how long before it got here?" the Nord asked.

"It's hard to tell?" Tex said. "Depends on where they launched it from. I don't know why they'd have any in country, but I'm sure they have something up north, probably doing counter drug shit."

"Where are our cell phones?" the Nord asked.

"In the team room. Locked up. Why?"

"We need bodies," the Nord said.

"For what?" Mex asked.

"To fool the drone. Our only way out is if we make them think they killed us."

"Alright, but what bodies?" Tex asked.

"Mex, you miss your mom?" The Nord asked. "Want to make a call?"

Mex just looked at him, then nodded slowly.

THE NORD SAT in one of the spinney chairs feet up on the desk, and watched Mex as he paced back and forth, cellphone to his ear, on the phone with his mom. They'd used the computer as a hotspot for the cellphone and turned the VPN off.

Mex asked how she was doing. How the treatments were going. He was calm and reassuring. At last, he was done. He hung up with an "I love you," a "goodbye," and tears in his eyes. He set the phone down on the table.

Tex sat at the computer. "Well?"

"The treatments seem to be working," Mex said.

"Not you," Tex said. He looked at Nord. "What's this about?"

"Chinese SIGINT," Nord said. "Ukraine was a fucking mess because everyone was snooping on everyone else's cellphone use."

"So that was bait," Tex said.

"If they are half as on it as anyone else is it will be," Nord said. "Now they know where to find us. That boat that got away is still out there somewhere. They'll be wanting to get even."

Nord sat concealed in the tree line, brush and tree branches pulled up around him. The others sat several feet off, equally well concealed. The water in the cove below lapped easily at the shoreline. The sun sunk lower in the sky.

"What if they don't come?" Tex said over comms.

"Then we'll have to play what we were dealt to begin with," Nord said.

"They'll come," Mex said. "After what we did on the GOPLAT. They'll come."

Night fell and with-it darkness, and still they sat under the cover of the trees. Nord flicked his NODs down over his eyes. Beneath the trees they were hidden from the eye of any drone that would be sent, even in IR, it couldn't penetrate the dense shield of foliage. For this to work they had to get lucky. The timing of it all worried him.

And then they arrived, as shadows on the water. Eight heads gliding just above the surface of the water. The Nord spotted them first, he whispered into his mic. "Eight tangoes in the water."

The Nord shouldered his rifle, and peered through the M4s scope. He placed his reticle on the head of the lead man.

"We need three of them alive," the Nord whispered. "I'll shoot to wound the first four that get out of the water. You take the rest when I stop firing."

"Rog," came the reply.

He was surprised they'd gotten here so quick. They must have already had a good idea of where they were set up. There were only so many places along the coast that fit the bill. The phone call was probably the final piece of the puzzle.

The enemy fighters approached the bank. Then they paused, and suddenly IR strobes emanated from their rifles as they readied their weapons.

They slowly walked up out of the water, wet suits shiny and dripping water. IR strobes from the rifles crisscrossing in front of them. They moved as one unit, all well trained fighters.

Nord inhaled slowly and drew a bead on the hip of the foremost man. A shot through the pelvis would drop him instantly, and he didn't want to risk a leg shot where he might hit the femoral. The shoulder and gut were also an option but finnicky with body armor. His finger closed around the trigger. He released his breath slowly and evenly and squeezed.

Thwap! The first man crumpled.. He followed up quickly on the next two, again aiming for the pelvis. His rifle thunked loudly, the silencer coughing. Two more men collapsed.

Nord scrambled backwards from his position as a torrent of bullets shredded his former hidey hole.

Mex and Tex both engaged then. Mag dumping the remaining men, and dumping them where they stood. The whole engagement took no more than fifteen seconds and was over nearly as soon as it had begun.

The Nord circled around for a flank. The ones he had shot to wound were squirming, but still armed and still dangerous. They dragged themselves up onto the shore of the beach and fired blindly into the tree line.

The Nord glided quietly through the soft undergrowth, picking his way carefully. Finally free of his trees, his boots found the soft sand, and he circled well behind the three wounded so they wouldn't see him.

They were shouting to each other in Chinese. One was howling from the pain.

Nord slunk along in a crouch behind the commotion. They still hadn't seen him. The one that was screaming was fully out of the fight. The other two were frantically trying to pry their mags free, their arms failing them as they went into shock.

Nord made his move then. He took two flash bangs and tossed them out, letting them clatter across the stony shore.

He turned away as they went off and then made his charge.

He struck one with the butt of his gun, knocking him unconscious. He kicked the other in the face and felt his nose crunch. The other tried to pull his pistol but Nord slammed a booted foot down on his hand.

THE FIRE WAS LIT, and the Chinese operators slowly came to around the blaze. They were battered and bloodied, but alive, tied hand and foot to the lawn chairs. Their wounds mashed full of quick clot. They looked terrified at the sight of the three Americans before them.

"Confused as fuck," Mex said. "Poor fuckers."

"Alright, let's get back to the trees," Nord said.

"Fucked up to fix them up like that," Tex said.

"We need em to stay alive."

Mex pulled out his IFAK, and broke out several morphine syringes.

"What are you doing that for?" Nord asked.

"Ah shut up," Mex said as he dosed them. "It's the least we could do. Besides maybe they'll last longer."

They spent the next ten minutes dragging the dead out of the water and concealing them beneath the trees. When they were done, they made their way back to the tree line and the safety of the foliage.

The three Chinese soldiers dozed next to the blaze, dosed out of their gourd on the painkillers.

"That was a good idea," Nord said.

They sat and watched them. Sometimes the men would wake up screaming and stuttering. Two hours passed and nothing happened.

"Do you think they are dead yet?" Mex asked.

And then they heard it. A low hum. Like a distant lawnmower. Sound traveled far out here, and there was not enough ambient noise to cover the sound of the engines. It was very low, and barely even perceptible, presenting itself as a vibration and a feeling more than a noise.

"Do you think that's it?" Tex asked.

"You heard it too?" the Nord asked.

"Yeah, I think so."

"I don't hear shit, just tinnitus," Mex said.

"I think it's on station," Tex said.

There was a sharp crack, a snap a split second before impact, that made them all jump. It was the sound an AGM-114 Hellfire made right at the moment it went supersonic.

NODs went white, blinding them and drawing shouts of pain.

Nord clinched his eyes shut and peeled his NODs off. There was nothing but fire and roiling smoke and dust where the three figures had sat just moments before. The whole cove bathed in the explosion's orange light. Debris from the explosion splashed down in the water, and then all was silent.

"It fucking worked," Mex said suddenly. "It really fucking worked."

"Congratulations, we're all dead men walking," Nord said.

"How long should we wait here?" Tex asked.

"Until morning at least," Nord said. "Figure they'll go off station as soon as they can confirm nothing is left down here to kill. No use moving sooner."

He sat back then, crossed his arms and leaned against a tree behind him. The weariness found him, and the adrenaline from the last twenty four hours was wearing off. And he slept. They all slept.

Chapter Twenty-Seven

My lips were cracked and bleeding, my throat dry, and my head thumped from dehydration. I stumbled among the rocks on the beach looking for an outcropping. Anywhere rainwater had collected.

After about an hour of this, I found a small puddle set back in a jumble of boulders. I lowered myself to my belly and lapped the water up out of the rocks like a dog or wild beast. It was warm. Hot even, and tasted stale, but not salty. I had no idea how long it had been stagnant, but sickness seemed the least of my worries at this moment. I'd chance shitting my brains out. Dehydration had that affect.

I continued my path North with no idea where I was headed. I recognized none of the land, for I had not studied the area the way I now wished I had.

Late in the afternoon, I came to an area of the beach littered with trash. I found a burlap sack and briefly thought of cutting holes in it to use as a shirt. My wetsuit had begun to chafe and I felt in a bad way. In the end, the thought of the scratchy burlap sounded even more unbearable. I did however find half a tarp, weather-eaten and brittle, but still useable, and I washed it off in the ocean.

I was tired. Tired and weak and thirsty. My training had been hard. All of it. The rucks for miles on nothing but a steady diet of MREs. The Crucible at the end of Bootcamp. Selection for Marine Recon. The Basic Reconnaissance Course itself. None of it had left me so drained. Never had I been so close to death physically, and yet... so far away spiritually. There was a fire in my bosom now. The fire of life and yearning. I could not die, because my spirit would simply refuse to leave.

I found a spot on the beach near the tide line and dug a donut shaped hole that would fill with water at high tide. I picked through the debris that had washed ashore for a container of sorts, but only found a half empty bottle of bleach. I poured out the contents, and then cut the top off. I washed it with seawater and then stumbled back up to the beach where I scrubbed the inside with sand.

I did this several times. until I was confident that contamination was minimal. Bleach would only be harmful in large amounts anyways, in fact, one could even add a few drops of bleach to a gallon of water to decontaminate it. I wondered if I should have saved some of it. But satisfied at last with my container, and not wanting to wait for high tide, I used it to fill the hole with seawater. This took the better part of an hour, weak as I was.

The hole held the water well for the sand was already waterlogged. I placed the container in the center of the pit, spread the tarp out over the top and secured the edges with sand. I placed a fist sized stone in the very middle of the tarp, right above my container. The tarp would hasten evaporation and catch the condensation on the bottom.

The condensation would run downwards guided by gravity to the low spot with my stone, and drip into the container. It was a little over midday now, so I would wait until evening to retrieve my water.

I took shelter among the rocks, finding a spot with shade, and took my time clearing a place to lay down. The sand was cool to the touch and still damp. I curled up in the fetal position, overcome with weakness.

It was dark out when I awoke, and what had been a bed of loose, cool sand was now heavily compacted. It left my body stiff and aching. My head throbbed and my mouth and throat were bone dry. Sand clung stubbornly to my skin and chafed when I moved. I stumbled down to the beach and bathed in the water.

I checked my still. It had produced no more than a cup of water, which was to be expected, but still depressed me. I drank it down, and it did nothing but leave me wanting more. Instead of dying of thirst, I was now simply dying of thirst more slowly.

I wrapped the tarp over my shoulders and wandered on again. I was a vagabond. I would travel at night when it was cool, using my movement to warm me. When day broke, I would set up the still, and find a place to sleep, sheltered from the sun's rays.

My thoughts turned to those of my friends, and I wondered if they were dead. They did not feel dead. I had always heard stories of the souls of close ones visiting you one last time before they departed. Of men on business trips, seeing the apparition of their sickly mother in their hotel room, and the dreaded call coming only a few minutes later. Or a parent rushing to a school where their child had just been seriously injured, driven by some feeling of dread, an intense panic of the soul, only to get a call from the school nurse when they were halfway there. I had always found comfort in these stories and believed them to be true. How many times had I thought of an ex-lover, or dreamt of them, and the next day they called. I prayed that the others had somehow made it.

I had no idea how far I walked in those first hours, but when I turned around the faint shadows of the debris field on the beach were still in sight. I refused to look back again, and vowed to only move forward, no matter how slowly.

The sand was coarse beneath my feet, and the webbing between my toes began to bleed from so much chafing. My soles felt as if they were on fire. My head pounded with every beat of my heart, and my tongue swelled from dehydration. When I breathed, I whistled, and when that grew annoying, I breathed through my mouth, which in turn just hurt my throat.

At the first sign of dawn and the gentle graying of the sky, I scurried vampirically around the water's edge to build my still. As the sun broke the horizon, I hurried to the rocks and hunted for a place that would remain shaded for most of the day. I wandered high up into the boulders looking for a place to hole up, but the land had changed, and these stones were smaller. Finally, at the very top of the small hill where the beach and the rocks transitioned to the land beyond, I found a crag of boulders and a patch of grass to lay my head.

I WOKE WITH A START. Something breathing on me, warm, and wet on my cheek. I was face to face with a cow. I slowly pushed myself up to a sitting position and the cow took two startled steps back. It blew forcefully, as startled by me, as I was it. Several other cows grazed nearby. They watched me indifferently as I emerged from the small crag I'd crawled into. Storm clouds had moved in during the day and it was just starting to drizzle.

" Quién eres?" a voice behind me said.

I turned around to see a rider. He was a cowboy, or a gaucho. His horse stomped impatiently as he rode closer, keeping a tight rein. The horse was a beautiful buckskin with a golden hide and black stockings.

I tried to speak, but no more than a grunt came out. My tongue so swollen and mouth so dry, words refused to form. The rider slid out of the saddle and produced a canteen from beneath his slicker. He handed it to me and I struggled with the cap for a minute. Finally, tired of watching me fumble with it, he took it back and unscrewed it for me.

I had barely taken a single pull at the water, when he shook his head and snatched the canteen back saying something in Spanish.

I started to get mad then, but his eyes were kind and the lines on his face concerned. His eyes matched the color of his brown flat brimmed hat. Sandy blond hair stuck out from the sides of it in tufts. Creases around his eyes spoke to life in the sun, but he was not old. About thirty or so, I guessed. He eyed me up and down, then motioned for me to sit while saying something in Spanish that I could not understand.

He retrieved his bedroll from the horse and unrolled it to reveal an extra set of clothes.

When I had changed into the clothes, he let me have another drink. I wrapped the blanket around my shoulders, feeling some sort of warmth for the first time in days. I still couldn't form words, so I nodded awkwardly as he talked to me in Spanish.

He built a fire and set up a tarp to protect us from the weather. I sat with my back to the rock and watched as the flames lapped at the driftwood. The drizzle turned to rain, and then back to drizzle. I was thankful to have been found by this stranger when I was, for I had been all but naked out here, and this rain would have likely ended me. Ironically, it would have solved my water problem at the same time. The elements were like that, either too little or too much.

After several hours of slowly nursing the canteen. I felt my tongue break loose from the top of my mouth.

"English?" I asked, finally able to form words.

His face lit up and he smiled.

"What's your name?" he said in broken English.

I thought for a second. The question had caught me off guard. "John," I said, saying the first thing that came to mind. I couldn't risk using my real name anymore.

"I'm Luis," he said and stuck out a hand. "You are fortunate I found you."

"I am. Thank you."

"Feeling better?"

"A little," I nodded.

Dinner was beans, and by nightfall the storm had broken. I fell asleep by the fire and woke in the middle of the night having to piss. Luis lay asleep, arms crossed over his chest, and hat over his eyes.

I wandered some ways off and relieved myself. The night was quiet. Peaceful, and the fog in my head had started to lift. I stared out at the stars and could just barely make out the sound of the ocean.

The next morning, Luis showed me his small remuda. He picked out a gentle looking chestnut and helped me climb onto her back. He cut a bit of rope and made a hackamore, then handed me the makeshift reins. He didn't have an extra saddle, so I rode bareback.

I sat the horse and helped him drive the cows as best I could, mostly trying to stay out of his way. By the end of the first day, my hips and groin were sore from straddling the horse, but I felt good. The food and water, and clothes had made me a new man, and I could feel my strength returning in waves.

It was sundown when we got the cows back to his ranch. Luis herded them into an old pole corral. We led the horses to a barn that looked new but smelled old. He'd kept it in good repair. There were lights on in the farmhouse, and an old flatbed pickup truck parked in the yard.

"You can stay with us," Luis told me. "Rest up, and then I'll help you get where you need to go."

"Thank you," I said.

"Do you need to call someone?"

"No. No one. And you don't call anyone either?" I said.

A look of understanding crossed his face. "I understand. You are on the run." He turned heel and took off at a brisk walk across the yard. I followed behind.

His wife greeted him at the door, throwing her arms around his neck and I stood awkwardly trying not to impose on their reunion. She was a small woman, perhaps a foot shorter than him, and pretty.

She asked him something in Spanish while looking at me.

"John, this is my wife, Esmeralda," he said.

I reached out a hand and she shook it, giving me a small welcoming nod.

Luis guided me inside. Dinner was already on the table when we entered, and Esmeralda hurried to set another place for me.

Two children barely a year apart ran to greet their father and hugged him at the door. One, a girl no more than five years old, and the other a boy who looked slightly older. Luis gave both a hug and then ruffled their hair.

Dinner was breaded flank steak and green beans, with a generous helping of chimichurri and corn chips on the side. It was perhaps the best meal I had ever had in my life. I only made it halfway through the pile of food before calling it quits, for I was painfully full.

Afterwards, Luis led me outside to the porch and handed me a cigar. He showed me to one of the rocking chairs.

It was dark out now, and the milky way

stretched out above us in all its glory. In the wilderness, away from the light of cities, the true beauty and vastness of the stars was on display. I felt a profound humility, and smallness, beneath the stars.

I rolled the cigar between my fingers and then took the cutter to it. Luis handed me the torch and I roasted the end. When I had puffed mine to life, I took a heavy pull, and the buzz hit me like a brick wall. I'd been without nicotine for the last three or four days, which likely explained some of my throbbing head.

"It's beautiful isn't it," Luis said.

"I always forget how many stars are out there," I responded.

"It's cities," Luis said. "The are of Cain."

I nodded, slightly confused.

"His inheritance. He was the first city builder."

"I've never given much thought to God," I said. "I was raised Christian sure, raised right for the most part. But it never really stuck. Never really felt God."

"He's all around you," Luis said. "Everywhere, and in everything. You can feel him most outside of cities."

"You really hate cities, huh," I said.

"Abominations. Leave me out here, alone." He took a pull on the cigar then, and the red-hot end briefly illuminated his face. "Tell me what happened?"

"I can't," I said. "I wish I could, but I can't. All you really need to know is that I died out there and you've never seen me."

"So, John is a fake name?" Luis said.

"Yeah,"

"You come up with a last one?"

"Not yet," I said. I took a pull at the cigar. "John Mars," I added, and chuckled.

"That's a good name," Luis chuckled. "Has a ring to it."

"It's a riff on an old pulp novel," I said. "John Carter of Mars."

"You can take the truck," Luis said.

"I really can't," I said. "You've done enough."

"You can't stay here," Luis said. "There is a mechanic shop in Del Mar, you can drop it off there."

"Del Mar?" I said.

"You've heard of it?"

"I've been there. How far from it are we?"

"No more than an hour away. Just south of it." Luis said.

"That's good," I said.

Chapter Twenty-Eight

Early the next morning, I drove the old flatbed into Villa Del Mar. A few locals sat in front of the grocer. Some old men chatted on the stoop of the Barbero. I passed the turnoff that would take me near the sea, and up towards Valentina's house, and the knot in my stomach traveled up to my throat.

I shook it off and drove forward. The mechanic had not opened yet, so I simply left the truck and a note that said: *Luis will come to pick it up.*

The mechanics was on the edge of the town, so I walked off towards the beach and the docks, my hands in my pockets.

The less I showed my face around here the better. I pulled the old trucker hat Luis had given me down lower on my head. I looked like quite the sight, I was sure. Blue jeans, old tennis shoes, a button up with pearl buttons, and a trucker hat.

Along the shore, I stopped by the place where Valentina and I had shared the night. Her house, I knew, was just over the ridge to my left. My feet begged me to let them take me, but I didn't budge.

I couldn't risk it. Not now. If they were still on

the lookout for me, they would surely have this place under surveillance, since Psycho had been snitching to Mike.

Mike would know about the girl. She was ok. She was safe as long as I stayed dead.

I continued walking up the shore, putting some distance between myself and the backside of Valentina's house. I walked past the bar where I'd first seen her. Where she'd first whisked me up off my feet and not the other way around.

I climbed the steps to a rickety boardwalk, that ran along the marina. Buildings backed all the way up to the beach stretched out to the right, boats and water to my left.

I felt the presence before I heard it. I turned quickly, catching the shape of two men in my peripheral.

They closed quickly, one from the shadows of the buildings and another from his hiding spot on one of the boats. But the man immediately behind me, had a gun. I clocked that first.

I whirled, ready to fight.

"I knew you come back," the man said. His speech heavily accented and English only slightly broken. He was Argentinian through and through, and I just glimpsed the edge of a tattoo peeking above his collar. Black hair greased backwards. But in his hand was an old revolver by the look of it, and he had been smart enough to keep a safe distance.

I froze. His friend circled.

I didn't recognize him, but I put our connection together in an instant. This is who had clubbed me in the bar on that first night. The one that was jealous over Valentina.

As my recognition dawned, he smiled to reveal a set of gapped teeth, and his two friends grabbed me. I didn't resist even as I felt the zip ties go around my wrists, and the black bag over my head.

WHEN THE BAG was finally pulled free of my head I sat tied to a chair. I was in an old shed of some sort. Fishing nets hung on the wall to my left, and to my right was a pile of junk and old tires. A single bulb flickered above us and bathed the place in a dull yellow light.

Dust floated in the air, and almost immediately I felt the impulse to sneeze. I stifled it until my eyes watered. I'm not completely sure why I stifled it. Something about sneezing didn't really project strength. Which was a funny concern considering I was zip tied to a chair.

Across from me was Armand. His boys sat on an old, junked couch positioned by the door.

I continued to scan my surroundings. They'd left me conscious for the ride, and while I couldn't see through the black bag, I had counted off the minutes in my head. Wherever they'd taken me was about 20-25 minutes from Del Mar. I'd felt the ride go from asphalt to gravel, and I intuited that this was a somewhat isolated location.

What was it that Valentina had said? They were smugglers of some sort or another. This was likely where they offloaded their goods. Near the coast no doubt.

The smell of the saltwater stung my nostrils—on the coast.

What kind of goods did they smuggle? Goods as in drugs, because I couldn't imagine what else they could be smuggling. Humans maybe, they seemed small fry, so I doubted it.

This was the second time in a week I'd found myself a prisoner and truth be told I was getting tired of it. I probably could've taken them if I'd been back to full health, but I was still weak from the wilderness. Still sluggish too, and while my spirit was vigorous my body was not. My head had just barely healed from the last bottle Armand had smashed across it. I wasn't in a hurry to add a pistol whipping to the list.

"Do you know why we brought you here?"

"I have no idea," I said.

Armand stood up and sat on the edge of the desk. "I know who you are."

"And who's that?"

"We've heard the stories," Armand said. "About the mercenario killing the fishermen."

"I don't know anything about that," I said. "I'm a Marine Biologist."

"Company men," Armand said.

I gave him a confused look.

"CIA, pendejo," Armand said.

"I don't know anything about that," I said slowly.

"You know Valentina will never talk to you again," he said. "Because she will never see you again."

My heart dropped.

"You love her?" I asked.

He said nothing, but I saw the flicker of pain cross his eyes.

"She doesn't see you that way huh?" I said. I was wading into dangerous territory now. "You really want my sloppy seconds?"

He punched me hard across the mouth, and my head went to ringing. "I would have let you go if you agreed to never come back, but I have a feeling that's not a promise you can make."

"Yeah, you're probably right."

"So, I've got to kill you." He pulled the slide back on the Glock.

The front door suddenly flew open and sunlight bathed the inside of the shed. I clinched my eyes against the sudden change. Three figures streamed through the door. Silhouettes with rifles. They were shouting.

Armand turned and started to raise the Glock but a firm voice said, "Don't." He slowly lowered the weapon, setting it back on the table, before raising his hands.

The lead gunmen walked towards me, and I squinted against the sunlight.

I recognized his voice before I could make out the face. "You're getting pretty good at getting captured," the Nord said.

"What the fuck," I said, in equal amounts of shock and joy.

The Nord walked towards Armand, and picked up his pistol as he slung the rifle.

"Sit," he commanded.

Armand sat.

The Nord pulled a knife from his boot and cut

me free with one hand while maintaining his aim on Armand.

"How'd you find me?" I asked.

"We were waiting for you in Del Mar," the Nord said. "We watched them take you."

"And you didn't stop them?"

"We need them," the Nord said.

"Need them?" I said, rubbing my wrists.

Nord handed me Armand's gun. I checked the chamber, and then jabbed it towards Armand. "Who's the pendejo now?"

He didn't flinch, didn't cower, and I respected him a little more for it.

Tex and Mex had put the others on their faces.

"Fuck am I glad to see you," I said. "How the fuck did you get away?"

"Very carefully," Tex said.

Back to Nord: "You said you need them. What for?"

"Papers. New ID's," Nord said. "You told us Valentina said they were smugglers."

"Ah," I said. "How'd you get away?"

"They sent a drone. Long story," Nord said. "With any luck they think we're dead."

"Can't wait to hear it," I said. Back to Mex: "Can't believe you fucks are alive."

"Back atcha," Mex said.

"You look like shit," Tex said.

"Thanks, but I feel like a million bucks."

"You're about the only one."

"What?" I asked.

"Mike robbed us. The stupid fuck."

One of the guys on the floor squirmed, and Mex kicked him in the ribs.

"He robbed us," I said, still confused. "The crypto accounts?"

"Yeah," Mex said.

"Did you change the password on yours?" Tex asked.

"No," I said. "Was I supposed to?"

"Yeah, apparently."

"I didn't even think about it," I said. "So, what do we have for money?"

"Been pimping Mex out," the Nord said.

"Rich dudes pay top dollar," Tex interjected.

"Fuck off," Mex said. "Tex has been givin' handies for beer money since he was ten."

"Dark," Nord said.

I looked at Armand. "Can you get us new papers?" I asked.

Armand stayed silent.

"Look, I don't really want to kill you," I said. "But you already know we ain't got money, so it looks like your life is our currency."

"What do you need?" Armand said, finally.

"Passports. Driver's license. All of it," Nord said.

"For four of you?" Armand said. He looked exasperated.

"Yeah," I said.

"That costs money," Armand said.

"You better sponsor us then," Tex said.

"Look, that's like half a million dollars easy," Armand said.

"What crime don't pay." I said. I stepped forward and put the barrel of Armand's gun to his forehead. Our eyes locked, and I kept it there until he looked away. He hated me. Hated everything about me.

"Fine," he said.

"These fucks trustworthy?" the Nord asked, motioning towards the two men on the ground.

"They're my brothers," Armand said.

"Nice, which one is the youngest?" Nord asked.

"Martin," Armand said.

One of the men looked at us. "Is that Martin?" I asked and Armand nodded.

"Cool, you and Martin, are going to stay with us."

"And you," I pointed to the other. "What's your name?"

"Miguel," the man said.

"Miguel is going to get us our shit. And if there is anything funny that happens, Martin is gonna get it first." I turned back to Armand and asked, "how long?"

"A week maybe," Armand said. "Documents take time."

"Then we better get started."

WE HOLED up in the shed for a week. Miguel set up the appointment with the man they referred to as "el falsificador," or the counterfeiter, and then returned. They were real creative with names.

The shed where they had taken me was about 30 minutes from Del Mar, hidden along a small inlet that created a sort of natural harbor. In the back of the shed was a door.

It was only when Mex had opened it that he had found that the shed backed up to the mountain. It was placed such to hide the mouth of a cave. Along the small peninsula was an extravagant cave system, which the smugglers used to offload and stash the drugs smuggled in from the sea.

Armand assured us that they were not expecting any visitors for at least two weeks, but we had no idea if that was true or not. So, we took turns keeping watch at the very tip of the peninsula.

There was a high point, where the land rose sharply just before falling off completely into the sea, and if stationed at the top of it, one could see for miles.

Day one, we swapped stories of our respective escapes. I told them about being dumped in the sea, and floating for hours, how I had been close to dying, and then reluctantly, for I barely believed it myself, that a pod of Orcas had saved me.

Nord was convinced it was a hallucination. Mex believed it wholeheartedly. And Tex had simply said, "sometimes the universe has a way of reaching a hand out when you need it most," which was surprisingly philosophical for someone that once poached alligators.

But then the Nord suggested my new nickname be *Free Willy*, and I didn't really have any sort of comeback, so I decided to never bring up the Orcas again.

The others told me about their trap. How they'd baited the Chinese to attack them, and then used the bodies to fake out the drone. It was a clever ruse, and not one that I would have thought of in such a short time. But that was the Nord, calm, even, deceptively humble, and the smartest one among us.

"You know you didn't have to keep them alive for it?" I said when he had finished.

"What do you mean?" the Nord said.

"The soldiers, you could have killed them and still used them by the fire."

"We needed the heat signature though?" the Nord said. "It was nighttime, so the drone would've been in IR."

"Yeah, but next to the fire the bodies were always going to look cold, didn't really matter as long as they looked like bodies."

"That's fucked," Mex said. "Why would you point that out?"

"I don't know," I said. "You know for next time."

"I'll add that to the list of things that keep me up at night," Nord said.

"Do we have any idea where Mike went?" I asked. It felt like all the air had been very suddenly sucked out of the room.

"I got a lead," the Nord said. "I hit an old Army buddy up on a burner. He owes me a favor. Works at Langley now."

"How big was the favor?"

"The I saved his life kind," Nord said.

"Good," I said. "Mike's gonna pay."

"Yeah," the Nord said. "We know."

Day two, I sat on the peninsula. Tex approached from behind me. A cool breeze was blowing in off the ocean, and the air smelled fresh, like salt and spray. Tex sat down beside me.

"Go see her," he said. "I know you want to."

"I can't."

"Sure, you can," Tex said. "Don't make things more dramatic than they are. This isn't a movie. It's just life. A fucked up, weird life, sure—but you only get one. One go around this God forsaken planet, and for all the fucked-up shit that happens, it's the women in it that make it worth it."

I looked back at him. "You never struck me as the romantic type."

He smirked. An easy, wry smile that had likely broken as many hearts as it had captured. "Only been in love once. She broke my heart," Tex said, he pulled a pack of cigarettes from inside his blue windbreaker and packed them.

He offered me one, and I drew it like lots from the pack. Tex handed me the lighter and I cupped it against the wind. "Red hair, but natural like. Milk white skin and freckles," he said. "Big ol' tits," he held his hands out in front of him as if they were still there.

"Well, how'd you fuck it up?" I asked.

"I didn't," he said. "She liked to smoke, and you know what they say."

"That when you started?" I asked.

Tex held out the cigarette. "She was cool as fuck, honestly. We really vibed. She was funny too. Do you know how dangerous a funny woman is. That shit will completely fuck up your life."

"So, what happened?"

"Got drunk, fucked some other guy at a party."

"That sucks."

"She was nuts. Total freak, but holy shit did I love her."

"We don't get to pick do we?"

"No," Tex said. "They say we pick 'em like our mothers."

"Good mental image," I said. "Was she like your mother?"

"I didn't know my mother," he said.

"So... a yes?"

He laughed hard at that.

Day three, we again sent Miguel to go check on the falsificador. When he returned, he reported that the man only needed two more days and our papers would be ready. He couldn't make the passports, but he had a contact at the National Registry who he paid handsomely to make them under the table.

I uncuffed Armand from the bed we'd found further back in the shed.

"Eat," I said, handing him a plate of beans and beef.

Wordlessly, he took it from me. He shoveled the food into his mouth.

"You know, I'm not gonna kill you, but if I find out you ever do anything to harm Valentina—"

"Fuck you, pendejo." He spit a mouthful of beans at my face. I turned away, blocking most of his projectiles with my shoulder. "I love her! I will never stop trying."

I backhanded him across the face. "You fucking latin types. The machismo. My god."

Blood trickled down the side of Armand's chin from where my slap had split his lip. He glared at me, and I just shook my head. I didn't really get it. The hate for me. I'd fucked his ex not killed his dog.

Day four, I was feeling like my old self. Mex found a couple pairs of boxing gloves on the top shelf of a steel rack. It was set back in a corner of the shed, unreachable because of the junk piled in front of it. Mex spotted them from across the room, and then carefully climbed across the junk until he reached the steel rack.

We sparred after that. Passing the time, and it felt good to breathe the fresh air, and to move. The sun was high in the sky and felt good on my skin. I could feel power and vigor starting to return to my limbs. It was always incredible to me how fast the body could bounce back if given a steady diet and exercise.

Nord walked up to us and slung the burner phone over the cliff's edge and into the ocean. Mex slung a punch, and I slipped.

"He's in Mexico," the Nord said.

Both Mex and I stopped dancing. "Doing what?" I asked.

"Retired," the Nord said. "Lives on some sort of cattle ranch out there."

"Did you get his grids?" I asked.

"Yeah."

On the fifth day, Miguel came back with our papers. He returned late at night and passed each of us a manilla envelope. I gently pried the metal clasps open and scanned my documents. Birth certificate, driver's license, passport. They were all there. I glanced at the others. Nord, Tex, and Mex. Somehow, the four of us had all made it. We were just missing Hulk. The big bastard. May he rest in peace.

I looked at my documents. I was now officially John Mars.

Chapter Twenty-Nine

Current Day - A Ranch in the Sinaloa Mountains

"Hi Mike," I said.

He froze. His hand hanging loosely at his waist, like a gunfighter ready to draw, but the 1911 that had kept him company for the last 20 years was nowhere to be seen.

"Ryan." Mike said. Mostly because that's all he could manage. His voice cracked, and now his mind swam—frantically—searching for an angle.

"It's John now," I said, lowering the M4 I had aimed at his gut. "Where's your gun?"

Mex and Tex sidled up next to me from their places in the shadows.

"I'm unarmed," he said.

I laughed. "That never stopped you."

I slung the gun and pulled out a tin of Copenhagen.

"Look boys," Mike started, as I packed a lip. "I

tried to keep you in line. I tried to keep you all out of trouble."

Mex cocked an eyebrow.

"If you hadn't gone off halfcocked looking for Hulk, it would have been fine. After that it got too hot. They didn't think you could be controlled."

"Don't beg Mike," I said. "It's not a good look."

"Goddammit Ryan—John. Whatever the fuck you want to be called. You have to listen to me. I didn't want it to go down like this."

"Where's our money, Mike?" Tex asked.

"You want your money? I got your money."

"Good, because you are going to take us to it," I said.

"What then?"

"You betrayed us, Mike. You pay us and maybe we let you have a fighting chance. What about a boxing match for old time's sake?"

"I didn't though. I tried to protect you." He was lying of course. Lying as fast as he could, and even as he did it, he knew it would make no difference.

"Mike, you know your fatal flaw. The one thing that for all your competence, and even your courage, is you were faithless. You thought you were so tough. A one man show. What was it you said, hard power, fire power, will power. You didn't think you were king of the jungle, you thought you were the jungle. But you know what beats the jungle?"

Mike froze.

"The gang, Mike. The tribe beats the jungle. That's the whole story. Men burn out the jungle. We make farms, we take wives, we build cities. Men that are loyal only to each other. The gang turns the jungle into a city, and the city into a state. And when the state gets too big it turns everything back into a jungle. And then it starts all over. Well the gang's back, Mike, and you picked the wrong side."

"How do you want to do it?" he asked finally, shoulders slumping slightly.

"Get in the UTV," I said. "Take us to our money."

"It's not in crypto anymore," he said.

"Well what's it in Mike?" I asked.

"I'll show you," he said. "I'll take you."

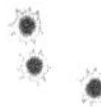

Mike slid into the driver's seat of the UTV, and I took the passenger seat. I stuck my Glock into his ribs. "Don't be stupid."

Mex and Tex walked back to the little Ford Ranger we'd parked down the hill.

Mike started the UTV and headed down the mountain back towards the ranch house.

"Easy," I said, anytime he got too much in a hurry. I didn't want him to even think about trying to crash it.

As he pulled up to the house, I watched as his jaw dropped. Flat on their stomachs were ten of his ranch hands. They were already zip tied, black bags over their heads. Nord sat in a chair on the front porch guarding them.

Also scattered around the front yard were several dead bodies. His guards. We'd made quick work of those that didn't want to surrender.

"What the fuck did you do?" he asked.

"What does it look like, Mike," I said, rapping him roughly in the side of the head with the pistol. "Get out."

He shimmied out of the UTV and wiped his hands off on the front of his shirt.

"Mike, you old goat," Nord shouted from the porch. "Long time no see."

"How did you fools make it out of there?" Mike asked suddenly. He looked at each of us one at a time.

I smiled.

"And you," he said to me. "How the fuck did you survive?"

It had finally set in. The unrealness of it all.

"Orcas," I said. "Would you believe it. It's a whole thing. Killer Whales is only if you are a seal, they save guys from shipwrecks all the time."

He just stared at me, dumbstruck.

"And you," he asked, turning towards Tex. "I saw the airstrike. I saw it."

"Ask Nord," Tex said. "He pulled us out of that one."

"Those were Chinese special forces you saw," Nord said. "We baited them in with a cellphone. You saw three bodies by a fire, that's all."

"Alright, reunion is over," I said, waving my Glock towards the ranch house. "Our money, now."

Mike led us inside. Nord stayed on the porch to watch the guards.

In the front part of the house, I clocked a gun cabinet with antique firearms. Two nice and shiny single action Colts front and center.

I walked to it and tried to open it but it was locked. I busted the glass and pulled the Colt's out.

Mike watched me do it.

"You got ammo for these?" I asked.

"The drawer," Mike said.

I flung the drawer open, and grabbed up a box of .45s. "Alright, where's our money."

"In here," Mike said. He led us deeper into the house until we reached what could only be described as a den. Books lined the shelves. And on one wall was a massive safe.

"It's in there," Mike said.

"Well open it," I said.

He crossed the room and I followed. I watched as he turned the safe's dial. He started to swing it open, but I clucked, "Nuh uh. I wasn't born yesterday."

He stepped back from the safe.

"There's a gun in there huh," I said.

He held out his hands and shrugged in a what did you expect sort of way.

I swung the safe door open and Tex whistled. The top shelf had at least ten gold bars. The 400 oz institutional kind. Several stacks of cash lined the second shelf.

I clocked the revolver laid next to them and turned to him. I shook my head, disapproving.

"Five of those gold bars is five million dollars," he said. "That's what I took. I'll even give you a sixth as interest."

Tex started laughing.

"Mike, this is called a hold up. You aren't giving us anything. We're taking it."

I stepped back, "get it."

Mex and Tex started forward. There were two

crumpled duffels in the bottom of the safe. They took these and started with the gold.

"Holy shit these are heavy," Mex said, hefting a bar. "They are like thirty pounds."

"Twenty five," Mike said.

"250 lbs of gold," I said. "Take it all. Even the cash."

It took Mex and Tex four trips to clean out the safe. I stood with my gun on Mike the whole time. I liked making him watch. I liked how long it took.

"Ok, outside," I said.

I SHOVED Mike out the front door and into the patio area. Mex and Tex followed us out with the last load.

"How much money does he have?" Nord asked as we passed.

"More than anyone working for the Government should," I said, shoving Mike forward.

The sky was all reds and oranges, the sun having just kissed the horizon. Mex tossed both duffels into the back of the truck. Tex sidled up next to me.

"Remember what you said," Mike started. He turned around to face me, even as he kept walking backwards. His hands were pleading. "About a fighting chance. You want to box, we can box.'

"Oh you'd love that," I said. "But I think you beat me for the last time. No, I think we play my game."

I pulled one of the single action Colts from my waistband, broke open the box of shells and loaded it. Then I spun the cylinder and handed it off to Tex.

I loaded the second gun, staring at Mike the whole time. His face had lost all its color.

"This ain't fair," Mike said. "I read your file. Three gun champion as a highschooler. What is this. You think this is a gunfight. We draw it out like its high noon."

I spun the cylinder and tucked the Colt into my waistband. Then I nodded to Tex.

He walked the second Colt over to Mike, and tucked it into his waistband.

Mike just stood there, his hands by his side, sweat beading across his face. "Damn you to hell Ryan. You fucking son of a bitch."

"This is it, Mike," I said.

His hand flew to his gun, but it snagged on his pants, or he grabbed his waistband. Regardless, something fucked up his draw because he never got it out.

I drew my own, a bit slower than I used to be, but it was still second nature. The Colt bucked, and my first one took him high in the chest.

He stutter stepped backwards, still grasping at the Colt in his waistband. Blood trickled out of his mouth, and he spasmed awkwardly, desperate to remain standing. Then his eyes rolled up into his head and he fell forward.

I STUDIED the still body of Mike. His blood pooling on the brick patio of his casa. I felt nothing for the man. There was no room for traitors.

Mex stepped forward. "Now what?" he asked.

"Whatever we want," I said.

"We should start a company," Nord said.

"And do what?" Tex asked.

"This," I said. "Plenty of merc work around."

"What would we call it?" Tex asked, a smile flickering across his lips.

"Something funny," I said. "And nonsensical like all the other PMCs."

"VIP Solutions?" Tex said.

"Executive Outcomes," Mex said.

"I think that's been used before," Nord said, with a wry smile.

"That was the joke, dumbass," Mex said.

"Strategic Solutions?" I said.

"Nice, yeah let's make our acronym SS," Nord said.

"And double lightning bolts our logo," I added, laughing.

"Strategic Advantages," Tex said.

"That's not bad," I said. "Let's put it on the list."

We walked towards the old Ford Ranger.

"Why are we taking that?" Nord said. "He has a brand new Hummer in the garage over there."

"Why the fuck didn't you tell us that before we loaded 250 lbs gold, pendejo."

I looked from Nord to Mex and shrugged. "Hummer seems like the better option."

"Dios mio, I hate you fucking guys. You can unload it then."

"Fine," I said.

"What about them?" Nord said, motioning towards our hostages.

"Leave them, they'll figure it out," I said.

THE END

A note from the Author

Thank YOU for reading. It is because of you that I can do this.

Indie books don't come with big traditional marketing budgets. We rely on word of mouth. One of the best ways to help me write more of the types of books you like, is to leave a review.

If you enjoyed this book or even if you hated it, please leave a review.

Stay in Touch

Author Updates, Short Stories, Essays and more!

Never miss a new release.

Join today at frankkiddauthor.com

About the Author

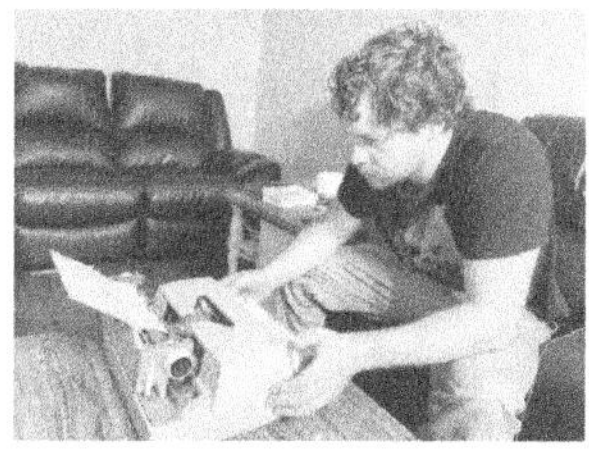

Frank Kidd is an American author and screenwriter living in Missouri. He writes across genres, but specializes in westerns and historical adventure. He is also a veteran, an outdoorsman, and an amateur historian. Some of his favorite authors include Louis L'Amour, Jack London, Richard Matheson, and Robert E. Howard. You can follow his work via his online publication, Pulp West, or on his website at frankkiddauthor.com.

www.ingramcontent.com/pod-product-compliance
Lightning Source LLC
LaVergne TN
LVHW020655110826
845149LV00012B/2014

* 9 7 8 1 9 6 6 8 4 7 0 3 8 *